THE VERDICT

of

US ALL

H. R. F. KEATING
(Photograph by Simon Keating)

THE VERDICT

of

US ALL

Stories by the Detection Club for

H.R.F. KEATING

Edited by Peter Lovesey

Crippen & Landru Publishers
Norfolk, Virginia
2006

Cover painting by Carol Heyer

Cover design by Deborah Miller

Crippen & Landru logo by Eric D. Greene

ISBN (limited edition): 1-932009-54-X
ISBN (trade edition): 1-932009-55-8

FIRST EDITION

10 9 8 7 6 5 4 3 2 1

Crippen & Landru Publishers, Inc.
P. O. Box 9315
Norfolk, VA 23505
USA

www.crippenlandru.com
CrippenLandru@earthlink.net

CONTENTS

FOREWORD BY DICK FRANCIS

My God, have you heard? HRF is eighty. But, hold on. He's looked the same for forty years. He's always been older than me but now I find he isn't. It must be the beard, and the gravitas and the adult sense of humour.

The day Harry turns eighty, I shall be eighty-six. We share the same birthday. We were born on October 31st – we are both Halloween babies. Perhaps that is why we do what we do. We share a fascination for the ghoulish and the creepy, we both have a love of the dark side of life – and death – and then there is our writing too.

I have known Harry for more than forty years. We first met in the mid-nineteen sixties when I was invited to join the august, select and discerning membership of The Detection Club. What an honour! How I was in awe of Agatha and Julian, and of Harry and the others, and, of course, of Eric, the skull, who presided over all the Detection Club meetings like Nelson over Trafalgar Square – always silent, but always … there.

Since those days, I have grown to know Harry somewhat better, but that has increased rather than decreased the awe factor.

Harry loves India – in this we differ. In India there are just so very many people that the concept of personal privacy simply does not exist. If you are sitting alone in an empty café in, say, Inspector Ghote's native Bombay, and an Indian gentleman enters the establishment, he will come and sit with you, at your very table. He would think that you would be offended if he sat elsewhere and if he did not keep you company. Harry is like that too – he comes and keeps you company all the time – on printed page and in person.

This wonderful collection of short stories is a veritable treasure trove, an Aladdin's cave of delights. It is a volume of respect and affection – nay, love – for one of our own. Harry is our leader, our muse – our friend.

Let's face it, Harry must be quite a guy to rouse Len Deighton to write his first short story for more than 30 years, and to have Simon

Brett, the current Ruler of the Detection Club, creating in verse to emulate Harry's novel *Jack, The Lady Killer*. The list is as impressive as it is extensive – no Morse code needed to decipher Colin's, just pop around to the post and meet Uncle Harry at the Garrick, but keep your head and watch out for Kali on the Titanic and, of course, the bearded wonder with Nikolaivich and the others. It sounds like a case for the Inspector, or his perfidious sisters.

Read on. Experience the mood – Happy 80th Birthday Harry. Still a youngster.

Dick Francis
Cayman Islands
28 May 2006

TUESDAY'S CHILD

Lionel Davidson

My first contact with Harry (a non-contact really) came from an approving review for an early book of mine. I was en route to Israel just then with a wife, two children and a household packed in crates. I couldn't write a grateful note at the time. But a few years later just before my return to England he reviewed another book, this time as a brief – but encapsulated so succinctly that the publishers plundered every word. This time I did write, and we met, and became friends. I am older than Harry but my occasional attempts to grow a beard have never been able to match his own capacious specimen. It isn't jealousy, but you know ...

Early morning; Mr Kintage out for a walk. He was an early-morning person, and *this* morning had wakened especially early, summoned by Bach. The great cantata *Wachet Auf* had roared in his head; but only in his head, for his wife Ashlie still slept. Considerately he had crept with his clothes elsewhere to dress. Now, dressing completed, ablutions completed, he walked.

He liked walking. In London he had walked from Kensington Gardens to Wimbledon and on other occasions had roamed still farther afield, mingling with high and low; in India with maharajahs, in California with hippies.

Now as he walked he pondered. Something puzzled him.

Mr Kintage – Heryn Kintage the writer – was a master of puzzles. His last work had won wide acclaim. ('Vintage Kintage', the critics had agreed.) But this was something else. He couldn't yet identify *what* was puzzling him. This was often the way when ideas stirred; and a good walk could clarify them, so on he walked. He was a large man, with a large beard, which he felt from time to time while dwelling on the problem.

The problem. Was it the *day*? A day was useful in a title. 'Solomon Grundy, born on a ...' But no. Julian had done *The End of Solomon Grundy*. In any case today was Tuesday. Monday, after the weekend, could be messy. On *Tuesday* one got into one's stride, and on he strode; to Bayswater Road, which he crossed, and at the first open gate, entered the park.

All to the left was Hyde Park and he traversed it, sniffing the fine nutty air. Autumn had come. The Fall.

Was it *that*? The Fall. Falling bodies. Falling angels. Something about this time of year – in fact the month, which was October, the very end of it – always made him reflective. Leaves on the ground had turned to gold, and dew glittered like diamonds. Mr Kintage was familiar with gold and also with diamonds. But his mind was now on angels, fallen ones. Lucifer. Prince of Darkness. But the name in fact meant light – *lux, lucis*. Well, Lucifer had once been Light. Rebelliousness had led to his fall. All the same, Darkness/Light. *Might* be something there. Ambivalence in one word; language infinitely complex, infinitely variable. Heryn Kintage had studied languages.

This mental activity and the walk now stimulated an appetite. He took an egg from his beard and ate it. A small salt cellar came from the same place, and after use he returned it to that place.

Yes, and not only language, he thought. Names too could be highly variable. He had several himself – those given at birth, those he had invented, and those interfered with in some way. His most popular creation, a small Indian detective, bore the forename Ganesh. Elephant. Heryn Kintage was attracted to the ways and the argot of the east.

Coming out of the park, he now encountered two eastern persons. A couple, evidently Japanese, and in difficulty. The man was gesticulating over a map, and at Marble Arch. Mr Kintage asked if he could help. His grasp of Japanese – sufficient only for correcting the odd literal in proofs – was by no means perfect; at about the same level, perhaps, as their English. The sole word he could pick out was Shelfridge.

'Ah. Selfridge. Yes. You are going the wrong *way*. It is *that* way. And on the other side of the street. *Other* side,' said Mr Kintage, pointing to the left side of Oxford Street. 'You first pass Marks and Spencer –'

'Hah! Markaspence!' This one they wanted too, and offered up thanks, the woman at the same time examining him intently. From rapid remarks to her husband Mr Kintage identified his own name.

'Oh. Hah. You are,' asked the male, 'Mr Heryn Kintage?'

Heryn admitted that it was he, was at once photographed with each of them in turn, then presented with a pen and the cover of the map for signature. He complied, and the trio parted with many tokens of respect.

The sun had barely risen when he left home. Now it smiled benignly, and Mr Kintage smiled with it. A happy coincidence, the Japanese! A case of beard recognition. He took a small pull at the beard, and wouldn't have minded another egg. But he never carried more than one.

He crossed to Oxford Street himself – and almost immediately here was a second coincidence. A group of young men, dancing. They waved at him joyfully, shaking tambourines, crying, 'Hari, Hari!' This was another of his names, and he responded graciously. The young men wore saffron robes. Mr Kintage was no stranger to robes. He had been President of a select club (the Reflection Club), and on occasion had been required to don a robe.

But time was now getting on. He'd had no intention of walking into Oxford Street. Just a walk in the park. Absentmindedness! Ashlie must be wondering where he's got to. And still the problem in his mind remained unresolved. It was not the *day*. He'd tried that. Not the *month*. Tried that too. From somewhere a clock chimed nine. Good Lord! *Wachet Auf* had hit him before seven. He had been up and about for two hours. Vaguely he recalled having heard another clock chime at some point in his walk. He'd missed the first strokes, but realised now that it must have been eight.

Eight. There was something there. The figure eight, like a skating figure, or like music – indeed like Bach – had looped about and about, deep in the subconscious. The subconscious frequently presented puzzles in this way. But what did it mean? Ashlie would be able to help. Ashlie was prodigiously able. Ashlie would be able, and he sped home to her.

He arrived at the house, somewhat out of breath, beard streaming, and observed the postman approaching.

'Mr Kintage! Quite a lot for *you* today,' said the postman.

And so there was. The post had been capricious lately. There seemed to be several weeks' supply here, secured by a stout elastic band. Had others experienced similar trouble? Or was there some misfeasance at the sorting office (perhaps bribery, corruption also)?

He took the bundle, took his key, but had not yet opened the door when Ashlie opened it for him. 'Where have *you* been?' she said.

Heryn explained where he had been, and the puzzle that had taken him there.

'Do you know what day it is?' she said.

'Tuesday.'

'Do you know what month it is?'

'October.'

'Do you know the date of the month?'

'The 31st. I've done all that,' sad Heryn. 'It wasn't any –'

'It's your birthday, you lovely idiot!' And she gave him a kiss.

'Oh. Ah. But the *eight* –'

'Your *eightieth* birthday. Today. Tuesday. But you were born on a Sunday. Your mother once told me. What's the rhyme for Sunday's child?'

The rhyme for Sunday's child. Heryn reviewed it. 'Yes. The child that is born on the Sabbath day is fair and wise and good and gay.'

Ashlie reflected. 'Well. You get seventy-five per cent for that. And for Tuesday's child?'

'Tuesday's child,' said Heryn with a blush, 'is full of grace.'

Ashlie gave him another kiss. 'For that I'll give you a hundred per cent,' she said.

(And so will all his friends at the Reflection Club, not least, and with affection, Loniel Nadsidov.)

SHERLOCK HOLMES AND THE TITANIC SWINDLE

Len Deighton

Cyril Connolly, in Enemies of Promise, *told us 'A great writer creates a world of his own and readers are proud to live in it.' Dialogue, setting, description and characterisation, to say nothing of plot, are important factors, but unless a writer is able to take us into a world that exists only in our minds, books are just an exercise in typing. Of all the novelists working today I know of no one who does this with the consummate skills and intellectual abandon that Harry Keating displays.*

It is little wonder that Harry is such a knowledgeable enthusiast for the Sherlock Holmes stories; in the matter of created 'worlds' they illustrate comparable brilliance. Doyle's plots are often predictable, his dialogue frequently wooden and unconvincing. We forgive him. The reason that Sherlock Holmes enchants readers all over the world, and has lasted so long, is because Doyle takes us by the hand and leads us into this foggy world of clip-clopping Hansoms, coal fires and an avuncular doctor with a strange and somewhat sinister friend. Harry has written a perceptive book about Sherlock's real and unreal world and I have read it again and again.

Television and the film industry have over the years provided irrefutable proof that you can't interpret the imagination of the novelist by means of photography. The writer can give us a world that invigorates our brain and refines our experiences. That's why we can go back to the same book time and time again and find a new reward when reading it. The difference between that book we enjoyed in childhood and the same book read last week, is us. So it is with Harry Keating's writings. Harry's worlds are many and various. They are there for all of us to share and I for one will never tire of them.

It was handwritten in a bold, attractive and well-formed writing style, on a cream-coloured heavy paper. There was a small crease on the corner but there was no sign of fading and the colour was the same on both front and back. Held to the light, this single sheet revealed a watermark of a floral design that I did not recognize. The upper edge of the sheet was slightly rough as if it might have been torn from a writing pad but it may have been because the paper was hand made. Most significantly, the writing varied in ink density. The sentences started in a strong dark grayish-blue and then faded slightly as happens when writing with an old-fashioned pen frequently dipped into a bottle of ink.

SHERLOCK HOLMES AND THE TITANIC SWINDLE.

It was a raw and foggy night in early December when Holmes and I sat either side of a blazing fire in our sitting room in Baker Street. Inspector Lestrade of Scotland Yard was there. He was likely to call in on us of an evening and Sherlock Holmes always welcomed him, as he liked to hear the latest news from police headquarters. On this particular evening Lestrade puffed at his cigar and was uncustomarily quiet. 'It's this terrible disaster,' said Lestrade, shaking his head sadly.

'Some fine old families will be mourning still,' I said.

'There are fears abroad that this failure of an unsinkable vessel could deliver a crippling blow to our whole shipbuilding industry,' said Holmes. 'I can reveal that I have already been in contact with the captain, the helmsman and several others who were on watch at the time. I am presenting my spiritual research to the directors of the White Star Line. There remain many unanswered questions.'

'Surely not?' said Lestrade. 'The Titanic *struck an iceberg, was ripped open and sank. How can there be a mystery concerning it?'*

'The Titanic, *was it?' said Holmes. He waited a long time before continuing. 'There is not one article; not one piece of flotsam or jetsam bearing the name* Titanic.' *He watched our faces and then answered the tacit question. ' "White Star Line" yes but not one item with the word* Titanic.'

He held up his hand to still our questions. 'To other matters,' he said.

'And where's the rest of it?' I asked.

'In his father's bank or in a private Swiss vault or in a tower of his auntie's Bavarian castle,' said Percy.

'Is that what's he's like?'

'Strong London accent; almost like an Aussie, carefully-trimmed black beard; brown corduroy suit; pompous, assertive; aggressive almost.'

'Could be any one of our authors,' I said.

'My authors are respectful,' said Percy.

'Because you send the aggressive ones to me.'

'And they are the ones that make the money,' said Percy. 'Ever since that piece in *The Bookseller*, they all want you to be their editor, you know that. Fiction writers do anyway.'

I read the sheet of paper again and said nothing.

'So what do you think?' said Percy after looking around the room. 'Bloody untidy; your office.' He had removed a pile of books in order to sit in the soft leather chair I put authors into when I have bad news for them. One leg was resting across the other to display a red cashmere sock and handmade Oxford shoe. Percy always looked like a page from a fashion magazine even on days like today, when the rain was thrashing against the windows, and the sky was so dark that all the office lights were turned on.

'Is it a parody or what?' I said. 'It has the same plodding style that I remember from all Conan Doyle's Sherlock Holmes yarns.'

'Is that a recommendation? Do you mean it's genuine?'

'We have quite a big list, and it will be too late for the new catalogue, no matter how fast we move. I think we should stay out of this. Send him one of your sad rejection letters.'

'Send him where? To HarperCollins? To Random House?'

'Why did he pick us?' I asked.

'He wanted to bring it to the last independent publisher in London, he said.'

'You didn't tell me he was a philanthropist.'

'Now, now, Carl. Don't let your nasty Teutonic streak show.'

'It's been a long day,' I said. Percy's Teutonic joke, a reference to my Christian name, had worn thin.

'And you've had your regular kick-boxing lesson from Princess Diana all afternoon.'

'Her agent told her our contract will have to be renegotiated.'

'More money. She can go to Hell and take "Footsteps to Heaven" with her.'

'We did rather well with her last Sharon du Parr,' I reminded him. 'And she has a new agent now: Freckles. Her other agent was not commercial enough for her. New agents, Percy, always want to flex their muscles.'

'Her last agent was a man,' said Percy who was high enough in the command structure to be in on the deals. 'Sensible enough to keep her feet on the ground.'

'Was he? I never met him.'

'Blonde lady bomber pilots and female secret agents toting machine guns. The art-work on her last dust-jacket haunts me. I don't know why we publish that crap.'

'You don't?' I enjoyed winding him up. 'She loved the dust-jacket. She wanted us to make it into a poster.'

'That wretched Freckles? Has she really started her own agency? Good grief.'

'I think we might be dealing with her for more of our lady writers before long. She wrote an amusing article in *The Author*. She said men authors always got paid twice as much as women authors and she was going to fight for them. And you'd better not call her Freckles to her face, Percy.'

'Let's get back to this Sherlock Holmes story,' said Percy. He put a finger on to his starched shirt cuff to sneak a look at his gold Rolex. 'You want me to tell him to get stuffed? He's demanding some 'token' money down before we see the rest of it.'

'That's just to keep us on the hook,' I told him.

'So I'll tell him we're not interested?'

'Not in as many words, Percy. You don't want to make headlines as the publisher who turned down a Sherlock Holmes story that has been locked away undiscovered for a hundred years.'

He wetted his lips and then sighed. 'Make up your mind, Carl.'

'Everyone loves Sherlock Holmes,' I said. 'If it's the real thing this will make news. Not trade news; big international headline news and TV.'

'The paper looks old,' he picked it up and looked at it and smelled it. 'But is it Conan Doyle's writing?'

'Well, I don't imagine he would bring us an autograph edition; he may have copied it out.'

'You'd think he'd put on a computer or something.'

'Not very secure, computers, Percy. Put something like that on the hard drive and it's only a couple of keystrokes away from going on to the Internet. And into the Public Domain as you lawyers say. Your – what did you say his name was – seems to be a careful chap.'

'He says he wants a definite answer, and cash on the table, by the fifteenth of the month.'

'The fifteenth? Next week.'

'He's out of the country till then; a business trip he said.'

'Writers all say that; they have a guilt complex about holidays.'

* * *

I was very busy over the next few days. One of our best line-editors had gone sick with what they suspected was chickenpox. Her daughter phoned us to say her mother might need hospital treatment. She was having blood tests. I knew that would mean a week or more out of action. The worst of it was that she lived in deepest, darkest Cornwall and there was a tall pile of typescripts sitting on her shelf. I couldn't find time to go down there, and Percy was frightened he might catch chickenpox. Finally we decided to wait and see what the medical tests showed. And Percy found an urgent need to visit one of our writers in Ireland. As usual, this meant a diligent exploration of the local pubs and Percy running at half speed for several following days.

Once back in action, Percy took his single sheet of handwritten Sherlock Holmes all around the building, swearing them all to secrecy, as he had before showing it to me. By Thursday he must have run out of people to consult for he came back to talk to me again.

'That young fellow who does the computer stuff in accounts had a good suggestion.'

'About Sherlock Holmes?'

'He said we must insist on having a sheet from the original, and then have the paper examined and tested in a laboratory to see how old it was.'

'No great problem getting your hands on sheets of old paper, Percy. We could probably find some in the store room, or the slush pile, if we rooted around long enough.'

'And I thought of that too, Carl. I'm not a complete fool. It might be better to get one of these computer people to compare the syntax against other stories.' I suppose I did not light up in the expected fashion. 'Verbs, adjectives; the length of the sentences and so on. That "customarily", for instance. Was that a word Doyle ever used?'

'It wouldn't be conclusive. We shouldn't assume that this fellow whatshisname is an untutored oaf. If he's a forger he will have looked at the stories: verbs, adjectives and the length of sentences.'

'You don't have to be so bloody sarcastic, Carl. I'm trying to see some way out of this situation.'

'Way out?'

'Yes, I didn't tell you but I've had the newspapers sniffing around, asking if we'd found some long lost manuscript.'

'Sherlock Holmes?'

'One of them said H.G. Wells – he'd heard it was a sequel to *Things to Come* and the other didn't have a clue about who wrote anything.'

'That must have been a senior literary editor. Let me guess which paper.'

'No, that's just the point. These queries are coming from the news desks. The H.G. Wells looney had heard that it was going to be a major film.'

'Why doesn't your punter just put it up for auction? One of the big boys might be willing to put it into their New York auctions.'

'Perhaps he's frightened of it being turned down as a fake,' said Percy. 'That could be a crippling setback for anyone selling it.'

'Will an auction house care too much whether it's a fake? They'll get their money; then it's *cave canem* for the bidders. I sometimes think half the junk put up for auction is bogus in one way or another.'

'*Caveat emptor*,' Percy solemnly corrected me.

'Same goes for the film,' I said. 'If some sharp film man grabs it, he could ride along on the publicity generated by a controversy about whether it's genuine. And if it turns out fake that will hardly dent the takings at the box office.'

'So you think we should publish it?'

'I didn't say that, Percy.'

'It's all right for you. You can just move on if the firm hits a rock. I'm stuck here.' Percy was determined not to be deprived of his crisis.

'I don't see why.'

'Because my uncle is the chairman, Carl. Be your age. You've made enough jokes at my expense.'

'Have I, Percy? I hope I have never been offensive.'

'I don't mind your jokes. You can be very humorous sometimes. It's the crap I get when people have to be sacked.'

'People say things they don't mean.'

'They mean it all right,' said Percy and I almost felt sorry for him. It was after all Percy who had got me the job. The ad agency let me go after they lost the breakfast food account I was working on. Percy got to his feet. 'Well, I must leave you now. I have an important lunch appointment.'

When I saw Percy later that afternoon he was roseate and ebullient. And it wasn't all due to the unspecified number of bottles of Chevalier-Montrachet he and his luncheon guest had consumed. 'There it is,' he said. He put a brown packet on my desk. His aim erred to the extent that it sideswiped my keyboard and put about three hundred zs across a letter I was concocting for the 'Princess' about the bewildering way her characters were apt to change names and/or appearance and then sometimes change back again. 'That's it.' He pointed. 'That's the Sherlock Holmes story. That's your Christmas bonus and my seat on the board.'

'He gave it to you?'

'It wasn't easy but lunch at the Ritz can have a magical effect upon authors. I've noticed that before.'

'And this is the only copy? No photocopies in your desk?'

He hesitated. 'He made me promise on my honour. I signed a piece of paper for him. It wouldn't have much effect in a court of law but he knows I wouldn't want him brandishing it if there was evidence that I'd cheated on him. So look after it. Don't leave it on the train or something. You remember how you went past your station and had to get a minicab home that night after the Christmas party?'

'Yes,' I said. I wished I'd never mentioned that journey home to him. At the time I was hoping he'd offer to reimburse the cab fare but instead of that he kept using it to beat me over the head with implications that I got everything wrong. 'So how much did you have to pay him?'

'Nothing. Not a penny.'

'He just handed it over?'

'I said the directors would have a meeting on Monday and have an offer and a contract ready for Tuesday morning. I thought that would give you a chance to read it.'

'What about you reading it?'

'I have read it,' said Percy. 'I read it as soon as I got back from lunch.'

I noticed that the packet had been torn open and then sealed up again, so perhaps he had.

'And?' Percy was not an avid reader.

'It's damned clever: almost too clever for a Sherlock Holmes yarn. *Corpus delicti* it all turns on that. You know what I mean?'

'You don't plough your way through a thousand whodunits without discovering what *corpus delicti* means,' I told him.

Percy was not to be denied a chance to display his legal qualifications. 'Body; but not necessarily a human body. It's the facts, money, physical substance, evidence of any kind that a crime has been committed.'

'How does the story read?'

'You'll have to read it for yourself but at the conclusion of the story, Holmes finds there is no written evidence, no substance, no witnesses, not even this gigantic ship, to prove that any crime was ever committed. Holmes ends up baffled but anyway you must read it.'

'Doyle was ingenious,' I admitted

'It's good,' said Percy. 'A page-turner. But you are the senior editor, senior fiction editor, anyway.'

'Ummm,' I said. I could see into Percy's mind. If it turned out well, the firm would make umpteen thousands, Percy would get his seat on the board – there was going to be a vacancy in January anyway- and I would get a small Christmas bonus. If it became the sort of fiasco that Percy feared, it would all be my fault.'

'Take it home. Read it over the weekend and let me know on Monday.'

'Monday is a difficult day for me, Percy.'

'Your day at home, I know.'

'It's the only way I can get through the backlog. Here in the office there is always something cropping up.'

'Like me.'

'It's not only that, Percy. I have to see Sergeant McGregor in the morning and so I asked him to come to my flat for a sandwich and a beer. I want to switch a couple of his chapters and I've drafted out a new beginning. It's not as much work as it sounds but getting an author to understand the need for revisions is always a delicate job.'

'Who the devil is Sergeant McGregor?'

'Peter Cardiff. He writes the *Copper's Diary* series. We've done six of them now. They have all been trade paperbacks but marketing think he's ready to go mass-market.'

Why do these fellows have to have nom de plumes? Isn't Cardiff a good enough name? Better, in my humble opinion.'

'Not for a police series about Glasgow criminals. And when he first started he was still on the Glasgow force. He had to have an assumed name.'

'Move him to Tuesday, Carl. This Sherlock Holmes decision is important.'

'He's coming all the way down from the other side of Aberdeen. And he is a widower; with a school-age child. He has to arrange for someone to collect her and look after her. I really wouldn't like to throw a spanner into his arrangements. And he's one of our best authors, Percy.'

'What is best about him?'

'He can spell; he puts a capital letter at the beginning of each sentence and a full-stop at the end. He knows an adjective from a verb and doesn't use flash-backs or dream sequences or try to write sexy scenes that he can't handle.'

'He's old fashioned, is that what you mean?'

'Yes, exactly.'

'And now I've annoyed you.'

'A few more old-fashioned writers like Cardiff and I would have a weekend to myself now and again.'

'A palpable hit, Carl.'

'Yes, well, he's not old-fashioned, Percy. He's a fine writer who stays within his capabilities, and understands instinctively the taste and intelligence of the reading public in a way that not many people in this building do.'

'I say, Carl. A streak of passion! You are always able to surprise me. Very well then; ten a.m. Tuesday morning. And don't leave it on the train tonight.' He rummaged around in the cupboard where unpublished books grow dusty before going into the bin and found a green plastic bag with a Harrods motif. He put the manuscript into it, and hung it on the bentwood stand with my raincoat.

'Red sealing wax and string.' I observed.

'I wanted it to be secure. On this floor, any wrapped parcel of A4 size gets thrown into the slush pile without being opened.'

'Is that your signet ring you used on the wax?'

'It looks good doesn't it? I'm going to start using it on letters too. What about on the contracts?' I gave him a wintry smile. 'We worked hard at college didn't we Carl? Not many parties; not very often drunk; work, work, work.' I nodded. 'Well I was going through the numbers with Uncle John last week, and I noticed that only one of our top earners even got into college, and she didn't graduate.'

' "There are only three things needed for writing a best seller; but no one knows what they are." Somerset Maugham.'

'Yes it's all very well for an old buzzard like that to be sardonic but he was sitting on a barrel of cash in his villa in the south of France and lunching with the likes of Winston Churchill.'

'Maugham was a doctor at St Thomas's Hospital. Doesn't that rather undermine your theory about illiterate best-selling authors?'

'And Conan Doyle was a doctor, too. So were a lot of best selling authors but that was all long ago. Now we all know what is needed for a best seller. Not three things, only one damned thing: TV. It doesn't matter what illiterate rubbish you write, if it becomes a TV series you'll be feted and feasted and rich, and people will say you are a famous writer.'

'Not always, Percy.'

'Yes, always. Good grief Carl, who would have guessed, in Maugham's day, that any silly little cookery book could be made into a best seller? Or a book about exercising, wriggling your *derrière*; like that one we did with that frightful athlete woman who insisted on having her photo on every page?'

'We did well with it, as I remember.'

'That was because the photographer did such wonders. Or his retoucher or someone at the printer. He made her look like Jane Fonda, that's why it sold.'

'For whatever reason. She asked for twice as much for her second book.'

'She didn't get it from us,' said Percy with some force. 'She didn't get another TV series. I could see that it was going to be the end of her. Her end, perhaps I should say.' He didn't need to remind me that she'd made a loud and angry scene in Percy's office before taking her book to another publisher. And they had advertised it in the Sunday papers and lost a great deal of money on it. He laughed. It was good to see him happy and there is nothing that makes a publisher happier than to have a rival company steal authors, and then lose money with them.

*   *   *

Peter Cardiff arrived at my flat on the dot. A result of twenty-five years on the force, I suppose. His books had the series title *A Copper's Diary* and everyone in the trade, including me, admired them as fast-moving, well-written stories. Judging by his mail, the police service liked them too. But the joke was that Cardiff had actually kept a diary right from the first day he joined up as a constable recruit. He retired with dozens of notebooks and was unhurriedly making them into a literary career.

He hadn't been to my flat before. After I took his coat, he moved around the room. There wasn't much furniture. He went to the built-in shelves and started looking at all my books in a systematic way. 'Reference mostly,' I said. 'Specialist dictionaries and encyclopedias, maps and so on. I do most of my editing work here, away from the telephones and interruptions.'

'I thought my stuff went off to someone in the country for corrections of that sort.'

'For line editing; yes it does, but if I can pick something up in the early readings I can call the author with a query. It's quicker like that.' I opened two cans of beer and poured them out. Then I opened the packets of smoked salmon sandwiches and arranged them on the plates. He bent to look at one of the photos on the fireplace. 'My wife,' I said. 'She's a wonderful woman.'

'I thought you were getting divorced,' he said. 'I'm sorry, it's the policeman in me.'

I had no doubt referred to my wife in one of my letters or emails; it was sharp of him to remember so well. 'We've had our ups and downs,' I explained. 'She went to see her family in Brisbane. My teen-age son is with her. She wants me to join her there. It's not something I want to rush into. On the other hand, if I decide to go, her fare back here and return would be money wasted.'

'Looks like you were there when you were getting married,' he said, pointing to our wedding photo in a silver frame on the hi-fi. 'The eucalyptus trees, the coastline and the man in the bush shirt just a guess, of course.'

'Ten years back. It can get very hot in summer and I'm very fond of hot weather.'

He smiled and we both listened to the wind howling in the chimney. Despite the heat turned fully on, it was cold in the flat and it had been raining on and off for almost a week. 'And my son wants to go to college there.'

'What will he study?'

'He'll try for a Ph.D. in surfing and sunning.'

'I'd miss you if you moved,' he said. 'You are painstaking and understand what I would like to be able to do. The editor they gave me at first scribbled all over my typing, scribbled in red ballpoint. That was before I got the word processor. It all had to be typed again. It used to make me livid.'

He was still looking around when I said: 'I like the new one very much. You are really exploring McGregor's character now. The indecision and the anger ... and that chapter with the kid who can't speak English. You've come a long way from your first book with the motor cycle cops.' It was enough to bring him to the table where I had my notes.

'So you went back and read my first one?' he said. He sipped some beer and bit into a sandwich.

'I try to see how writers develop. And I must keep you to the continuity. We don't want you slipping up about past references; things like the new inspector going to the staff college.'

'No, that was stupid. So you picked that one up? I wondered who had spotted it. I should have sent a proper thank you letter. I'm not in touch as closely as I should be.'

'You need a London agent,' I told him.

'That doesn't sound like a publisher speaking.' He was much more relaxed now and I could hear his soft Glasgow accent; the only Scots accent that I could recognize.

'Someone who knows the way around town could get you some radio plays and maybe TV too. It would get you known to a larger public and that's what publishing is all about nowadays.'

'Yes, I know but I'm a slow worker. You wouldn't believe how many hours I spend in front of that damned screen. And I've always liked to be outdoors.' He tucked into the sandwiches. He probably hadn't eaten since getting off the train. I should have offered him something more substantial.

'Peter, old pal,' I said. He looked up sharply. I usually kept to more distant forms of address. It made it easier to criticize if I made it a bit formal. 'I have a safe here. It was broken into over the weekend.'

He looked at me as if I had gone mad. 'How much did you lose?'

'There was no money there; just my lease and bank statements and passport and so on. Other than that: six silver spoons that were my mother's, and a packet.'

'Packet?'

'With a small manuscript inside. Keep it to yourself. I haven't told anyone at the office about it. I didn't go to the police either.'

'No, I understand. It's more or less useless reporting robberies to your local coppers. Can I look at the front door?' He got up. He was a policeman now.

We went and looked at the door and the surround. 'The door shows no sign of being forced,' I said. 'And all the windows look okay too.'

'What sort of safe?'

'Not very wonderful.' I went and opened the closet in the hall to show him where the safe was hidden behind the coats. 'Guaranteed fireproof; that was important to me. Four figure combination lock. No sign of it being forced either.'

He ran his hands round the back of it to see if he could detect damage of any kind. 'Only four digits. That's useless.'

'The salesman said it meant almost ten thousand variations.'

'Who else has the key to this place?'

'No one. At least, there is an extra one I keep in the main safe at the office in case I locked myself out and the cleaning lady has one.'

'Look at it like this,' he said as he sat down and swallowed the rest of his beer, 'most of these combination safes have locks that are quick to operate. User friendly. That means it's quick to swing through the numbers. Try and you'll see.'

'Ten thousand numbers.'

'Five hundred wouldn't be too daunting, would it?'

'No, it wouldn't.'

'Five hundred a day. Try it; click click click. You'd be through it in twenty visits. And your winning combination is unlikely to be at the very end. On average, a thief would find the number halfway through his search. That may not be in line with the science of probability but you see what I mean.'

'Yes, I see what you mean. But I don't know what I should do.'

'If it's insured you'd better report it as soon as possible. Insurance companies are always looking for an excuse not to pay out.'

'I'll speak to the cleaning lady. She's Estonian. She only comes in twice a week: She's a nice young woman. She's been doing the flat for almost a year.' I realized how stupid it all sounded but I suppose Cardiff knew that crime victims are likely to become a little disoriented.

'She probably met some tearaway. It's a familiar story, I'm afraid. They meet in a pub and he gets the key and makes a copy. She may not be in on it but I doubt if you will see her again. It's a nasty old world. That's why I was happy to retire to my little hovel in the highlands.'

We went quickly though some literals and questions that I'd sent him in advance. Then I got to my feet. 'Thanks, Peter. Your new book is very good. It will have to be finally decided by the money men and the marketing people but I would be amazed if there was any hitch about your next one going mass market. We will have the same artist. You said you were happy with the previous covers.'

'I leave all that to you London laddies,' he said. 'That's what a publisher does, isn't it?'

'That's what a publisher does if he's lucky enough to have a sensible author,' I said. Another beer?'

He shook his head but he didn't leave. He didn't even put his coat on, he picked it up and held it awkwardly and said. 'You'd better tell me about it. I might be able to help. The parcel. Why would anyone crack open a safe to get a manuscript? Is it valuable? Why?'

I didn't answer.

'Come along, man. I won't be telling any of your secrets to the sheep.'

'I didn't open it,' I admitted. 'I thought it was a photocopy of a manuscript but perhaps it's an autograph manuscript. If it's written by a famous writer from the past, it could be valuable.'

'How valuable?'

'I've no idea. Anything up to a hundred thousand pounds.'

'Glasgow's full of gentry who would slit their mother's throat for a crate of scotch. London's worse. You'd better tell your local law, or someone might start thinking it's an inside job.'

'That I've stolen it?'

'There's no evidence of a break-in, is there?' he reasoned.

I shivered. 'I'll give it another day or so. You'll keep all this to yourself, won't you?'

He nodded but he didn't say yes. Peter Cardiff was a decent chap but once a policeman always a policeman. I had a feeling he was wondering about me. Wondering if I was trying to use him to cover some ingenious theft. All the other times I'd seen him it was in the office; so why ask him to come here today? I could see that question written in his face as he shook hands and said goodbye.

'I don't have my cleaning lady's address or phone number,' I said.

He smiled and nodded and I went down to the street and said goodbye. By that time I believe he thought I was the same sort of accident-prone schlemiel that Percy thought I was.

*   *   *

Percy's office was almost directly below mine, so on the Tuesday morning I arrived early and then went down to tell him I was ready for the meeting. I was still wondering how I was going to tackle him and his uncle. I would have indulged myself in a stiff drink before leaving home but I didn't want to make things worse by arriving with booze on my breath. 'Percy not here yet?' I asked his secretary.

'Has no one told you? He never arrived yesterday.' She was flustered.

'What?'

'Poor Percy. He was waiting for a bus yesterday morning and a little car came out of nowhere.' She seemed to welcome the chance to relate the story again. 'The ambulance took ages apparently and you know how dreadful the rain was. They took him to the little cottage hospital near where he lives. It's not life threatening or anything. But his leg is broken. And he has what they call 'superficial injuries' – bruises and grazes. It didn't stop; the car didn't stop. What brutes people are. They're doing tests, of course, in case he has anything internal. But he sounded quite cheerful on the telephone this morning. I'll give you the number. He has a private line. You can visit him any time they say. It's only a little hospital. I sent him some nice things to eat. He's not on any special diet or anything.' Finally she ran out of steam.

'So, no meeting this morning?'

'It could be days,' she said. 'Next week perhaps. He's got his laptop and a dozen books he wanted from the London Library.'

The phone rang. When she answered it I could tell it was an author complaining about a late arriving royalty check. I waved goodbye and left.

*   *   *

At first I thought, hooray, reprieved. But then I thought of Percy in the hospital and I put aside the bundle of sentimental scribble that Princess bloody Diana expected me to transform into her next best-seller. Percy lived in a rather verdant neighbourhood on the edge of the green belt. The hospital was just half a mile away, a private one, situated in many acres of countryside. It was almost possible to forget the thunder and filth of the heavy traffic grinding along the nearby North Circular.

'I see our client is a publisher by the cruel look in his eyes. His well-nourished countenance reveals a convivial lifestyle, and the faint remains of a tan suggest either an army man lately returned from service in the orient, or a playboy who takes extended holidays in Provence. As for the casing on the lower leg, this reveals a propensity to cross the road without looking both ways.'

'Hello, Carl,' He was sitting up in bed with a cast on his leg and extensive dressings on one arm. I'd always thought of Percy as somewhat effete. He was continuously getting colds and was likely to be found pausing breathless on the landing when the lift was out order. He was only slightly younger, but I'd been in the army while he was getting his law degree and somehow that made a difference to our relationship.

But today I saw a new side to Percy. Despite having had surgery, he was energetically researching the world of Sherlock Holmes. On the bedside table he had his shiny new Sony laptop open and lit up. Beside it there was a tower of books from which grew a torrent of yellow sticky markers.

I decided that the best line of defence was attack. 'Look, Percy, the *Titanic* sank in April 1912 I looked it up and Doyle didn't become interested in spiritualism until long after that. Long after Sherlock Holmes was dead and buried.'

'If the old man offers you non-fiction editing, old lad, be sure to say no.'

'Then what?'

'First of all, Doyle joined the Psychical Research Society in 1893. That was the same year the *Strand* magazine ran 'The Final Problem' with Holmes tipping over into the waterfall. Doyle didn't stop writing about Holmes just because his hero had died. He wrote *The Hound of the Baskervilles*, perhaps his best and most famous, in 1902, and predated the events. He simply said that this story was something that had happened to Holmes before he wrestled with Professor Moriarty above the lethal torrent of the Reichenbach Falls.'

'I see.' I put a bottle of Johnny Walker on the bed and Percy grabbed it and hid it under his pillow. 'You've been working hard, Percy. What are you going to be like when the anaesthetic wears off?'

He beamed. Percy was enjoying it all. Sherlock Holmes had got to him as it has done to many thousands of readers over the years. And, from my point of view this was splendid. Anything that kept Percy explaining the manuscript to me, instead of the other way around, was a relief. 'Tell me what else you found out?'

'This is the interesting stuff, Carl.' He tapped one of the books. 'Can you believe it? A new Sherlock Holmes story was published in the August 1948 issue of *Cosmopolitan* magazine. August 1948. Doyle died in 1930, didn't he?'

'Maybe they got it from an Ouija board.'

'Very good, Carl. A very good joke,' he said solemnly. I think he hated jokes. He once told me that jokes diverted and diluted serious thought and conversation. He was right and that's what I liked about them. 'And I went on the Internet and found some *Titanic* nutters. It seems that Holmes got that one right too. None of the remains: flotsam, jetsam, anything-elsesam, had the name *Titanic* on it. Nothing! Nothing so far retrieved can be positively identified as from the *Titanic*.'

'What are they saying then? That some other ship struck the iceberg?'

'Yes. The *Olympic*. But let's not get into that just yet, Carl. *Corpus delicti*, remember what I told you? Our concern is the story we are offered. Let me tell you about another situation that might – at law – be comparable with the one we find ourselves in.' Percy was really enjoying himself. 'This one surfaced in 1948. This was a Sherlock Holmes story called 'The Man Who was Wanted'. It wasn't written by Sir Arthur Conan Doyle; it was the work of another Arthur; a hard-up English architect named Arthur Whitaker. He sent it to Doyle. Feeling sorry for him, Doyle sent Whitaker a check for ten pounds and a sarcastic note telling him to invent his own characters rather than using Sherlock Holmes and co. Doyle tossed the story into the waste paper basket and forgot it. But someone – Lady Conan Doyle probably, or perhaps Doyle's secretary – rescued it and filed it away with Doyle's other papers.'

A woman in a white starched overall came in, bringing a tray bearing two cups of tea and four chocolate biscuits. She wanted to adjust his pillows but Percy waved her away so he could get on with his story.

'Ten years after both Doyles are dead, someone finds 'The Man Who was Wanted' tucked away in the Doyle archives. It's unpublished and the law says that trustees are obliged to maximize the income of the estate. In good faith, they sell it to Hearst Newspapers. In England the *Sunday Dispatch* published this 'new unpublished story'. January 2nd, January 9th and January 16th, 1949. It's a big circulation booster for all concerned.'

'But your story hasn't come from the Doyle estate,' I pointed out to him.

'I wish you would stop being such a damned wet blanket.'

'I'm trying to stop you setting yourself ablaze.'

'In fact, Carl, old bean, you are the one who struck the match. What you said about controversy, about a lot of people who will care less about authenticity than about wallowing in the financial benefits that widespread controversy will bring well, that's it.'

I held up my finger in tacit protest. 'It's all very well to say that to
me, Percy. But you must be very careful in expressing such ideas to
other people. You're a lawyer; I don't have to tell you the implications.
Conspiracy and so on.'

He vigorously waved away my objections with his bandaged arm.
'Just tell me one thing, Carl. Did you like the story?'

'It's all right,' I said cautiously.

'It's not just all right; it's marvellous, isn't it? It would make an exciting
film with all the exteriors that film people call production values. It's
not just two old Victorian dinosaurs chatting by the fireplace in a Baker
Street sitting room. You have the shipyards, the squalid Liverpool back
streets and signing the contract in the fabulous Belgravia home of the
White Star chairman. New York, too. It has enough to expand the
American end of the story.'

'Well, that would need a lot of extra writing and dialogue. A lot.'

'Film people don't mind that, Carl. They love extra writing. It gives
them a chance to make the sort of film they prefer to make. Is that tea
all right?'

'Yes, the tea is fine,' I took a biscuit and bit into it. 'The film end is a
long shot,' I cautioned him.

'Ah. That's what you think. One advantage to having this private
room is I can talk to New York and Hollywood while they are still
awake out there.'

'Hollywood?'

'Yes, Hollywood, you damned Jeremiah. A film production company
has been phoning everyone they can think of to ask about the new
Sherlock Holmes story.'

'A big company? How did they find out?'

'Big enough to be talking about half a million dollars. And a share of
the profits. What do I care about how they found out?'

'But why?'

'They need to schedule it. They need time to get the stars they want.
They don't want to wait around while we stage some prolonged kind
of auction. Cash: up front.'

'You talked to them?'

'It's better than that, Carl. These film company idiots in California
have made enough phone calls to stir up our cousins in New York.
I now have two publishers – one quite small, I admit – who want to
do a deal. The word will soon get out. World volume rights; film

and TV rights. There are all these disks and things nowadays. It could add up to a fortune.'

'I've never been a party to that sort of thing, Percy. I just edit the books.'

'And if the manuscript is in Doyle's hand, it could bring an immense price at auction. It's only in the last few hours, on the Internet, that I have learned how many rich collectors of Sherlock Holmes material are still active. There's money in every aspect of this deal.'

'Really?'

'Yes, really, you old misery. And don't tell me that the whole manuscript is a forgery, because I think it's kosher.'

'Well, I don't know.'

'Let me put it another way. Is there anything at all to suggest it's a fake?'

I pulled a face, not knowing how to proceed. 'I'm not an expert.'

'It's real, isn't it? It's exactly like Doyle's handwriting even to the sloping words on the title page ... I was able to compare the writing with pages and pages of Doyle's. I went carefully through every line of that facsimile edition of a Doyle manuscript that was published in Santa Barbara in 1985.'

I nodded.

'Yes, you know the one I mean: "The Adventure of the Priory School".' Percy gave a triumphal grin. 'You remember, do you? I've got it here now. My secretary found it. And do you know where my secretary found it? On the floor in your office.'

'I was sorting through my books to throw some out. I need shelf space.'

'On the floor in your office, Carl. On the top of a pile near the door. That's where she found it.' He laughed indulgently. 'You need shelf space, do you? You probably didn't even look at it.'

'I was working at home yesterday.'

'With that policeman, Peter Cardiff. Yes, I know. Well, now you can drop everything like that until we get this story contract in the bag. I'll want you with me when we face the board.'

'You'll buy it?'

'We don't want the Americans to share the purchase. If we can get it for half a million sterling, perhaps even more, we can't lose, perhaps even six. It's better that we have it to ourselves, and then sell it piecemeal according to the best offers. The film people are in contact with New

York and desperate to conclude. We have to move fast, Carl. And, let's face it, you are not renowned as a fast mover.'

'I've always been a cautious animal.'

'That's why you are still an editor. I do believe that if it was up to you, you wouldn't buy this story.'

'It's a lot of money, Percy.'

'Uncle agrees with me. It's a business opportunity. You don't have to have a degree in English Literature to see that.'

'What about provenance?'

'You are not to be swayed, are you? Personally I think this is a genuine story written, and hand-written too, by the master himself. But let's suppose it's not. You don't imagine that this fellow Whitaker was the only one ever to have sent Doyle a Sherlock Holmes story, do you?'

'I see what you mean.'

'Yes, now at last, you are getting to see what I am driving at. I contend that, at the worst, this is a story that Doyle read and grudgingly approved. A story that perhaps Lady Doyle rescued and that people in his office filed away in his archive.'

'Umm.'

'And that's at the worst.'

'We'd better keep this conversation to ourselves, Percy.'

'Everyone will make money.'

'And the Doyle Estate?'

'I will provoke them into denying that it's genuine, or that they have ever seen it, or handled it.'

'I'm glad I'm not a lawyer, Percy.'

'That's not nice. That's the sort of joke I resent.'

'I'm sorry,' I said. 'Having a wife in Australia is not very good for the morale.'

'A bonus and a long weekend will restore your morale. That new advertising girl is rather sweet on you, Carl. The one with the long blonde hair who wears those white sweaters. Did you notice that?'

'I hadn't even noticed there were girls in the advertising department.'

'Exactly,' he said with the triumph of a diagnosis proved correct. 'It's no good sitting at home moping, Carl.'

'I might go to Australia, Percy.'

'That would be a blow, Carl.'

'It's my marriage, Percy. She has her family there and her parents are getting old. And my son doesn't want to come back here.'

'What work will you do?'

'There's an ad agency there. They would probably like the idea that I'd worked for a big London agency.'

'You haven't been negotiating all this on the sly, have you?'

I shook my head and he smiled. I think he would have thought more of me if I'd said yes, I had.

*   *   *

When I phoned my wife, I did it on a public phone from a railway terminal. It was better done that way. It was evening in London but noon in Los Angeles where she had a temporary secretarial job in a big movie production company. At noon Irene's boss was always at lunch.

'I sold our lovely Volvo. I didn't have many offers. It went for a song but I'm using it for another few days and we did rather well on the lease of the flat. The new tenant moves in next week.'

'Are you managing all right, darling?'

'It's not much fun without a cleaning lady – the dishes pile up – but it was better to let her go well in advance. She's gone home for a few weeks. I gave her half towards her plane ticket and told her it was time she visited her mother.'

'Well, in that case I shall give notice this afternoon.'

'You should have seen Percy,' I said. 'He was like a small child.'

'We are going to ask for six. My brother is sure they'll pay another hundred grand. They are very keen indeed. You are so clever, darling. A regular Sherlock.'

I was silent for a minute or so.

'Are you there, darling?' she asked.

'It was just a goodbye joke,' I said. 'You remember what we agreed.'

'Why are you always such a wimp, darling? This is six hundred thousand pounds. This is a new life of high-living in a new land. We start again.'

'Just a goodbye joke,' I said. 'Taking the money would be ... I trailed to a halt.

'Would be wonderful,' she completed her version of the sentence. 'Your son could go to Harvard the way you said you would have liked to have done.' She took a deep breath and became charming. 'We will live a life of ease. Be sensible.'

'No, Irene. It was just an idea for a story. Then it became a joke to play on Percy.'

'No *corpus delicti*, darling. It's foolproof. No manuscript as evidence. No witness to the negotiations. All concerned disappear to the other side of the globe with no forwarding addresses.' There was a sudden note of concern: 'Your policeman swallowed the robbery story?'

'Everything went okay,' I said. 'But the answer is still no. No, Irene. Do you hear me?'

'Don't "no Irene" me, Carl. My brother and I have worked damned hard on this one. And spent good money on airline tickets. All you did is scribble a silly story and sit on your ass in London. It's going ahead no matter what you think about it. So have an aspirin and go to bed. Tell the office you have a virus and by the weekend you will have vanished.'

'Very well, Irene. But I don't like it.'

'You have your airline ticket. Don't forget your passport. See you on the beach, darling.'

'Poor Percy,' I said.

*   *   *

And when, six months or so later, the letters started arriving, Percy's letter was one of the first. No hard feelings he said. No crowing. I read the letter several times; I had the feeling that he was half inclined to offer me some money towards my legal costs. But he could afford to be generous. He'd got the greater part of the money back, and the world rights on my 'silly story' was eventually added to that. And there is to be a movie, too, they say. Nature follows art, I suppose.

There was no point in putting more money into my lawyer's pocket. When Irene's brother, Gordon McPhail, confessed, I had no alternative but to fill in the gaps. Most of the people who heard about it got it wrong and the newspapers did too. Even Percy, who should have known everything about it, thought that the Bali bomb in October had destroyed our 'lovely restaurant'. Some latecomers to the bad news thought we were victims of the tsunami, which came two years later. In fact we never did buy the restaurant we were negotiating for in Bali. We found a place we liked better; in *Surabaja* – Irene always said that I went for it only because of the Brecht song lyrics – and we were doing quite good business when the blow fell. 'We got it for a song,' she used to say before telling everyone that we had paid almost double the real value.

It was the terrorist bomb in Bali that did for us, of course. The Indonesian cops opened up the bank records to the Australian security service and they noticed the big money transfer. They became really excited. Sydney told London and Washington, and before I knew what was happening I was locked up in a prison in Jakarta with dozens of cops giving me hell on a shift for shift basis. Either they were convinced that I was the moneyman for the terrorists or they put on a wonderful act. They were rough and kept saying they'd hold me for ever and they didn't care about giving me a lawyer or bringing me to trial. They put Gordon through the wringer too. He was treated worse than me.

But ours had been a good plan. Even when they had Percy identify photos of Gordon and got their tame experts to agree about Gordon's signatures it still made a flimsy case to bring before a jury.

But my mind was changed by an avuncular old Aussie detective: 'I'll tell you this much, Mohammed, old son, the only way you can avoid serving fifty years in an Indonesian clink as a terrorist is to convince me you are a thief.'

I shook my head.

He gave a mirthless grin and said: 'The locals tell me there are 365 islands out there. That's bullshit, of course, but there are plenty of them, fever ridden and overgrown, some of them no bigger than a football field. Ideal in fact to use as high security prisons. I went to one of them once. The local coppers were showing us how they handled local law-breakers. It was a stinking hole: dense jungle; everyone as skinny as a rake, even the guards. One of the jokers there said that either the prisoners ate the snakes and rats, or the snakes and rats ate them. It was a good joke but it didn't get much of a laugh from any of our boys. The cons never come back. The guards only do six months at a time. Any questions asked and the pen-pushers at headquarters say the paperwork got eaten by termites.' He sat down and mopped his brow. 'You wouldn't think it was still winter, would you?'

Perhaps it was a contrivance. No doubt the same cop did the same fatherly routine with Gordon, and they were all determined not to let us discover who cracked first. I could see it might all be a bluff at the time but I didn't feel like betting my life on it.

And all through this, Percy was decent. He told the police he'd known me all his life, and that I couldn't be a terrorist. But he wouldn't lift a finger to help Irene's brother. It was understandable really; Gordon was the one who had duped him. He didn't have the same animosity towards me. He told the cops I was a weak character who had been drawn into crime by a shrewish domineering wife and criminal brother-in-law.

So I have no resentment concerning Gordon's confession. It was just bad luck and he managed to get Irene totally exonerated. They treat me quite decently now that I've got the transfer back to the UK, but I'll never eat rice, boiled fish or any of those damned fiery sambals for as long as I live. The governor here is a Sherlock Holmes devotee, so he likes to talk and display his knowledge to me, and I think I've persuaded him to try his hand at a pastiche of a Sherlock Homes story. I'll help. We are going to invent 'The Adventure of the Tired Captain', a case that Doyle mentions in passing at the beginning of 'The Naval Treaty' but never used. We won't be the first to have a go at it but no matter. There is no pressure of time and Percy says if it's good enough he'll publish it. And why not? He published my previous Sherlock Holmes story, didn't he?

Mind you, that's not going to be the end of the story. Next week I have a lawyer coming in to see me and that kind of visit doesn't have some big-eared warder sitting in to hear what we say. The court found me guilty of a whole string of offences, and writing that damned *Titanic* story is only one of them. So what are Percy and his uncle going to do when I claim copyright and my share of all the money they have put away? I'll get legal aid, so I won't have to find the money for the lawyers.

It's only now that I can understand why writers were always complaining to me about the way publishers treat them. Why should we writers be exploited?

UNCLE HARRY

Reginald Hill

So you've made it to 80, Harry! Let joy be unconfined. Here is occasion for congratulation, and celebration, and gifts – though of course you do present your friends with the problem of what to give to a man who has everything!

There's only a decade between us, but when we first met I was very much the tyro while you were already a crime writing legend – critic, scholar, editor, as well of course as brilliant novelist, breaking new ground with your Ghote series after starting off with four or five beautifully quirky books including A Rush *on the* Ultimate *which stands high in my list of titles I wish I'd thought of first. To gild the lily of your perfection, you'd also reviewed my own first efforts with your customary generosity and insight. So I approached you in a near rapturous state of awe and admiration. The awe didn't last long – you were far too amiable and unassuming to be comfortable with that – but the admiration has remained and indeed grown over the next three decades in face of your demonstration that true talent doesn't fade with age but continues to obey the great heroic injunction – to strive, to seek, to find, and not to yield!*

That first encounter took place at a Writers' Conference in Harrogate, Yorkshire in May, 1973, an event I still recall with pleasure a third of a century on.

But I'm no closer to solving that problem I mentioned earlier.

What can I possibly offer the man who has everything?

Nothing … except, perhaps … an alibi?

What I need to make clear and you need to get clear is, any resemblance between me and a real terrorist is purely coincidental.

We've nothing in common, me and those guys. My thing was personal, not ideological. The only common ground was putting the thing together, which did teach me one thing about their line of business that I'd never realised before.

The trouble with being a terrorist is that you experience a lot of terror!

Not perhaps if you're one of those mad sods who reckon that blowing up a busload of people on their way to work is a first class ticket to a world full of warm sunshine, sweet music, soft couches and doe-eyed virgins.

But for a middle-aged rationalist atheist humanist who claims to believe that this life is all you get – *finito* – good night Vienna – this is the end there is no more – then sitting in your flat trying to follow the instructions on your laptop which will turn the motley assembly of chemicals, wires, batteries and clock parts strewn across your kitchen table into a lethal weapon is fraught with terror, believe me.

You will note I say *claims* to believe.

It never really goes away, does it, all that religious stuff you get drummed into you when you're a kid? Mature logic and experience may seem to wash it all out of your mind, but scrub as hard as you like, it you look carefully under a bright light you can still find the faint outline of an indelible *what if?*

And a laptop screen showing a DIY bomb recipe casts a very bright light indeed.

Now this may not be so bad if your *what if?* tunes in images of all that sweet music and doe-eyed virgins stuff. The trouble is no matter how I cut it, the *what if?* my upbringing has left me with produces pictures of fires that burn but do not consume, grinning devils, souls in paroxysms of pain, eternities of agony.

Killing people is wrong, my dad used to say. Doesn't matter who, how, why, when or where, take a life and your soul belongs to Satan.

Of course being a preacher, he would say that, wouldn't he?

Not necessarily, you may think. There are plenty of preachers able to trot out any number of exceptions to the sixth commandment. Where would politicians be without them? But my dad was a fundamentalist which was surprising, seeing that he was C of E from a good old traditional Middle England background. When he got up in the pulpit you'd have looked for skeins of soporific platitude followed by a pre-lunch sherry at the vicarage. Instead he made most Welsh chapel sermons sound like Christopher Robin saying his prayers.

'Ten commandments there are!' he'd thunder. 'Just ten. Not a lot to remember, not a number to over-tax even the mind of a poor stockbroker wending his weary way home on the five-fifty-five after a long hard day breaking stock. No! God reviewed his Creation and He thought, *these humans look all right, most of them, even the stockbrokers, but I've got to face it, I did skimp on the brain power. So best keep it simple. Ten fingers they've got, so surely they'll be able to count up to ten?* And that's how we got the Decalogue. Ten simple commandments. No riders, no subclauses. You do what they say, or else! There's no Fifth Amendment saying, *honour thy father and thy mother until you become a teenager, then anything goes.* There's no Six-and-a-halfth Commandment that says, *Thou shalt not kill except in the following circumstances.* NO! These are God's rules!! Break them, and, believe me, YOU WILL BURN!!!'

I found that gem in a bundle of his old sermons which had turned up in the Bombay Mission. They'd been moving premises and dad's papers would have been burned with all the other rubbish if Sister Angela, the Mission's chief administrator, hadn't spotted them. She always had a soft spot for me and we've kept in touch, even though she knows I've strayed a long way from my father's path since last we met. Possibly she thought that forwarding a small selection of the sermons might nudge me back. Sorry, Angela, no deal, though they certainly brought dad back to me, and that early one at least gave me a laugh as I imagined how sentiments like these must have gone down in the rich Surrey parish where he started his ministry! No wonder it wasn't long before his bishop suggested his talents might be better employed in a more challenging environment, i.e. one a long way away from Surrey. He probably meant anywhere north of Watford, but dad never did things by half and that was how he came to be pastor of the Ecumenical Mission settlement in Mumbai, or Bombay as it still was back in the seventies.

So if we look for first causes, it was the dear old bishop who was responsible for putting my father into the predatory path of Uncle Harry. He's dead too, the bishop, so in the unlikely event of their mythology proving true, dad will have eternity to harangue the poor chap for not letting him continue his God-given task of bashing the brokers.

I suppose by the same token we could say that ultimately it was the bishop's pusillanimity that led to me setting out on my long bus journey from Battersea this morning, gingerly clutching an eight by four by two brown paper package on my knee.

Dad had got it wrong, you see. In my view there definitely is a Six-and-a-halfth Commandment, and what it says is, killing's OK when the target has enjoyed the rewards of his villainy for decades and looks like he's heading for the winning post so far ahead of the Law, he no longer even bothers to glance back over his shoulder.

Religion, if you've got it, might be a comfort here. *Vengeance is mine; I will repay, saith the Lord*, dad liked to thunder, meaning don't worry that there's no justice in this world, there'll be plenty in the next. Well, I'd like to believe that, dad, but despite those residual *what-if*s I mentioned earlier, I really don't. Meaning, unless I take care of the bastard, no-one else will.

So there I was carrying a bomb through the streets of London to rid the world of the villain who'd destroyed my family.

Does that make me a terrorist? In the eyes of the Law, I suppose it does. To me what I was planning to do was an act of justice, but I suppose that's what all the doe-eyed virgin boys say too. Though I must confess it did occur to me as I sat on the bus that if I'd got something wrong – an ingredient too volatile, a connection too loose – and we bounced over a pothole a bit deeper than the norm even on this stretch of the Earls Court Road, none of these innocent people around me would be interested in making fine distinctions.

I had learned to clasp my package a bit tighter as a stop approached. This driver must have missed the bit on his training course about gradually applying the brakes. By this time I only had one more stop to go. I was glad to see most of the other passengers had got out. Only a perspiring bald man and his glossily veneered companion remained, and they didn't look too innocent.

I glanced down at my package. It looked good. I never throw anything away and when I decided it would be both convincing and appropriate if the instrument of Uncle Harry's death seemed to have come from the site of his infamy, I had dug out the brown paper Sister Angela had wrapped the sermons in. Of course I couldn't simply re-use it, not with my address all over it in the Sister's fine copperplate. But with infinite care I had been able to remove the stamps and enough of the Mumbai post mark to be convincing, and transfer them to my own parcel.

An Indian fan, he would think, an admirer on the sub-continent who has remembered my birthday. How terribly kind! And full of anticipation he would rip the package open …

Surprise!

I hoped he'd have time to take in the writing on the inside lid of the box before the bang. I'd cut it from the title page of one of my father's sermons and pasted it there.

It read: *On Divine Retribution* by D.L.P. Lachrymate DD.

Yes, he was a three initial man too. Perhaps that was why it was so easy for Uncle Harry to ensnare him. *Three forenames means a man comes from a family with a pride in their past,* dad would say. *You can always trust a man with three initials. Never buy a used car from a one initial man. Hesitate to lend money to someone with only two. But give your hand and your trust when you see that third initial!*

Four he felt a little ostentatious except in the case of royalty.

I have three, of course. P.D.L. Same as my father's only the order is changed.

That's me all over. All the same elements as my father only the order is changed.

I too believe in retribution and hellfire, but I want them now!

I wouldn't like you to think that I have spent my life obsessing about my poor father's fate. I was only six when he died. To me one day he was there, the next he wasn't. Everyone talked about him being in a better place, but how a place could be better that didn't have me and mum in it, I could never fathom. As to how he got there, throughout my youth I was well protected from any real knowledge of what had actually happened. Certainly without him the place we were in seemed a great deal worse. My mother continued to work at the Mission. I don't think she really had a wage, just the occasional subsistence level hand out. I expect it was the same for the rest of them. It was probably believed that any complaints about wage levels could be answered by pointing to the squalor and abject poverty around us and saying, 'How can you look at that and still complain?'

Myself, I don't think mother gave a toss about remuneration levels. I don't even think she had any real interest in the Mission's work. All she wanted was see me through to the age of independence then, with a sigh of relief, give up the ghost and go to join her lost husband, which is exactly what she did.

It was after the funeral, in dribs and drabs, that Sister Angela told me the story. She had to support her own memory of events from a report she had written for the Mission Trustees at the time. It was couched in a curious mixture of Indian Civil Service jargon and King James Bible English. It went something like this.

The comprehensive recording procedures installed at the Mission by the present writer acting on the excellent advice of C.K. Bannerjee (Bachelor of Law-University of Bombay) by the grace of God our legal officer, enable us to trace precisely the first appearance of the subtle serpent, Keating, on our premises. For it is clearly written in the Book of Visitors that he was a guest in our midst at tea-time on the fifteenth day of May in the year of our Lord, 1974, as testified by his own signature, H.R.S. Keating.

As her narrative unfolded, it took me some time to realise that this serpent she was talking about, the architect of all our woes, was in fact Uncle Harry.

Not really my uncle, of course. But within a very short time of his first appearance at the Mission, that's what I was calling him. I remembered him very well, and all my memories were pleasant ones. He was a merry, voluble man in his late forties, always willing to spend time with me and treat me to ices from one of the street vendors that my mother warned me against but whose wares I adored. (In fact I never had any stomach trouble all my life till I came to England and tried a Shepherd's Pie out of a pub microwave.) I knew vaguely that he was some kind of writer and Sister Angela now confirmed that the fraud by which he gained access to the Mission was that he was gathering material for a book about the disenfranchised, destitute and often criminal classes that my father worked amongst. Certainly he had real creative talent. Often when his visits coincided with my bedtime, he would fill my head with marvellous stories of high adventure and wild excitement. These were a rare treat. Mother had no narrative gift and for father any story that did not come from the Bible was so much factitious frippery.

Curiously, it is dad's tales of Samson pulling down the temple, and the death of Jezebel, and the slaughter of the Benjamites, that remain with me while Uncle Harry's marvellous stories have all faded. But at the time I waited like a drug addict for the next instalment.

But the real evidence of Uncle Harry's powers of invention lies in the way he took in my father.

I think the trouble was – and Sister Angela confirmed this – that dad believed his life was directed by God. When he asked a question, God answered it with the result that in decision, he was incisive and in judgment absolute. And for the twenty years of his adult life, this had worked.

So when he asked God about Uncle Harry and he thought he heard God telling him *Harry's OK*, that was it. In my father's eyes friends, and enemies, were forever.

Thus when Uncle Harry came to him in a distracted state, he didn't hesitate. The pitch was that Harry's widowed mother who lived in the States was seriously ill and her only chance of survival lay in a new transplant procedure which only one hospital in the country could offer. Harry was on his way to see her now. He had realised his assets and managed to raise most of what was needed to pay for the procedure. But he was still short, and though he would have the rest in a fortnight's time when an investment bond matured, by then it might be too late.

I can remember Uncle Harry's distraction though its alleged cause was of course unknown to me till Sister Angela filled me in. My reason for remembering was purely selfish. It was May 19th, my sixth birthday, and I felt I ought to be the centre of everyone's attention.

Not that Harry's pretended agitation prevented him from bringing me a splendid present, a wooden locomotive big enough for me to straddle which made whooping noises just like the real thing when you pulled a cord.

It might have been this generosity, plus of course the three initials, that made my father rise to the bait.

'How much do you need?' he asked.

'Fifteen hundred pounds,' said Harry.

Now you should understand that the Mission finances were on a very hand-to-mouth basis. Only the big charities could afford to do national appeals in those days, and even they weren't yet the streamlined corporate machines for extracting money from the public they have since become. So the Mission relied very much on local charitable donations and there was rarely much in the kitty. But just the day before, a rather dodgy local businessman had decided to spring-clean his conscience by donating a couple of lakhs of rupees. He'd been on the brink for a week or so, and the proposed act of charity had almost turned into a bazaar haggle with my father as to how much, or rather how little would see him right with the Christian God. My father had probably entertained Uncle Harry with a description of the man's hesitations. Finally the previous day, a threat of police investigation had made the vacillating villain decide he needed help from all the deities available and he'd turned up with the cash which was now in the Mission safe.

How much cash?

In sterling, about fifteen hundred pounds.

Surprise.

To my father this was evidence of God's handiwork.

To Angela, with hindsight, it was evidence of Uncle Harry's brilliant opportunism.

Dad who had a key to the safe – why wouldn't he? – gave Harry the money on the promise that it would be paid within two weeks. Harry left that night with protestations of eternal gratitude and the cash. Probably his gratitude was genuine enough, or does a con man simply despise his mark? Whatever, Uncle Harry and the fifteen hundred pounds quickly vanished from Bombay and our lives, never to be seen again.

It evidently took my father a whole month to admit that neither was about to reappear. So that was it. A sting. Not a particularly big one in the grand scale of stings, though fifteen hundred was worth a lot more back then. The trustees of the Mission took it, if not in their stride, at least with the resigned philosophy of men long accustomed to dealing with humanity at its worst. They read Sister Angela's report and, judging that chances of the police catching up with Uncle Harry were remote and of recovering the money non-existent, they decided it was better to hush the whole thing up rather than risk putting off other potential benefactors.

So, all in all, an unpleasant experience which many men after the first shock might have treated as a rough but salutary lesson.

Not dad.

You see it undermined that supremely confident belief in his own God-backed judgment which had been the mainstay of his being these many years. If he'd got this wrong, what else had he got wrong? It pulled away or at least seriously damaged one of the mainstays of his faith.

Within a fortnight of recognising he'd been conned, a fortnight during which by Angela's account he worked like a man possessed, he went out on some errand of mercy one night and that was all that anyone saw of him till his body was pulled out of the Mazagon Docks a fortnight later. The fish had worked at it so much that cause of death could never be established. Suicide? I don't like to think so. I want to believe he just took a risk too far and paid the price.

All these memories rolled through my mind as I sat on that bus, and the violent jolt as the vehicle crashed to a halt at my stop took me by surprise and I almost dropped the package. As I stepped onto the pavement, despite the cool autumn air I was sweating. I had walked the route before while making my plans so I set off at a brisk pace towards my destination. Getting the package delivered without arousing suspicion was always going to be the hard part, but I'd worked out a method. It was not without risk, but apart from knocking at Uncle Harry's door and handing it over to whoever answered, I couldn't think of anything better.

Now the end was near, I felt only relief. Like I say, at the time of dad's death, I'd been a child, and was devastated like a child, and then had adapted like a child. Mother's death had hit me harder. And when I learned from Angela that Uncle Harry's chicanery had ultimately been the cause of both of them, I got very angry.

But I was only eighteen and at eighteen you're very angry at a lot of things. The main long term effect of learning the true facts was to finally make me dump the religious baggage I'd been dragging after me all my short life. I looked around and saw that the world was full of goodies and the only way to get your share was to go in hot pursuit.

So that's what I did, mainly in the sub-continent where I'd grown up, with occasional forays to Malaysia and the Antipodes.

Then with youth well behind me and my fortieth birthday lumbering ever closer, I got the chance to come and work in England.

Why not? After all I was English, that's what my passport said. So back I came to this cold damp unwelcoming country. After six months I was beginning to think it was a mistake. I reached the dreaded fortieth in May and in this dreadful climate, it felt more like fifty. I had to get out, but my contract bound me here at least till Christmas. By the end of September I was feeling desperate. I looked back at my life and it seemed a wasted journey, and I looked forward and saw only a road to nowhere. Then one evening as I travelled back to my lonely apartment, I picked up a bookshop magazine that someone had left on the train.

Now I'm not a reading man myself, and it was in a mood of cynical mockery that I glanced down a list of newsworthy forthcoming events in the literary calendar. Who the hell could really be interested in dinners to award prizes to novelists or the publication of a ghosted life of some idiot sportsman too thick to write his own biography?

Then something leapt out at me.

Notable Anniversaries
On October 31st, the distinguished crime writer and well known figure
on the London literary scene, Mr Harry Keating, best known as the
creator of the famous series of books featuring Inspector Ghote of the
Bombay Police, will be celebrating his eightieth birthday, to general
rejoicing.

Keating ... Bombay ... it couldn't be coincidence. This had to be Uncle Harry!

When I arrived at my station I popped into the bookshop.

Quite a lot of his books were on the shelves. I bought a couple and took them back to my flat.

I raced through them. The detailed knowledge of Bombay life and topography could only have come from a man who knew the city inside out. And when I looked at the author photo on the back cover of the book, I knew I was right.

He had attempted to change his appearance by growing a rather fine bushy beard, but there was no disguising that splendid hook nose.

Uncle Harry. The subtle serpent who had destroyed my family's personal paradise.

I thought of my dead parents. Then I thought of this man, approaching eighty, basking in the love of friends and family, acknowledging the applause of the world of literature. And suddenly it seemed to me that here was fate offering me a chance to do at least one meaningful act before I died! I told you that dad used to believe God spoke directly to him. It must be in the genes. For the first time in my life I heard a voice speak in my head.

Let him get to eighty. But make sure he gets no further!

God? I didn't think so. After all, I don't believe in God. I refuse to believe in God!

But as I approached Northumberland Place I found myself thinking, this is the real test, this is where things need to go absolutely smoothly or it's all in vain. If the Almighty really reckons this is a good idea, then the next few minutes will be a stroll in the park.

And a few minutes later, I knew I had the divine seal of approval.

The post van which I'd watched for five mornings on the trot the previous week showed up within the usual fifteen minute range. And about five minutes before it turned into Northumberland Place, it parked in its usual spot outside a block of flats. The driver got out with an armful of letters and packages and went into the building. On previous evidence he would be in there a good five minutes, sometimes longer. Perhaps someone gave him a cup of tea, or something. I moved forward, checked there was no-one watching me, opened the van door and leaned inside. There were several bags filled with mail. I pulled a couple of envelopes out of the nearest one. I was really on a divine providence roll, for they both bore Uncle Harry's name and address! As I'd anticipated from all I'd read about him, the world was so overcome with joy at the great man's eightieth birthday that his numerous gifts and greetings merited a separate bag.

I dropped my packet into it, closed the door and went on my way.

I thought of hanging around to listen for the bang, but there was no way of foretelling how long it would be before he opened his last present, and I didn't want to be picked up on CCTV loitering in the area. So I came home and waited for the news to come over the airwaves. *Famous writer killed by bomb on 80th birthday.* That must make the headlines surely?

Instead after nearly three hours just as I was getting really impatient, the doorbell rang, I opened the door, and there you were holding up your ID, and I knew things had gone seriously wrong.

But not so wrong, Detective Inspector Gospill, that you need to treat me as a terrorist! So why not get that out of the way, then perhaps you won't need to sit here any longer waiting for this Commander Grisewood who seems to be such a very bad time-keeper.

You could start off by telling me exactly what's happened. And where did it all go wrong?'

After my arrest, I'd been brought to Scotland Yard and left sitting in an interview room for well over an hour with a blank faced constable for company.

Finally DI Gospill reappeared, the constable left, and I waited for the interview to start. When nothing happened, I asked him what the hold-up was. He said that we were waiting for his superior, Commander Grisewood, who was returning from a conference in the Midlands. I said surely there must be enough senior officers sitting around on their thumbs in Scotland Yard for one of them to deal with the matter. What was so special about this man Grisewood anyway?

And that was when he told me, in a tone of some irritation not totally aimed at me, that Commander Grisewood was in charge of the unit which dealt with terrorist acts by British nationals and that for reasons best known to himself he wanted to conduct my interview personally to which end he had given strict orders that nothing was to be done until he arrived which should have been half an hour ago.

I might have been amused by the thought that Gospill was clearly missing a very important date because of this, but one word had caught all my attention and there was nothing amusing about it.

Terrorist!

That's what had launched me into my long defence and justification..

Gospill tried to interrupt me a couple of times, presumably to point out that the tape wasn't on and I'd have to say it all again. But once I got started, out it all came, and finally he sat back and listened. He never switched the recorder on but after a while he did start making notes.

When I finished he made no attempt to answer my concluding question but sat with furrowed brow in complete silence.

Then his phone rang.

He listened, said, 'Jesus H, Christ!' and switched off.

I said, 'What?'

'Accident on the motorway,' he said, not really in answer me but in accusation against some malevolent fate. 'Twenty mile tailback. Jesus!'

Then he picked his notes and without another word rose and left the room, to be replaced by the silent constable.

Another hour went by. I tried to provoke the constable to speech by requesting a drink. He went to the door and bellowed, 'Tea!' and that was all I got for my effort at social intercourse, except for a cup of tea so foul there'd have been a riot if it had been served in India. By the time Gospill returned I was feeling very irritated and ready to be extremely uncooperative.

'Now listen, inspector,' I said. 'Either you start answering my questions or you'll get no answers when you start asking yours.'

To my surprise he smiled.

'Certainly, Mr Lachrymate,' he said. 'Now let me see. I seem to recall the last question you asked me was, where did it all go wrong? Where indeed? My problem is knowing where to begin. You made more mistakes than Tony bloody Blair! But let's start with the biggest one of all, shall we? You clearly didn't stop for a moment and consider who it was you were dealing with!'

I said weakly, 'Sorry, I don't understand …'

'Clearly! Well, listen and learn. Now, I like watching detective series on the box as much as the next man, and I've read quite a lot of crime novels too, and I can tell you, from a professional point of view, they're mainly very ripe farmyard manure. What most of them writers know about real detection you could write on the end of a gnat's cock without arousing it.

'But this Mr Keating, he's different. He's been at it so long, there's stuff he could teach us!' So there he is, on his eightieth birthday, opening his prezzies, and he sees this package from India. Or at least it looks as if it's from India. Except that he can't see a Customs Declaration.

'Funny, he thinks. So he looks closer. Now he gets a lot of mail from India, does Mr Keating. He's big out there, it seems. And he's got lots of young relatives and friends who collect stamps so he takes note of the postage. So here's what his sharp detective mind gets puzzling over. He knows the Indian Post Office Speedpost rates to the UK are 675 rupees for the first 250 grams and 75 for each additional 250 grams. So why should a package which weighs about 1200 grams only have the basic 675 rupees postage on it?'

He paused. If his intention was to alleviate his own irritation by making me feel foolish, he was succeeding. Seeing this, he smiled malevolently and pressed home his advantage.

'But there was something else, something much more basic. The very first thing that attracted his keen detective eye was the fact that you got his name wrong.'

'I don't believe that,' I said indignantly. 'I'm absolutely sure I didn't misspell Keating.'

'No, you got that right,' he admitted. 'It was the initials you cocked up. It's H.R.F., not H.R.S.'

I checked my memory bank which is usually pretty reliable. It definitely printed out Uncle Harry's initials as H.R.S.

'Are you quite sure?' I asked.

'Dead sure. Look for yourself.'

From his pocket he produced one of the Keating paperbacks I'd bought and dropped it on the table.

He was quite right.

H.R.F. Keating.

'I don't know how I got that wrong,' I muttered disconsolately.

'I do,' he said smugly. 'As soon as we were alerted to this attempt on

Mr Keating's life, we contacted our colleagues in Mumbai to check if the postmark was genuine and to ask if they might be able to throw any light on the outrage. They got back to us about forty minutes ago. And it was the thing about the wrong initial that put them on to it. Very efficient record keepers, those boys. It seems that about thirty years ago, in 1973 to be precise, they had their eye on a suspected con-man who was using the name Keating. Our Mr Keating's name was already getting to be well known in literary circles over there, and this fellow was obvious trying to cash in on it by implying that he was the distinguished British crime writer, without actually saying it.

By using the famous three initials he put the idea into people's minds, but by changing the last one from F to S (which sounds very much the same if you say it fast) he put himself just out of reach of a charge of personation. Clever that. Of course from what you say, in your parents' case it probably didn't matter as they don't sound the types to be interested in anything so worldly as detective novels.'

'No, I'm pretty sure they thought Agatha Christi was a nun,' I burbled as I tried to come to terms with what he'd just said. 'I'm sorry, inspector, but are you telling me that H.R.F. Keating the writer isn't the same man as H.R.S. Keating, my Uncle Harry, the con man?'

'Of course he's not, you moron,' snapped Gospill. 'Do you think a man like Mr Keating would go around conning people out of money? In any case, what happened to your father happened in 1973, right? Well, it's on the record that our Mr Keating didn't make his first visit to India till a couple of years later!'

'No, that can't be true,' I objected. 'From the dates on those books of his, he'd been writing about Inspector Ghote for a whole decade by then. How could a man show such an intimate knowledge of a country without visiting it? Who's to say he didn't make an earlier trip before this official one he admits to?'

'You are,' he cried triumphantly. 'You mentioned it was your birthday, your sixth birthday, on the day that your father let Uncle Harry con him out of them rupees. And that would be the nineteenth of May, right?'

'Right.'

'Well, by one of those quirks of fate which protect good innocent people and put toe-rags like you in jail, Mr Keating who is a meticulous record keeper was able to tell us exactly where he was on that date. He was at a Crime Writers' Conference in Harrogate on the weekend of

Friday 18th to Sunday 20th May 1973, and he was able to give us the names of several other writers of unimpeachable character and unfaultable memory who were delighted to confirm what he said. So there it is. You picked on the wrong man, stupid!'

I was beginning to be seriously annoyed by his attitude. I mean, I might be a murder suspect, but there was no need to be rude!

And in any case, now I thought about it, I wasn't actually a murder suspect, was I? From the way he was talking, the attempt must certainly have failed.

For the sake of certainty, I continued to ignore his rudeness and asked, 'So Mr Keating is all right, is he? I mean, from what you say, the bomb didn't go off?'

'Yes, I'm glad to say Mr Keating is alive and well and at this very moment no doubt entertaining his friends at his birthday party with the story of the idiot who tried to blow him up. Of course, what he doesn't know yet because the bomb squad only confirmed it an hour ago was that he never was in any real danger. Don't know where you got your recipe from, Mr Lachrymate, but the experts say there was as much chance of your bomb going off as there is of Mr Keating's birthday cake blowing up when they light the candles!'

I suppose I should have felt relieved, but all I felt at that moment was an utter incompetent fool.

'So,' I said wretchedly, 'I got the wrong man and I made a dud bomb.'

Then cheering up a little because it's not in my nature to be down for long, I went on, 'But if my bomb wasn't really a bomb and no-one actually got hurt, I can't have committed a crime, can I? Certainly not a terrorist crime. In fact, nothing more than a slap on the wrist, ASBO, two weeks community service kind of crime!'

He laughed.

If Bloody Judge Jeffreys laughed as he was handing down sentences, it probably sounded like that.

'Never believe it, sunshine. We've got you bang to rights. That's another little error you made. A pro knows that you burn all the stuff that could be evidence against you as you go along. But with you we've got the lot. All them notes you made planning out the attack, the hard disk from your computer showing the terrorist sites you accessed, not forgetting the bomb itself. OK, it might be a Mickey Mouse device with as much chance of working as a chocolate teapot, but it's got your prints all over it.

This government may not have done much but they did pass some legislation that makes the intention as culpable as the deed. As the very old bishop said to the actress at the third time of asking, it's intent that counts, darling. Way people feel about terrorist threats these days, I'd say you're looking at ten years minimum.'

The shock nearly made me faint. *It's intent that counts.* That's what my dad used to say about sin. I never knew it applied in law too.

Ten years ... I'd be fifty by the time I got out ... I'd be an old man!

Gospill's phone rang.

He growled, 'Yeah?', then suddenly sat up to attention and said, 'Yes, Commander! I'm with him now, Commander. No, I haven't started the interrogation. Definitely not. Yes, I've collected all the physical evidence, and I've put it on your desk so that you can take a look at it before you start. Yes, sir, it's confirmed the device is quite safe. Commander, can I suggest ... yes ... what I meant was ... thank you, sir. See you soon. Look forward to it, sir. Goodbye.'

I got the impression the Commander had cut him off short and the last few phrases were for my benefit.

He caught me looking at him and snarled, 'That's happy hour over, Lachrymate. Commander Grisewood's just coming into the building and he'll be along here soon as he checks out the evidence bags on his desk. And that's when your troubles are really going to begin, believe me.'

I believed him. So much so that for the first time since I was a child, I found myself saying a little prayer to God. To dad's God. Something on the lines of, 'OK, God, after the crap you heaped on my mum and dad, you owe the Lachrymate family. I'd really appreciate it if you could come through now.'

My lips must have moved.

Gospill said, 'What?'

I said for the want of anything else to say, 'So how did you get on to me so quick?'

'Easy,' he said. 'That sermon title you pasted on the lid of the box. *Divine Retribution* by D.L.P. Lachrymate DD. Not many Lachrymates in London, believe me. In fact, you're the only one. With the same initials in a different order. And as soon as you opened the door, I saw you were our boy.'

He looked so smug and self satisfied, I offered another little prayer, this time for a thunderbolt to come down and destroy him.

At the same moment we both heard a distant bang, like a birthday balloon being punctured. Perhaps God had taken aim and missed.

For a moment nothing happened then came the distant shrill of an alarm bell.

Gospill sat looking at me for a moment then he rose.

'Wait there,' he commanded and went to the door.

He closed it firmly behind him but I didn't hear a lock click.

After a little while I stood up, went to the door and opened it a crack.

I could see Gospill at the end of the corridor. He was talking to a uniformed sergeant who had a phone to his ear.

I opened the door a little further so I could hear them.

'What's going on, sarge?' I heard Gospill ask.

'Not sure, sir. Just checking it out. Think there's been an explosion.'

'I gathered that!' snapped the DI. 'Where?'

'Hang about, sir, I'm getting something now … yes … yes … you're sure? so no evacuation … that's good … that's very good … OK, thanks.'

He switched off his phone and said to Gospill, 'It's OK, sir, Seems a device went off, and there's been a bit of a fire and quite a lot of damage, but it's all been confined to one room and no-one's hurt. So no panic and we can stay put. Reckon someone's head's going to roll though. Doesn't look good, letting a bomber get right into the heart of the Yard!'

A pause, then Gospill asked too casually, 'Whose room?'

Even at a distance I could here the tremolo in his voice.

'Not absolutely sure, sir, but they think it was Commander Grisewood's. Made a right mess from the sound of it. All those lovely water colours his missus did and he was so proud of, they'll have gone. Oh, someone's in real trouble, believe me!'

I closed the door quietly and went back to my seat.

Things were looking better. I'd been very stupid but there wasn't a commandment saying *Thou shalt not be stupid*. And now with nothing of what I'd said so far on tape, and all the physical evidence against me probably burning merrily away with the Commander's desk, all I needed to do was continue to look stupid and say nothing.

Thank you, dad's God. You came through!

The Ghote novel Gospill had produced still lay on the table.

I picked it up and looked at the author photo.

No longer could I see much resemblance to the plausible crook who all those years ago had touched on my family's life then gone on his way. Probably he'd been dead for years. Probably he died without ever having had had the slightest awareness of the consequences of his sordid little deception.

OK, there was a slight similarity in the nose of the man in the book photo, but the eyes were the giveaway. Uncle Harry's eyes had been restless, always looking round as if in search of something worth lifting, or the best escape route, or the approach of the Law.

The deep-set eyes of the man on the book jacket were steadfast and resolute, bright with intelligence. They gazed out at me as if they could actually see me and for the first time I felt the glow of a truly avuncular benevolence and affection.

I don't suppose I shall ever get to meet him, but I felt at that moment as if there were a strong and very real relationship between us.

I raised my cup in a toast. It was only that filthy cold tea, but in this respect too it's intent that counts.

And I said, 'Happy Birthday, Uncle Harry.'

THE CASE OF THE CURIOUS QUORUM

Colin Dexter

I reckon the spotlight's been on Harry long enough. What about shifting the focus a bit? Not lower (certainly not!); but to the side, perhaps, and on to someone never far away from HRFK.

I have been pretty deaf since my late twenties, and very deaf for the past two decades or so. Listening and understanding – and especially pretending to understand – has been a difficult old job for me; and the theatre, TV, radio, lectures, even the AGM of the Detection Club, have been a great trial.

Yet over the years there have been voices which in some strange way have been comparatively easy for me to follow – voices with a degree of lucid articulation and tone colour perfectly suited to my ever-waning hearing. And supreme of those voices for me was that of Harry's wife, Sheila, whose many radio performances were sheer delight for me.

Triply marked had been the white envelope, Personal Private Confidential; and after reading its contents, Inspector Lewis's forehead registered considerable puzzlement. Furthermore, after re-reading the two-page letter, such puzzlement appeared compounded with each succeeding paragraph.

53 Cumberland Place
London W2 5AS
0207 3736642
10 April 2006

Dear Inspector,
My only connection with you is via the late Chief Inspector Morse, who once came to talk at the Detection Club's annual jamboree at The Ritz. We had known of him because one of our number had written

accounts of some of his high-profile investigations, particularly into murder, a crime ever nourishing the life-blood of our distinguished membership. Morse spoke rather stiffly, we thought, although after his speech he was somewhat more relaxed with his plentiful supply of single-malt Scotch.

It was at that point he came to speak of you, and in a most complimentary fashion. Clearly you formed an illustrious partnership and I know you will have learnt a great deal from him about the solving of crime. Indeed, one of our cruciverbalist members wrote an anagrammatic clue about his rank and name: 'Person with crimes to resolve (9, 5)'. And it is in order to resolve a crime that I write to you now. Please, Inspector, consider the following facts.

I was myself, until a few years ago, the President of the Detection Club, during which time I naturally held an open cheque-book on the Club's account. I attended a committee meeting two weeks ago in the hotel lounge at Paddington Railway Station, taking with me the cheque-book and intending (belatedly) to surrender it to the current President. There were five of us there, all male: our President, myself, and three other senior members. The business was conducted expeditiously; and before repairing to the bar with my colleagues, I collected up my own material, consisting of a few personal letters, the minutes of the last meeting, the morning's agenda, my notes, etc, and stuffed them into my brief-case.

On returning home and taking out these papers, I found that the cheque-book was missing, although I clearly remember that I had forgotten (yet again) to hand it over. Was my memory playing cruel tricks on me? I am certain this was not the case. My brain cells have not let me down for many a decade, to be frank – eight of them almost! I did not allow this matter to disturb me unduly, but it should have done. Why? Because two days ago I learnt that a considerable amount had been withdrawn from the Club's account on a cheque from that very book, a cheque ostensibly signed by me.

My mind has been going round whirlygigwise this last forty-eight hours, since I am certain that it was one of us at the committee meeting who was responsible for the theft, as well as for the criminal usage made of it thereafter. One of those men is a complete monster – bit of one, anyway! One of them is an d – arrant robber! One of them ought to be roasted under a grill – he deserves it! Do I sound a little incoherent? So be it.

Where does this leave my reputation? I used to be called the Crime King – Father of Detection! And now I am left in much anger and despair as I see myself the victim of a person who is that most despicable thing – faker of cheques! He would need a cheque, of course, as well as a copy of my signature, which he could (did) practise. It may therefore be of some help to you to have a list of those members to whom, reasonably recently, I wrote and *signed* semi-official letters: Len Deighton, Anthony Lejeune, Simon Brett, Lionel Davidson, Peter Lovesey, James Melville, Reginald Hill, Robert Barnard, Jonathan Gash, John Malcolm, Ian Rankin, John Harvey, and Robert Goddard. All men. But it *was* a man. And the only reason I am not listing the names of those members attending the committee meeting must be fairly obvious. I find myself unwilling to point a finger at any specific person.

Now that Morse is no longer with us, I am looking to you, Inspector, feeling confident that after working for so many years with that remarkable man, some of his skills will have rubbed off on you. Yes, I am certain you can help me, if you will. Alas, the resolution of this sorry affair is urgent and imperative. We need no private eye on the assignment: let's have it under your eye – let's prove, between us, who this villain is!

Yours truly,
H.R.F. Keating

PS On looking through what I have written, I notice that the phrase 'I am certain' is used three times. Please know that what I tell you three times is true.

Later that morning, rather more quickly than Lewis, it had been Detective Sergeant Hathaway who read the letter.

'Puzzling, don't you think?' queried Lewis.

'Well, yes. I don't suppose everybody knows what a cruciver –'

'*I* know,' interrupted Lewis sharply. 'I worked with a chronic cruciverbalist for twenty years.'

'Sorry, sir.'

Lewis pointed to the letter. 'Don't you find it all a bit of a mystery?'

Hathaway hesitated. 'To be truthful, sir, I don't, no. It seems pretty clear that either it's all a joke or else this fellow's more than halfway round the twist.'

'Really? Doesn't read much like a joke to me. And I don't reckon the fellow's lost his marbles, either. I remember Morse talking about this Keating chap. Said he'd got one of the shrewdest brains in the business.'

'But no one could expect us to take this sort of stuff seriously. He's told us next to nothing –'

'Except his home address and his telephone number.'

'So?'

'So ring him up.'

'And say what?'

'You think of something. You're a university graduate, remember.'

Lewis pushed the telephone across the desk; and a few moments later both men could hear the words: 'This number is not receiving incoming calls. I repeat, this ...'

'Never mind,' said Lewis. 'The President – ring him.'

'How do we know –'

'The Club'll be on Google, man.'

Hathaway looked up from the screen a minute later. 'Fellow called Simon Brett. There's a telephone number, too.'

But again both men were shortly to hear an automated voice. 'The person you require is not available. Please try again later.'

Lewis grinned wryly. 'They all seem to be telling us next to nothing, just like you said.'

But his eyes remained steadfastly on the letter as he wondered what Morse would have thought in the same situation ...

Was still wondering a few minutes later when Hathaway interrupted whatever might have been going through the inspector's mind.

'You remember we're due out at ten o'clock, sir?'

'Yep. But just you get a copy of that letter and take it home with you tonight. You see, I'm beginning to think we may be wrong about it not telling us anything. If I'd said that to Morse, do you know what he would have said?'

Hathaway shook his head indifferently.

'He'd have said that fellow's probably told us *everything*.'

'Not told us how the guilty party sorted out the transfer of the money; not told us which bank it was or how much dosh was taken out ... Ridiculous, really, that letter!'

Lewis made no reply, and Hathaway continued:

'Tell you something else, sir. My old tutor once told me that if I kept on using as many exclamation marks in my essays as this fellow's done, he'd refuse to read 'em. And any writer who kept on using those long dashes all the time hadn't much idea on how to write the Queen's English.'

Again Lewis made no reply, but something – some small, vague idea – was struggling into birth in the depths of his brain as Hathaway spoke again.

'I wonder whether Morse would think he was much of a writer, our man here. Things like "arrant monster" –'

'Arrant *robber*,' corrected Lewis.

'Ugh! Would your old boss have written that?'

'Dunno. He never wrote much. And if he had to *read* a lot of bumph, it was always the commas he was most particular about.'

'Wish I'd known him, sir,' said Hathaway with gentle irony as he closed the door behind him.

'A lot of people would!' said Lewis quietly to himself in the empty room.

Hathaway had finished his supper, and was looking through the evening's fare in the *TV Times* when his mind drifted back to the Keating letter. He'd won himself no Brownie points when he'd misquoted 'arrant robber' from the letter. 'Robber' ... not all that different from 'Robert', was it? And Lewis's Christian name must surely be Robert, with his senior colleagues always calling him 'Robbie' ... He took out the letter from his jacket-pocket: yes, there it was, 'arrant robber'. What *was* this stupid bloody letter all about?

But suddenly something clicked in his mind and his eyes were gleaming as he wrote out the letters of 'arrant robber' and crossed them off one by one against a name on the members' list. One letter short, agreed. But there it was, immediately before those two words: the letter 'd –', which he'd assumed to have been the way some people who'd never sworn in their lives expressed 'damned'.

'Wow!'

It was 8.45 pm and he rang Lewis immediately. Almost. But if one of the four names was hidden there in the text, in 'anagrammatic' form (the very word Keating had used), yes! If one of the names was nestling there, what about the other three?

Lewis was watching the 10 o'clock News on BBC1 when Hathaway rang.

'I went through that letter line by line, sir, letter by letter, and I've found them, found all of them. All four: 'd – arrant robber' is an anagram of Robert Barnard. Next one: 'monster – bit' is an anagram of Simon Brett, our honourable President. Then we've got 'grill – he', not quite so clear, but it must be Reg Hill. The last, near the end, is 'eye – let's prove', which works out as Peter Lovesey. I checked all then other names on the list, but there's no one *else* lurking there. No one!'

After finally replacing the receiver, Hathaway felt an inner glow of forgivable pride. Yet he realised that four names didn't help all that much when the problem was deciding on just *one* name. But the other four would go down to three if the President (surely) could be shunted along with Caesar's wife into the above-suspicion bracket. Which left him with Barnard, Hill, Lovesey ...

When Hathaway had rung, Lewis had only just got back from hearing Papadopoulos conducting the Oxford Philomusica at the Sheldonian. He felt pleasingly tired, and would have welcomed an earlyish night. But he knew he would have little chance of sleep with Hathaway's clever findings topmost in his mind, and with the idea that had begun to dawn on him that morning still undeveloped an unexamined. Unusually for him, he was aware of a strongly competitive urge to come up with something that could complement his sergeant's discovery. But who *was* that one crook on the committee? One of the four – or perhaps one of the three – for he (like Hathaway) felt prepared to pass over the President.

Think, Lewis! Think!

How would Morse have looked at the letter? Probably looked at it the wrong way round, say? How do you do that, though? Read it back to front? Ridiculous. Read the PS before the salutation? But where had he read the PS's 'what I tell you three times is true' before? From Lewis Carroll, wasn't it? He located the words immediately in *The Oxford Book of Quotations*, from 'The Hunting of the Snark'. So what? What had *that* got to do with anything? Just a minute. Three suspects ... but Keating hadn't mentioned any single one of the suspects three times. He hadn't mentioned *anything* three times.

Or had he?

Well, even if he had, it was past midnight, and he was walking up the stairs when he remembered what Hathaway had said about punctuation. Morse had once told him that Oscar Wilde had spent two hours one morning looking through one of his poems before removing a comma; and then spent a further two hours the same afternoon before deciding to re-instate the said comma. And after standing motionless on the third step from the top of the staircase, Lewis finally retraced his steps downstairs and looked at the letter for the umpteenth time, now paying no attention whatsoever to what things were being said, but *how* they were being said.

And suddenly, in a flash, eureka.

Thank you, Hathaway! Thank you, Morse!

Lewis took a can of beer from the fridge and drank it before finally completing his ascent of the staircase. Hathaway may have fallen asleep that night with a look of deep satisfaction on his face, but with Lewis it was one bordering on the beatific.

It was three days after the aforementioned events that Mr H.R.F. Keating received a letter at his London address with the envelope marked 'Thames Valley Police HQ, Kidlington, Oxon'.

13 April 2006

Dear Mr Keating,

I write to thank you for your letter of 10 April 2006. You asked for my help.

Between us, my sergeant and I finally fathomed the anagrammatised names of the committee quorum; and leaving aside yourself, and giving the benefit of the doubt to your successor as President, we were left with three names from the list you gave us: Messrs Barnard, Hill, Lovesey. The clues were there and we spotted them. But this didn't get us very far. Which of the three men was it?

It was more difficult for us to spot the vital clue, but in reality you had made it quite complex. The three names we had, as well as the President's, were each signposted by two items of punctuation: the long em-dash and the exclamation mark. It was cleverly done. But we were a bit slow to notice the full implication of this. These two punctuation marks were each used, always closely together, not four times, but *seven* times, and used nowhere else in your letter. Why had our suspect-list suddenly grown so much longer? The reason eventually became clear. The name of the perpetrator of the 'crime' was *not included* in the list of club-members. But there he was, three times: 'frank – eight'; 'King – Father'; 'thing – faker'; and each of the three is a perfect anagram of the man responsible for the alleged theft of the chequebook: a man, as I say, who was not listed among the suspects. A man named H R F Keating. *You*, sir!

Only one problem remains, a more difficult one than that posed by your letter. Why on earth did you go in for all that rigmarole? What was the point of it? If, as we suspect, it was for sheer amusement, please remember that irresponsible wasting of police time is liable to be interpreted as a crime, and as such be liable for prosecution.

Please satisfy our curiosity about your motive, although we trust that your reply can be rather shorter than your original communication.

Yours sincerely
R Lewis
(Detective Inspector)

16 April 2006

Dear Inspector Lewis,
Thank you so much for your letter, and heartiest congratulations on your cleverness.

An American philanthropist was one of our guests when Morse spoke to us, and the two of them got on finely. This same person revisited us a month ago, and was naturally saddened to hear of Morse's death. He remembered Morse mentioning to him the work of the Police Service of Northern Ireland Benevolent Fund, and expressed the wish to make some donation to this fund. But on one specific condition. Together we amused ourselves by jointly composing the letter I originally sent to you. The agreed condition was that the police should prove themselves still able to exhibit the high degree of mental acumen and flexibility that Morse himself had shown with crossword puzzles, and with criminal cases.

It was also agreed that I should write to you to explain the whole thing should you have shown no interest, or have been utterly flummoxed by our letter. Had such been the case, we had decided to consider the merits of the next two charities on my friend's gift-list: the Salvation Army, and the Donkey Sanctuary. I rang him immediately on receipt of your wonderfully welcome letter, and a cheque is now on its transatlantic flight to the police charity: a cheque for $25,000. This I hope should compensate in some degree for the time you and your colleague spent on the puzzle, and perhaps you can now cross my own name off the list of those potentially liable for prosecution. It remains for me only to subscribe this letter, which I now do.

A right nerk? – Ay!
PS Please note the punctuation.

HEARING GHOTE

P.D. James

I have known Harry and Sheila for so many years that it isn't easy to remember when we first met. I have, however, a recollection that I was included in a dinner party they gave at which Nina Bawden and her husband were also guests, an event which was the beginning of a warm friendship between all four. Harry is one of the most versatile of writers and I have always particularly admired him as a brilliant critic of the detective story. No one is more knowledgeable about the history and achievements of the genre or celebrates them with more discernment, elegance and wit. On the occasion of this momentous birthday I hope he will do so for many years to come.

Today is my twenty-seventh birthday and by happy coincidence also the publication day of my first novel. It never occurred to me to begin my writing career with other than a detective story, largely due to my fascination with my detective hero, Inspector Ghote, and my admiration for his creator, H.R.F. Keating. My name on the book is shown as F.R.H. Charlcourt. The initials stand for Francis Raymond Hugo but, as Mr Keating chose to use his initials, so have I. I regard it as a happy augury that mine are the same, if in a different order. It was Inspector Ghote who helped to make me a detective novelist but there was something else which I doubt whether I share with Mr Keating. If interviewers – assuming I get any – ask me if I have ever witnessed a real-life murder, I shan't tell them the truth. But it was Ghote and that one unforgettable night when I saw a man done to death that has formed me as a man and as a writer.

I was twelve years old, in my last year at prep school in Surrey. My father was a diplomat, serving in India at the time, and my mother was with him. I am their only child. I spent my holidays with a widowed grandmother in her small manor house in Cornwall, and was due to go there for the Christmas of 1991. The rail journey was tedious, requiring two changes and there was no local station, so she usually sent her own car and driver to collect me. But this year was different. The headmaster called me into his study to explain.

'I've had a telephone call this morning from your grandmother, Charlcourt. It appears that her chauffeur is suffering from influenza and will be unable to fetch you. I've arranged for Saunders to drive you down to Cornwall in my personal car. I need Saunders until after lunch, so you will be leaving later than usual. Lady Charlcourt has kindly offered him a bed for the night. And Mr Michaelmas will be travelling with you. Lady Charlcourt has invited him to spend Christmas at the manor, but no doubt she has already written to you about that.'

She hadn't, but I didn't say so. My grandmother wasn't fond of children and tolerated me more from family feeling – I was, after all, like her only son, the necessary heir – than from any affection. She did her dutiful best each Christmas to see that I was kept reasonably happy and out of mischief. There was a sufficiency of toys appropriate to my sex and age purchased by her chauffeur on written suggestions from my mother, but there was no laughter, no young companionship, no Christmas decorations and no emotional warmth. I suspect that she would have much preferred to spend Christmas alone than with a bored, restless and discontented child and I don't blame her.

But as I closed the door of the headmaster's study my heart was heavy with resentment and disgust. Didn't she know anything about me or the school? Didn't she realise that the holiday would be boring enough without the sharp eyes and sarcastic tongue of Mike the Menace? He was easily the most unpopular master in the school, pedantic, over-strict and given to that biting sarcasm which boys find more difficult to bear than shouted insults. I know now that he was a brilliant teacher. It was to Mike the Menace that I largely owe my public school scholarship. Perhaps it was this knowledge and the fact that he had been at Balliol with my father which had prompted my grandmother's invitation. My father might even have written to suggest it. I was less surprised that Mr Michaelmas had accepted. The comfort and excellent food at the manor would be a welcome change from the Spartan living and institutional cooking at school.

The journey was as boring as I had expected. Instead of the elderly Hastings at the wheel, who would have let me sit in the front seat beside him and kept me happy with chat about my father's childhood, I was closeted in the back with a silent Mr Michaelmas. The glass partition between us and the driver was closed and all I could see was the back of the rigid uniform hat, which the headmaster always insisted Saunders should wear when acting as chauffeur, and his gloved hands on the wheel.

Saunders wasn't really a chauffeur but was required to drive the headmaster when his prestige demanded this addition to his status. For the rest of the time Saunders was part grounds-man, part odd-job man. His wife, frail, gentle-faced and looking as young as a girl, was matron at one of the three boarding houses. His son Timmy was a pupil at the school. Only later did I fully understand this curious arrangement. Saunders was what I had overheard one of the parents describe as 'a most superior type of man'. I never knew what personal misfortune had brought him to his job at the school. The headmaster got Saunders's and his wife's services cheaply by offering them accommodation and free education for their son. He probably paid them a pittance. If Saunders resented this we, the boys, never knew. We got used to seeing him about the grounds, tall, white-faced, dark-haired and, when not busy, playing always with a red yo-yo. None of us boys possessed one, and I wonder now whether that regular rise and fall, the feeling of the yo-yo in his hand, was a comfort, a defence against anxiety.

Timmy was an undersized, delicate, nervous child. He sat always at the back of the class, neglected and ignored. One of the boys, a more egregious snob than the rest of us, said, 'I don't see why we have to have that creep in class with us. That's not why my father pays the fees.' But the rest of us didn't mind one way or the other, and in Mike the Menace's class Timmy was a positive asset, diverting from the rest of us the terror of that sharp, sarcastic tongue. I don't think in Mr Michaelmas's case his cruelty had anything to do with snobbery, or even that he recognised his behaviour as cruel. He was simply unable to tolerate wasting his teaching skills on an unresponsive and unintelligent boy.

But none of this occupied my mind on the journey. Sitting well apart from Mr Michaelmas in the back of the car, I was sunk in a reverie of resentment and despair. I had brought with me a paperback and a slender torch and asked him if it would disturb him if I read. He replied, 'Read by all means, boy', and sank back into the collar of his heavy tweed coat.

I took out my copy of the Ghote novel *Dead on Time* and tried to concentrate on the small moving pool of light. Hours passed. We were driven through anonymous towns and villages and it was a relief from boredom to look out at brightly-lit streets, the decorated gaudy windows of the shops and the busy stream of late shoppers. In one village a little group of carol-singers accompanied by a brass band were jangling their collection-boxes. The sound followed us as we left the brightness behind. We seemed to be travelling through a dark eternity. I was, of course, familiar with the route, but Hastings normally liked to drive down in daylight. Now, sitting beside that silent figure in the gloom of the car and with blackness pressing against the windows like a heavy blanket, the journey seemed interminable. Then I sensed that we were climbing, and soon I could hear the distant rhythmic thudding of the sea. We must be on the coast road. It would not be long now. We should be at the manor in less than an hour.

And then Saunders slowed the car and bumped gently onto the grass verge. The car stopped. He pulled back the glass partition and said, 'I'm sorry, sir, I need to get out. Call of nature.'

The euphemism made me want to giggle. Mr Michaelmas hesitated for a moment, then said, 'In that case we'd better all get out.'

Saunders came round and punctiliously opened the door. We stepped out on to lumpy grass and into black darkness and the swirl of snow. The sea was no longer a background murmur but a crashing tumult of sound. I was at first aware of nothing but the snowflakes settling and drying on my cheeks, the two dark figures close to me, the utter blackness of the night and the keen salty tang of the sea. Then, as my eyes became accustomed to the darkness, I could see the shape of a huge rock to my left.

Mr Michaelmas said, 'Go behind that boulder, boy. Don't take long. And don't go wandering off.'

I stepped closer to the boulder, but not behind it, and the two figures moved out of sight, Mr Michaelmas walking straight ahead and Saunders to the right. A minute later, turning from the rock-face, I could see nothing, not the car or either of my companions. It would be wise to wait until one of them reappeared. I plunged my hands into my pockets and, almost without thinking, took out the torch and shone it over the headland. The beam of light was narrow but bright. And in that moment, instantaneously, I saw the act of murder.

Mr Michaelmas was standing very still about thirty feet away, a dark shape outlined against the lighter sky. Saunders must have moved up silently behind him on the thin carpet of snow. Now, in that second when the dark figures were caught in the beam, I saw Saunders violently lunge forward, arms outstretched, and seemed to feel in the small of my back the strength of that fatal push. Without a sound Mr Michaelmas disappeared from view. There had been two shadowy figures; now there was one.

Saunders knew that I had seen; how could he help it? The beam of light had been too late to stop the action, but now he turned and it shone full on his face. We were alone together on the headland. Curiously I felt absolutely no fear. I suppose that what I did feel was surprise. We moved towards each other almost like automata. I said, hearing the note of simple wonder in my voice, 'You pushed him over. You murdered him.'

He said, 'I did it for my son. God help me, I did it for Timmy.'

I stood for a moment silently regarding him, aware again of the soft liquid touch of the snow melting on my cheeks. I shone the torch down and saw that the two sets of footprints were already no more than faint smudges on the snow. Soon they would be obliterated under that white blanket.

I can recall that moment as clearly as if it were yesterday. My first thought was, what would Ghote do? But Ghote was a police officer, a man dedicated to justice. I couldn't expect him to help. But it did seem that I heard his voice. 'Make up your own mind, boy. But remember, there is no turning back.' And I did make up my mind. I was prompted by my dislike of Michaelmas, sympathy with the silent man at my side, but most of all by an intoxicating sense of power. I didn't recognise it at the time; it is, after all, an adult perception. But it was there all right. Oh yes, it was there.

Still without speaking, I turned and we walked back to the car together, almost companionably, as if nothing had happened, as if that third person was walking by our side. I have a memory, but perhaps I may be wrong, that at one place Saunders seemed to stumble and I held his arm to steady him.

When we reached the car he said, his voice dull and without hope, 'What are you going to do?'

'Nothing. What is there to do? He slipped and fell over the cliff. I switched my torch on and I saw it. He was standing half-bent, and then suddenly he swayed and fell forward. You weren't there and nor was I.'

He said nothing for a moment, and when he did speak, I had to strain my ears to hear. 'I planned it, God help me. I planned it, but it was fate. If it was meant to be, then it would be.'

The words meant little at the time, but later, when I was older, I think I understood what he was saying. It was one way, perhaps the necessary way, to absolve himself from responsibility. That push hadn't been the overwhelming impulse of the moment. He had planned the deed, had chosen the place and the time. He knew exactly what he meant to do. But so much had been outside his control. He couldn't be sure that Mr Michaelmas would want to leave the car, or that he would stand so conveniently close to the edge of the cliff. He couldn't be sure that the darkness would be so absolute or that I would stand sufficiently apart. And one thing had worked against him: he hadn't known about my torch. If the attempt had failed, would he have tried again? Who can know? It was one of the many questions I never asked him.

He opened the rear door for me, suddenly standing upright, a deferential chauffeur doing his job. As I got in I turned and said, 'We must stop at the first police station and let them know what's happened. Leave the talking to me. It's important to say that it was Mr Michaelmas, not you, who wanted to stop the car.'

I look back now with some disgust at my childish arrogance. The words had the force of a command. If he resented it he made so sign. And he did leave the talking to me, merely quietly confirming my story. I told it first at the police station in the small Cornish town which we reached within fifteen minutes. Memory is always disjointed, episodic. Some impulse of the mind presses the button and, like a colour transparency, the picture is suddenly thrown on to the screen, vivid, immobile, a glowing instant fixed in time between the long stretches of dark emptiness. At the police station I remember a tall lamp with the snowflakes swirling out of darkness to die like moths against the glass, a small room which smelt of cigarette smoke and coffee; a sergeant, huge, imperturbable, taking down the details, the heavy oilskin capes of the policemen as they stamped out to begin the search. I had decided precisely what I would say.

'Mr Michaelmas told Saunders to stop the car and we got out. He said it was a call of nature. I went to the left by a large boulder and Mr Michaelmas walked ahead. I waited but no one appeared. Then I switched on my torch and he was caught in the beam. I saw him stumble and fall. I called out to Saunders and he came walking from the direction of the car. I told him what had happened and we explored. We could just see footsteps to the edge of the cliff but they were getting very faint because of the snow. We still hung around for a minute or two and called out, but Mr Michaelmas didn't reappear. I didn't expect him to, the cliffs are very high there.'

The sergeant said, 'Hear anything, did you?'

I was tempted to say, 'Well I did think I heard one sharp cry, but I thought it could be a bird', but I resisted the temptation. Would there be a seagull flying in the darkness? Better to keep the story simple and stick to it. Ghote would have seen a number of men sent down for life because they had neglected that simple rule.

The sergeant said that he would organise a search but that there was little chance of finding any trace of Mr Michaelmas that night. They would have to wait for first light. He added, 'And if he went over where I think he did, we may not retrieve the body for weeks.' He took the phone numbers and addresses of my grandmother and the school, and let us go.

I have no clear memory of our arrival at the manor, perhaps because recollection is overshadowed by what happened next morning. Saunders, of course, breakfasted with the servants while I was in the dining room with my grandmother. We were still in the middle of our toast and marmalade when the maid announced that Superintendent Trevelyan had called with a woman police constable. My grandmother asked that they be shown into the library, and left the dining room immediately. Less than a quarter of an hour later I was summoned.

And now my memory is sharp and clear, every word remembered as if it were yesterday. My grandmother was sitting in a high-backed leather chair before the fire. It had only recently been lit and the room struck me as chill. The wood was still crackling and the coals hadn't yet caught fire. There was a large desk set in the middle of the room where my grandfather used to work and Superintendent Trevelyn was sitting behind it, the WPC at his side. In front of it stood Saunders, rigid as a soldier called before his commanding officer. And on the desk, precisely placed in front of the Superintendent, was the red yo-yo.

Saunders turned briefly as I entered and our eyes met and held for a second before he turned away. But I saw in his eyes – how could I not? – a wild mixture of fear and pleading. But Saunders needn't have worried: I had relished too much the power of that first decision, the heady satisfaction of being in control, to think of betraying him now. And how could I betray him? Wasn't I now his accomplice in guilt?

The superintendent was stern-faced. He said, 'I want you to listen to my questions very carefully and tell me the exact truth.'

My grandmother said, 'Charlcourts don't lie.'

He kept his eyes on me. 'Do you recognise this yo-yo?'

'I think so. If it's the same one.'

My grandmother broke in. 'It was found on the edge of the cliff where Mr Michaelmas fell. Saunders says that it isn't his. Is it yours?'

She shouldn't have spoken, of course. And I wondered at the time why the superintendent should have allowed her to be present at the interview. Later I realised that he had no choice; a juvenile could not be questioned without a responsible adult present. The superintendent's frown of displeasure at the intervention was so brief that I almost missed it. But I didn't miss it. I was alive, gloriously alive, to every nuance, every gesture.

I said, 'Saunders is telling the truth. It isn't his; it's mine. He gave it to me before we started out, while we were waiting for Mr Michaelmas.'

'Gave it to you? Why should he do that?' My grandmother's voice was sharp. I turned towards her.

'He said it was because I'd been kind to Timmy. Timmy is his son. The boys rag him rather.'

Superintendent Trevelyan's voice had changed. 'Was this yo-yo in your possession when Mr Michaelmas fell to his death?'

I looked him straight in the eyes. 'No, sir. Mr Michaelmas confiscated it during the journey. He saw me fiddling with it and asked me how I came by it. I told him and he took it from me. He said "Whatever the other boys may choose to do, a Charlcourt should know that pupils don't take presents from a servant".'

I had subconsciously mimicked Mr Michaelmas's dry sarcastic tone and the words came out with utterly convincing verisimilitude, but they probably would have believed me anyway. Why not? A Charlcourt doesn't lie.

The Superintendent asked, 'And what did Mr Michaelmas do with the yo-yo when he'd confiscated it?'

'He put it in his coat pocket.'

The Superintendent leant back in his chair and looked over at my grandmother. 'Well, that's plain enough. It's obvious what happened. He made some adjustment to his clothing ...'

He paused, perhaps feeling some delicacy, but my grandmother was made of tougher metal. She said, 'Perfectly plain. He walked away from Saunders and Francis, not realising that he was dangerously close to the cliff edge. He took off his gloves to undo his flies, and stuffed them in his pockets. When he pulled them out again the yo-yo dropped. He wouldn't hear it in the snow. Then, disorientated by the darkness, he took a step in the wrong direction, slipped and fell.'

And then I swear I did hear Ghote's voice. Did it mean he approved of my lies? No, I rejected that. Perhaps, knowing that it was too late for me to turn back now, he wanted to help. I heard his voice speaking the one word *fingerprints*. And then I remembered. They wouldn't have had time to take prints from the yo-yo yet. Didn't they need fingerprint experts for that?

In a sudden movement I stretched out my hand and grasped the yo-yo, and handed it to Saunders. I said, 'You can have it back, Saunders. It's unlucky. I don't want it now.'

Did I imagine the frown of displeasure on Superintendent Trevelyan's face? But he didn't speak, and nor did anyone else in the room. Saunders put the yo-yo in his pocket. After a second's pause the Superintendent turned to him. 'It was a stupid place to stop, at the edge of a cliff. Didn't you realise that?'

My grandmother replied. She said, 'Normally my chauffeur collects my grandson. The road is, of course, familiar to him.'

Saunders said, through lips almost as white as his face, 'Mr Michaelmas asked me to stop the car, sir.'

'Of course, of course, I realise that it wasn't your place to argue. You've made your statement. There's no reason for you to stay on here. You can go back to the school and your duties. You'll be needed for the inquest, but that probably won't be for some time. We haven't found the body yet. And pull yourself together, man. It wasn't your fault. I suppose by not saying at once that you'd given the yo-yo to the boy you were trying to protect him. It was quite unnecessary. You should have told the whole truth, just as it happened. Concealing facts always leads to trouble. Remember that in future.'

Saunders said, 'Yes sir. Thank you, sir,' turned quietly and left.

When the door had closed behind him, Superintendent Trevelyan got up from his chair and moved over to the fire, standing with his back to it, rocking gently on his heels and looking down at my grandmother. They seemed to have forgotten my presence. I moved over to the door and stood there quietly beside it, but I didn't leave.

The Superintendent said, 'I didn't want to mention it while Saunders was here, but you don't think there's any possibility that he jumped?'

It was then that I realised that Superintendent Trevelyan and my grandmother knew each other. But then, was there anyone in a position of authority in that part of Cornwall that she didn't know?

Her voice was calm. 'Suicide? It did cross my mind. It was odd that he told Francis to go over to the boulder and he walked on into the darkness alone.'

The Superintendent said, 'A natural wish for privacy, perhaps.'

'I suppose so.' She paused, then went on, 'He lost his wife and child, you know. Killed in a car crash soon after they married. He was driving at the time. He never got over it. I don't think anything mattered to him after that, except perhaps his teaching. My son says that he was one of the most brilliant men of his year at Oxford. Everyone predicted a shining academic career for him, and what did he end up doing? Stuck in a prep school wasting his talent on small boys. Perhaps he saw it as some kind of penance.'

'No relations?'

'Not as far as I know.'

The Superintendent went on, 'I won't raise the possibility of suicide at the inquest, of course. Unfair to his memory. And there isn't a shred of proof. Accidental death is far more likely. It will be a loss for the school, of course. Was he popular with the boys?'

My grandmother said, 'I shouldn't think so. Highly unlikely, I would have said. They're all barbarians at that age.'

They stood for a moment in silence. Still unnoticed, I slipped out of the door and closed it quietly behind me.

I began to grow up during that Christmas week. I realised for the first time the intoxication of power, the exhilaration of feeling in control of people and events, the insidious satisfaction of patronage. And I learnt another lesson, best expressed by Henry James: *Never believe that you know the last thing about any human heart.* Who would have believed that Mr Michaelmas had once been a devoted father, a loving husband? I like to believe that the knowledge made me a better person, a more compassionate writer, but I'm not sure. The essential self is fixed well before the thirteenth birthday. It may be influenced by experience but it is seldom changed.

Saunders and I never spoke about the murder again, not even when we attended the inquest together and heard the expected verdict of accidental death. Back at school we hardly saw each other; after all, I was a pupil, he a servant. In boyhood I shared the snobbery of my caste. And what Saunders and I shared was a secret, not a friendship, not a life. But I would occasionally watch him pacing the side of the rugger field, his hands twitching as if there was something he missed.

And did it answer? A moralist, I suppose, would expect us both to be racked with guilt and the new master to be worse than Mr Michaelmas. But he wasn't. The headmaster's wife was not without influence and I can imagine her saying, 'He was a wonderful teacher, of course, but not popular with the boys. Perhaps, dear, you could find someone a little gentler – and a man we don't have to feed during the holidays.'

So Mr Wainwright came, a nervous, newly-qualified teacher. He didn't torment us, but we tormented him. A boys' prep school, after all, is a microcosm of the world outside. But he took trouble with Timmy, giving him special attention, perhaps because Timmy was the only boy who didn't bully him. And Timmy blossomed under his care and patience. He hadn't been stupid, only terrified.

And the murder answered in another way – or I suppose you could argue that it did. I lost touch with Timmy Saunders after I left prep school but met him briefly when we were both at Oxford. We were at different colleges and had nothing in common except those prep school days, so made no attempt to get in touch again. I believe he went into teaching. He did, however, tell me that his father had died five years previously from cancer. He, too, had passed out of my life. Back at school after the murder, before I left for my public school, we saw each other every day but met as strangers. But one thing was different: I never again saw Saunders playing with his yo-yo. Yet strangely, when I think of him – which isn't often – I see him walking slowly across the school grounds, his head bent, the red yo-yo jerking from his hand and flicking up and down, a bright bauble shining in the sun.

KALI IN KENSINGTON GARDENS

Liza Cody

The Kali story was inspired by Harry's wonderful Ghote series which sets a standard for humanity and humour I can't hope to reach.

In Hindu mythology, Kali is the destructive, vengeful, black-faced incarnation of the mother goddess. In one of the myths she has an epic battle with the demon Raktabija – Rak in my story. Sara S. represents Sarasvati who is a goddess revered by all types of artist and especially those concerned with the spoken word. Harvey is simply 'a great companion' – a characteristic he shares with Harry. The similarity ends there because Harvey isn't very bright whereas Harry most definitely is.

Harry was at the very first Crime Writers' Association meeting I ever attended. I'd been told at the door that I was on the short-list for the John Creasey Memorial Prize, so by the time I was introduced to the great man I was over-excited. When he too congratulated me I said, 'Who do I have to suck up to to win the thing?' He ducked his head, smiled that sweet unreadable smile and replied, 'Well, that'd be me, actually.'

'Are you mugging me?' I always thought when this moment came, if this moment ever came, I'd be scared. I wasn't. I was insulted. Outraged.

'I'm robbing you.' She corrected me with bored contempt. 'Gimme your purse and your phone, oh and shut up.'

I hit her with my sandwiches. And woke up on a bench with a tanned, blond rollerblader bending over me, brow creased with concern.

'You okay?' He felt for my pulse in all the wrong places. I sat up groggily. My jaw burned and my teeth wobbled. There was a growing, soggy lump on the back of my head.

'You went down like a tree in a hurricane. He must've packed one helluva wallop.' He helped me to a bench dedicated to 'Harvey – a great companion.'

74

'She,' I said.

'She? Wow. Good punch. No, look sorry. I called the cops anyway.'

Like being whacked by a woman didn't count. I said, 'Go home. I'll be all right now.'

'The cops say I'm a witness. I'm supposed to wait.'

Some witness, I thought. Can't tell a guy from a girl – fat lot of good you'll be.

'Erm, was she black?' The rollerblader looked uncomfortable enough to be a tactful, if unobservant, lad.

'Indigo,' I said. 'Tattoos all over her face.'

We sat in silence then. It was a beautiful winter afternoon: just right for the last picnic of the year. I looked around. 'Oh bugger.'

'What?'

'She stole my sandwiches. Bloody cheek!' There was painful drumming at the base of my skull and spasms of nausea. A nice salt beef, chilli and dill pickle sandwich might have settled my stomach or even my nerves.

'Which way did she go?' I asked my handsome rescuer.

He pointed towards the setting sun. I staggered to my feet.

'You can't leave.' He was shocked. 'The cops will be totally pissed with you.'

'I'm not too pleased with the cops. Where are they?'

The rollerblader looked up and down the avenue. It was remarkably empty of officers of the law. 'Where are you going?'

I limped southwards. 'I'm following a trail of breadcrumbs.'

'You should sit down,' he said. 'You were unconscious for one minute, forty seconds.' He was trying to be accurate now. Too late.

I said 'No one can eat my sandwiches but me.'

'Shouldn't you be more worried about your purse?' He was tagging along, crunching laboriously through dead leaves. A rollerblader trying to walk on grass is a heroic sight. But not a sensible one.

'Salt beef, chilli and pickle? Seriously, no one eats my sandwiches but me.'

One minute you are walking past the Italian fountains observing with amusement the statue of Jenner with a book in one hand and a seagull on his bonce, and the next you've been violently floored by an indigo-faced thuggette.

'Cobwebs,' I said, remembering suddenly. 'Cobwebs and skulls.' I stopped. 'The design on her face was one dense spider's web and there were skulls tattooed round her throat like a necklace.'

My companion said. 'Then she's unmistakable. All you have to do is describe her to the cops. You don't have to find her yourself. Not at your age.'

'Oops,' he added, catching what was undoubtedly my most incensed expression. 'Not that you aren't great for your age … whatever that is – but she was big, strong and fast. And violent. Look, I know about girl gangs – they scared the brown stuff out of us boys at school. They don't seem to have any rules, see.'

'I don't see any gang,' I said. 'What rules? Are you talking about articles of war? The Geneva Convention? Those sophistries that are supposed to make brutality more palatable?'

'A pacifist as well,' he muttered. 'Could today be any more perfect?'

'As well as what?'

'I don't mean to be rude, and please don't jump down my throat, but you're a woman of a certain age, and you obviously don't dress to impress …'

'I dress to distress.'

'And you're, forgive me, gobby, and you can't cook for shit …'

'I have an ex-husband who knows less about me than you do,' I said.

'So most likely you're a feminist as well as a pacifist,' he went on as if I hadn't spoken.

'And you're young enough to make all that sound like an insult.' I looked up and saw three crows watching us from the bare, tip-tilted branch of a chestnut tree. 'Also you're trying to walk on grass with your skates on so you probably aren't in further education …' I broke off, thinking, Why do I feel the need to retaliate? How many guys under thirty would stop to help an old pacifist feminist who can't cook for shit? I might have met the only one in Kensington Gardens.

'Harvey,' I said, 'you're right, I'm gobby. I'm sorry.'

'Who's Harvey?'

'A great companion', I told him. 'You should learn to read the backs of park benches. They're as good as books for feeding the imagination.'

Three crows screamed and rose as one, beating heavy black wings in the delicate blue air. A grey squirrel sat up, alarmed, and folded demure hands over her belly. I watched. The crows flew west and then circled twice. Beneath them was the little stone-built folly known as the Queen's

Temple. They circled once more over the cupola and then dived behind it. After a few seconds they rose again, bickering loudly, competing. Then without warning they shrieked and parted, each flying off at top speed in a different direction.

I pointed. 'My sandwiches?' I suggested.

'Well, bugger off!' Harvey said. 'Whatever they picked up, they couldn't get rid of it fast enough.'

'Definitely my sandwiches then,' I said, starting off towards the temple. 'If you're coming, Harvey, for goodness sake use one of the paths.'

The setting sun was in my eyes, dazzling me. It reminded me that this was the shortest day and also the day of the longest shadows – they striped the green grass like the hide of a tiger. I squinted along the shadows and saw dogs as tall as ponies sparring clumsily. I saw walkers, and mothers with children. I saw another rollerblader and two skateboarders. But I did not see an indigo-coloured thuggette fleeing with my wallet and phone.

From the tiny temple came the sound of someone playing the banjo. I heard a high voice singing, 'It's not too far to India, the tour bus leaves at seven ...'

The temple is only three small connecting rooms with no doors, all facing the rising sun. Like any other public place in every city in this country it smelled strongly of male pee and was decorated with graffiti and gang tags. The most aggressive piece of writing proclaimed, 'Kali Rocks & Rules.'

Sitting cross-legged on a square of cardboard was a girl, no more than eleven or twelve years of age. She was singing, 'And every nutter gets off at Calcutta ...' The surrounding stone made her weedy young voice ring. She stopped when she saw me. A tattered blue beanie was pulled down over dirty hair and she regarded me with bright rodent eyes.

'Spare a little change?' she suggested hopefully, 'for a cup of tea and a sandwich.'

I said, 'Someone just stole my purse so I'm flat broke. She also stole my sandwiches so I can't give you anything to eat either.'

'They was your ...' She stopped abruptly, glancing shiftily from left to right. There was a crumb of pumpernickel visible on her chin. I was in no doubt now that this malnourished child had received and rejected my stolen snack.

'They was indeed mine,' I told her. 'Where did she go?'

'Who?'

'You know who. The girl with the big tats.'

'Dunno whachoo talking about.' But her eyes shifted automatically towards the wall which read 'Kali Rocks & Rules.'

I said, 'The cops are coming. Tell me which way she went and maybe I won't bring them here to you.'

The young girl laughed. It was not the politest sound I'd ever heard. She said, 'Whachoo gonna do then, old lady? You wind her up, she'll chop you down and lick your blood off of the floor. You don't want to meet her when she's off on one.'

'Your problem is that if I don't meet her I become your problem.'

Harvey arrived then, out of breath. He was wearing trainers and his blades protruded from his backpack.

'Have you found her?' He was as sharp as a sofa cushion, was Harvey.

'Yes,' I said. 'This girl assaulted me and took my purse and phone. Call the cops, Harvey. Tell them it was robbery with violence and we've caught the perpetrator.'

'You lying old cow!' protested the girl with the banjo. 'I never touched you. I never even seen you before. Don't you call nobody,' she pleaded with Harvey who had pulled his phone out of his pocket. 'Don't listen to her. She's picking on me cos I won't tell her ...'

'Won't tell her what?'

'She won't tell me where Kali went,' I said.

'I swear I never even said her name.' The girl squeaked like a mouse. Harvey crouched down next to her.

'Why not?' he asked gently. The girl stared at him. His fair hair seemed to glow in the dying winter light. He was a stunning lad, now I came to look at him properly. And much nicer than I was.

The girl obviously thought so because she leaned towards him confidingly. 'I can't say nothing,' she whispered. 'She protects me.'

'Who are you?' Harvey asked. 'Who does she protect you from?'

'From people who hit me.' She turned huge eyes towards him. 'They call me Sara S.'

'Who hits you?' Harvey's handsome brow was furrowed with sympathy.

'She does,' the girl said simply, glancing at Kali's writing.

I laughed and my headache went away. 'The classic protection racket,' I said. 'Give me your lunch money or I'll hit you. Only in my case she took my lunch and she hit me.'

'You don't understand,' the girl said. 'Everyone used to hit me till she came along. Now no one does, not even me bruvvers.'

I looked at Harvey and Harvey looked at me. He shrugged and we walked out of the temple into the dusky park. There was still no sight of any cops. We exchanged addresses, and Harvey walked away. He looked a lot cuter on rollerblades.

I waited for a few minutes, listening. But the girl did not start singing. All I could hear was the sound of chainsaws as the park tree-surgeons lopped off dead branches.

The next day was Friday and I went to see my friend Min. The neighbourhood is infected with a creeping rash of cheap hotels. Min's house is one of the last to remain private but someone has bought the freehold and Min is worried.

She buzzed me in and I found the new landlord's son in the hall doing semi press-ups against the wall. He didn't move when I said, 'Excuse me.' I had to step over his feet.

He said, 'Hey lady, wait till I finish.'

I said, 'Maybe you should do your exercises at a gym.'

He said, 'Maybe you should suck dick.'

Upstairs, Min said, 'That's Rak – I wouldn't suck an ice-lolly in a heat wave if he gave it to me. He's a hooligan and a mental midget.'

So I told her about Kali in the park because a trouble shared is a trouble doubled and we were both at the mercy of young toughs.

'The police weren't interested,' I said.

'Nobody's interested in Rak either,' Min said. 'But he's such an intimidating presence that Edith and Stephen downstairs have already moved out. We were all going to stick together but what can you do when people get scared?'

'I had to stop my credit card,' I told Min, 'and you know what, it was used within fifteen minutes of being stolen.'

'Where?' Min asked.

'The supermarket. She spent a small fortune on food – enough to feed a very large family.'

'How odd.' Min's kindly eyes creased in puzzlement. 'From your description I'd have thought her more likely to buy a Harley Davidson or a load of Gangsta music.'

'I was surprised too. But buying food for a family doesn't turn her into a good person. She robbed me and she hit me.'

Min got up and poured more tea for both of us. Her teacups are a harlequin set of pieces she inherited by being the last survivor of her family. Her furniture's like that too: it's good but mismatched and there's too much of it. She was hoping she would never have to move again, but that hope is looking more and more forlorn.

I said, 'We're giving up far too much territory to bullies. You don't want to leave your flat, and I want to keep on walking in Kensington Gardens without fear of violence.'

Min has a wayward streak which I've always found entertaining. She handed me a steaming cup of tea and mused, 'If there were a fight between your Kali and my Rak who would you bet on?'

I pictured the hulking tattooed mass of Kali and remembered the ferocious speed with which she retaliated when I hit her with my lunch. But Rak was an arrogant young man with a lot of muscle. I shook my head. 'What a good thought,' I said.

Min took a ladylike sip from her floral patterned cup and said, 'They could beat the shit out of each other and leave us alone.' She is a translator of novels from Spanish to English. I used to restore antique clocks and watches before my fingers got too stiff.

By today's standards I suppose you could call us thinkers.

I said, 'It shouldn't be beyond us to arrange something of the sort.'

'Beware of old broads with brains.' Min smiled at me and I smiled back. Like a lot of people who work alone I'm attracted to a good conspiracy.

In the late afternoon I watched the Queen's Temple from a park bench fifty yards away. I wore my ex-husband's old raincoat which made me look poor, defeated and undeserving of attention from thuggettes. No one came or went. No song hung suspended on the cold air. An odd couple in white coats took a photo of the unnecessary little building, but apart from that and the furtive raids of squirrels through the dead leaves all was still and silent.

Just before sundown I crossed the grass myself and went into the temple. I took a can of scarlet spray paint out of my plastic bag, and in the room where the girl with the banjo had sat I wrote, 'Rak Rules, Kali Cowers.' Next, in girlie pink, I sprayed, 'Kali Luvs Rak 3-30 Monday xxx.' Then I hurried away for tea and toast at Min's.

'I was a bit more direct,' she said, proudly handing me a single sheet of typed paper and a plateful of hot buttered toast.

The toast was delicious and the writing on the paper was libellous. Both were just what I'd hoped for.

Min wrote, 'Theres a girl who plays banjo says you got good pecs and do it for money. She says you'll do that filthy thing with a soupspoon your famous for and it'll only cost a fiver. I like a guy whoos dirty and cheep. Meet me at Queens temple in Kensington Gardens 3.30 pm Monday. Roger.'

'Roger?' I said.

'I don't approve of anonymous letters.' Min took a prim nibble from her toast. 'If you're still up for it, put your stake money under the candlestick.'

'Ten pounds on Kali to win.' I flourished my money.

'Ten pounds on Rak. Winner buys supper.'

On my way out of the house I thumb tacked Min's letter to the front door where anyone could see it and even Rak couldn't miss it.

The next day was Monday. Min and I sat on a park bench watching the Queen's Temple. Min brought the sandwiches – tuna and cucumber; I brought the thermos. Soon we were surrounded by indigent pigeons and squirrels. Even the crows looked approvingly at Min's crusts. I have to admit she has a way with food.

It was very cold and the sky was white with unshed snow. From the temple came the chug-chug-chug of a banjo, and a thin young voice sang, 'You warned me, never linger when your eyes are red with anger ...' Then the music was interrupted by the sound of a motor. A green van with City Suburban Tree Surgeons written on its side drove across the grass to a dead tree. Three men got out. Two of them cordoned off an area round the tree with orange tape. The third began to unload equipment.

There was no sign of Kali. Min looked at her watch and said, 'What happens if she doesn't show up and the kid with the banjo has to face Rak alone?'

'That'll teach her not to pay protection, won't it? She'll just have to get strong and look after herself.' I caught Min's expression and added, 'We'll intervene, of course. I brought my ball-peen hammer.'

I looked up at a sudden noise and there was Harvey rolling towards us on a skateboard. He stopped when he saw us, tipping his board back and hopping gracefully to the ground. Automatically, Min raised a hand to fluff her hair. I couldn't blame her – Harvey looked like a young god.

He said, 'Aren't you scared to come here again?'

'I brought a friend,' I said, and introduced him to Min.

'Sit with us and have a sandwich,' Min said.

'Who made them?' he asked suspiciously.

Min giggled like a girl and I suppressed an urge to wring her neck. 'Don't let us keep you,' I said. But he sat and munched a sandwich with obvious pleasure.

He said, 'I came to see if Sara S. was okay.' He gestured towards the song and its banjo accompaniment. 'I don't suppose you have a spare sandwich for her, do you? She's always hungry.'

I could see Min struggling between the twin snares of wishing to please and wanting to keep Harvey by her side. I was horrified, because there, striding towards the temple, pectorals bulging under a thin t-shirt, was Rak in a foul temper. I couldn't let Harvey take a sandwich to Sara S.

'Are you her protector now?' I asked rudely. 'How much does she pay you?'

'Excuse me?' Harvey said.

Min looked shocked. 'Of course you can take food to the kid.'

I stood up between Harvey and the temple. 'She receives stolen goods,' I said, 'she didn't give a toss about Kali hitting me.'

'She's just a kid,' Harvey protested. 'She was scared.'

Min, the traitor, gave me a defiant look and handed the rest of the sandwiches to Harvey. He kissed her on the cheek. A simple 'thank you' would have done just as well. Min blushed and cooed. I could've used my ball-peen on both of them.

As Harvey started off towards the temple, Rak disappeared inside.

'You idiot, Min,' I hissed, 'you could get him killed. Rak's here.'

'Why didn't you say?' We went in pursuit.

Twin roars split the winter air.

The first was a chainsaw. The other was Kali erupting out of the temple in a full shoulder-charge. Sheer momentum forced Rak backwards. He was a big, bullisome man but he couldn't match Kali for ferocity. She was terrifying – indigo skin making her primitive and tribal, eyes staring and insane.

Rak rained blows on her face and shoulders but she ignored them. Some found their mark for her lips and teeth turned scarlet with blood.

Harvey stopped, stunned. Min said, 'That girl hit you? And you survived?'

Harvey sprinted to the temple.

'Don't!' Min cried. 'You'll get hurt.'

I wrenched my hammer out of my handbag and followed.

'Wait for me,' Min wailed. It's all very well for her to make a decent sandwich and receive kisses from handsome blond guys but she doesn't have a clue about action. 'Use your phone,' I called over my shoulder. The police didn't come the first time so they were hardly likely to come now, but it'd keep Min out of trouble for a while.

Kali grabbed and hauled Rak towards her. She wound her arms around him so that he couldn't raise his hands to hit. She ran him backwards into the dead tree and began to ram his head rhythmically against the trunk.

The tree surgeons scattered out of her way.

'Stop her!' Sara S. screamed as she came running out of the temple. 'Stop her or she'll kill him.'

We all rushed forward. One of the tree surgeons caught at Kali's arm but she brushed him off like a dead twig and he went spinning to the ground.

She snarled, 'This is Kali cowering!' Bash. 'This is how much I love you!' Whack.

'Kali!' Sara S. shrieked. 'Stop!' She pleaded with us, 'Stop her. She goes mad. She can't stop herself.'

Rak crumpled to the ground. Kali whirled and with one hand snatched the chainsaw out of a tree surgeon's grasp. The chain howled as she held it poised over Rak's throat.

We all yelled at once. But she didn't hear us. Blood was in her eyes, her mouth, her ears.

My plan had careened out of control. We were about to see Kali tear Rak's head off.

And then Harvey, blond hair flying, threw himself on Rak's body. Clear blue eyes looked straight into Kali's. He said only one word.

I could hear nothing over the screams and the chainsaw. But Kali heard him. She stood stock still and for a second it looked as if she would kill Harvey too.

He spoke again, and I could almost see the blood-rage drain out of her like water from a bottle.

She tossed the chainsaw aside and reached down to help Harvey up. She looked almost human.

I was astonished and relieved. But I couldn't help myself: I was disappointed too. Under the blood-rage she had been terrifying. But she'd been magnificent as well.

Now she turned and ran. Huge, fast, she loped away from what was nearly a terrible murder and disappeared into the glare of the setting sun.

The rest of us gathered, shaken, around Rak's body.

'He's alive,' Harvey told us, and Sara S. sighed and smiled through her tears.

'An ambulance is coming,' Min said. She drew me away from the group. 'This is our fault,' she said. 'We made this happen. I wrote it in a letter; you wrote it on a wall – the power of words. If Harvey hadn't stopped her Rak would be headless.'

'A word stopped that too,' I said. 'One word.'

'I couldn't hear a thing,' Min said.

Harvey came over to ask if we were all right.

I said, 'You were incredibly brave and incredibly stupid. What did you say to her?'

'Nothing.' Harvey shook his beautiful hair out of his eyes and looked embarrassed.

'Oh God.' Min looked ill. 'We could've got you killed.'

'What do you mean?' Harvey stared at her in surprise.

'Timing,' I said hurriedly. 'She gave you a sandwich to take to your friend, which meant you were at the temple when Kali attacked Rak.'

'Who's Rak?'

'Oh dear,' Min said, her lip trembling.

'Yer busted.' Sara S. had crept up unnoticed and was standing close to Harvey. 'You old witch.' She gave me a knowing malevolent glance. 'Couldn't deal with Kali yerself so you set her up. She went critical when she saw what you wrote.'

Harvey's steady blue gaze fixed on me and made me blush. 'You should be ashamed of yourself.'

Min, I noticed, did not rush to my defence or explain her part in the near massacre. As I stomped away I said, 'You owe me supper. Your boy lost.'

Let her explain the bet to Harvey, I thought angrily. But she was too busy batting her greying eyelashes at him to own up.

I wasn't as disappointed with Min as I was with Kali. Min has a well-known weakness for handsome men. Kali, on the other hand, in attack, looked like a warrior: female strength in full flow. I couldn't help being thrilled by it when it was directed at someone other than me.

But one word from a gorgeous guy and she chucked down her weapon and ran away, tamed.

What was the one word? Obviously I couldn't hear it, but I had been watching Harvey closely, and from where I stood it looked as if his mouth formed the word 'Please'.

PERFIDIOUS ALBION

Catherine Aird

My most memorable encounter with Harry was in Gravesend Cemetery. No, we weren't auditioning for Great Expectations, *but being present, Harry as Chairman of the Crime Writers' Association and myself as a local author, when the grave of R. Austin Freeman was being marked for the first time with a tombstone by the R. Austin Freeman Society of America. The good doctor had in fact died in 1943, pre-deceased by both his wife and son – this, and the fact that there was a war on, had led to the grave being unmarked until then.*

Much, much later when I was on holiday in deepest rural France I happened on a three-day old English newspaper. Falling upon this with the enthusiasm of a Robinson Crusoe sighting rescue, I started to try to complete the crossword. Before I could do so, I came across a clue – based on a pun on a world famous fly-killer about an equally famous crime writer – to which there was only one possible answer and that was – oh, you've guessed – Keating.

Later still, when rootling about in a second-hand bookshop (very much my own favourite form of entertainment) I came across for a few pence a street map of Bombay – or was it Calcutta? I sent this to Harry only to learn that he found such establishments deeply dispiriting.

About Gravesend Cemetery I cannot write, about second-hand bookshops I must not. I have therefore settled for rural France.

You didn't need to be a psychologist to be aware that the poor woman needed to talk to somebody. Anybody. No, that was wrong. Not anybody. Anybody English. And we were English.

So, of course, were she and her husband. At least, we assumed, I think with some justification, that the man she was with was her husband. There is something quite indefinable about the chemistry which exists between man and wife, a sort of invisible mental and physical congress that does not lend itself to explanation. To my mind there was no doubt that these two shared it even though they were sitting well apart when we came across them just outside the village of St Amand d'Huisselot and the husband soon walked off to sit on a nearby hummock.

It was equally obvious that when it came to pouring out her troubles that her husband wouldn't do as the recipient of them any longer. It wasn't that he gave any sign of not wishing to listen to her, nor was he exhibiting that *noli me tangere* attitude of dignified unapproachability that betrays bereavement. It seemed to me rather that the pair were showing all the signs of a couple who had talked themselves to a standstill and had nothing more to say until they had got their strength back.

He perched on his hummock of grass for a while, his head sunk forward resting between his knuckles. In fact, you could say that those who stood 'Silent, upon a peak in Darien' had nothing on his physical isolation, not to mention his metaphorical aloneness, but he soon wandered further off and out of sight behind us.

There was no doubt at all about the Englishness of both. Quite apart from the fact that the English abroad stand out like so many sore thumbs there was the woman's instant recognition of us as fellow citizens of the United Kingdom. She fell upon my husband and myself as kindred spirits almost before we had even had time to put up our little picnic table and chairs, let alone unpack our simple mid-day repast.

Actually, it wasn't all that simple a repast, especially in comparison with theirs. A small Charentais melon was going to be followed by some good French bread, spread, as was our holiday wont, with that Normandy butter which is such a joy. It was to be accompanied by a sizeable segment of St André cheese, and a wedge of that splendid *fromage* Saint Paulin. Somehow this last tastes so much better when eaten *al fresco* in *la Belle France* than when bought from the cold cabinet of your average British super-market and consumed at home. Two ripe peaches were going to stay in the picnic basket in the car, which we'd parked in the shade under some trees until such time as they were required. We had just started to look for somewhere cool to leave the bottle of Perrier water when the woman had hoved into view. She averted her eyes from our *déjeuner sur l'herbe*, hastily thrusting her own modest luncheon out of our sight. It looked to me as if the couple were subsisting on nothing more substantial than the bread abstracted from the breakfast basket of wherever they were staying: 'A little bit of bread and no cheese' as the yellowhammer's song goes and yet they were not obviously poor. True, their car was a little French one but they were both decently dressed – neat but not gaudy, as the cliché has it.

She must have seen her piece of bread catch my eye because the first thing she said was 'We're not in the least bit hungry. Neither of us.'

'Good,' I said lamely, waving her into one of the picnic chairs.

'Not after last night.' She gave a long sigh, choosing the chair facing our car, leaving the quite magnificent view over the valley to me. 'Thank you.'

'Montezuma's Revenge?' I suggested delicately. Although as we were deep in rural France mention of Napoleon Buonaparte might have been more appropriate; he having been said to have had tummy trouble, too.

'No, no,' she said instantly. 'The food itself was all too lovely.' She sighed again. 'Especially the *quenelles de veau*.'

'You dined well?' I said, refraining from quoting anything about Heaven being 'eating *pâtés de foie gras* to the sound of trumpets', Dean Sidney Smith being all very well but only in small doses.

The woman gave a little groan. 'But not wisely.'

'Ah.' I cast about in my mind, trying to remember whether we had anything in the nature of a hangover cure in our luggage. 'I'm sorry but I don't believe we've got any ...' I searched my memory for the French word for it, feeling that would be more diplomatic than the distinctly Anglo-Saxon 'hangover cure' but soon gave up. Now that I came to think of it, I wasn't sure that the French nation have either the word 'hangover' in their vocabulary or ever suffer from the condition. '... *digestif*,' I finished triumphantly.

'I didn't mean we'd drunk too much,' she said at once. 'It wasn't that at all, although I never saw the bottom of the glass all evening. To be honest, the wines were quite superb.'

'Good,' I said warmly, on the general principle that there could be nothing wrong with superb wines. 'I've never tasted anything like them,' she said with patent sincerity. 'The very best that the restaurant had to offer, Monsieur Sarre said they were, and I believed him.'

'Ah ...'

'And we were in one of the best restaurants in Paris, too,' she said. 'We didn't need Monsieur Sarre to tell us that. I've never tasted food like it. Even something that sounded simple like their *Consomme a la Jardiniere* was out of this world.'

'Then you're on your way south, as well,' I said briskly, 'like us.' My husband, not by nature a sympathetic listener, could see that this tale was going to take time and had taken himself off for a preprandial stroll down the valley rather than stand around.

'South,' she echoed wistfully. 'We had been going to go south but not now ...'

I capitulated then. For one thing I didn't think any of us would get any luncheon until she had unburdened herself and for another I was curious to learn of any situation made worse rather than better by the best wines that a good Paris restaurant had to offer. 'Tell me,' I said resignedly, leaving our car and sitting down opposite her. I tried to look attentive.

'It was all to do with business,' she began. 'My husband's business.' I nodded sagely. Even I knew that that word covered a multitude of sins. Sins of commission, usually. 'That's why we came to France in the first place,' she said. 'Business and then a little holiday.'

'Business before pleasure,' I smiled, 'if you were going south afterwards ...'

'The Auvergne was where we had been going ...' There was no mistaking the emphasis on the past perfect tense. 'Really?' If the demeanour of the pair was anything to go by, the future was going to be imperfect, too.

'But not now.' She twisted her hands. 'Not now.'

'Not after last night?' I hazarded.

'Exactly. You understand, don't you?'

'All I understand,' I said, 'is that something went wrong in a Paris restaurant last night ...'

'Yes ... no.' She twisted her hands into a veritable bird's nest of muddled fingers. 'Not wrong, exactly.' I tried again. 'Unexpected?'

'You could say that.'

My mind went back to an unfortunate experience of my husband's near Cahors after infringing some unknown traffic interdict by an infinitesimal degree quite early one summer Sunday morning when there was no-one but the French motorway police about. 'Hefty on-the-spot fine?'

'You could say that,' she repeated with a hollow laugh, 'but only in a manner of speaking.'

'Did you dine alone?' I asked tentatively. Had the restaurant piled on the bill their own tariff for bad behaviour? This unmemorable couple didn't look the sort to have broken up the place but perhaps

their friends had been young and what some call impetuous and I call
badly behaved ...

'No, no. We were with some business people ...'

There was a whole philosophy of meaning in that response but in
spite of our being in the homeland of famous philosophers too
numerous to mention, I merely remarked something along the lines of
being able to choose one's friends.

She seized on this. 'Exactly. Monsieur Sarre and his partner were
just Frenchmen who Bill – that's my husband – had to do business
with. It was important that we got on well with them because Bill
needed something only they could supply.'

'Not many people can afford to quarrel with their bread-and-butter,'
I observed sapiently, hoping that her Bill hadn't made his needs too
apparent. It's never a good idea to let any supplier know that it's got its
customer over the barrel. You can abolish Duty-Free but human nature
transcends national boundaries ...

'No ...'

'Although – you must forgive me – I don't quite see where the fine
wines came in.'

'Afterwards,' she explained. 'When the men'd finished their business.'
That figured. We were, after all, in France where *terroir* was important.
She was still talking. 'Bill spent Monday in their offices – they're called
Sarre et Chislet et Cie and they design components for industrial
chemists ...'

'Really?'

'You see, Bill's firm makes specialised parts for United Mellemetics –
they're that big chemical engineering outfit in Luston in Calleshire. I
don't know if you've heard of them?'

I assured her that I had heard of United Mellemetics. My name would
have had to be Rip Van Winkle if I hadn't. If I hadn't actually seen the
firm's plant, I certainly saw their advertisements every time I opened a
newspaper. I didn't see the French connection, though, and told her so.

'Sarre et Chislet et Cie own the rights to a process which Bill needs
to use so that he can supply United Mellemetics with what they want,'
she explained, adding uncertainly, 'I think I've got that right ...'

'Sounds like it,' I said robustly, since time was passing.

'So Bill came over to negotiate with them for a short lease – a sort of
licence, he said it was – to the right to use their process while he did
this precision work for United Mellemetics ...'

'And he wanted to talk to them face to face?' I understood that, all right. Electronic communication can't take body language into account. Yet.

'Yes. I don't understand the details but I know it was important.' She added naively 'United Mellemetics are far and away his best customers.'

'Not a lot of room for manoeuvre then.'

'None ...'

'It's always useful to know on which side your bread is buttered,' I said, my mind on our own butter. It would be starting to melt any minute now.

'When Bill had finished his business with Jules Sarre on Monday – he was pleased because he'd arranged a good deal for the United Mellemetics job – Philippe Chislet came in – he's their money man ...'

'You can't do without money men,' I observed. It was a hard lesson I'd learned long ago. 'True. Well, Monsieur Chislet suggested that they took us both out for dinner that evening to celebrate clinching the deal.'

'So that's where the good wines came in?' At this rate, even our melon would have gone off before she finished her tale and we could get to it.

She shook her head. 'No. On Monday, they took us out to a perfectly adequate bistro near Montmartre.' She waved an arm. 'You know the sort of place, I'm sure, red striped tablecloths ...' I did. 'Candles in bottles ...'

'Exactly. *Vin ordinaire*, too,' she said. 'Not that there's anything wrong with that. It's what we have at home.'

'Tell me,' I asked pertinently, 'had the contract been signed by then?' In my experience the aphorism *in vino veritas* ought to be writ large over all business entertaining.

'Oh, yes. There was no problem there ...'

'So what would seem to be the trouble then?' I said, sounding rather too much like my dentist for comfort. The exact nature of the trouble was something the dentist always reserved the right to decide. It was usually in the next tooth along to the one I indicated.

'Our meal the next evening was the trouble,' she said warmly. 'When we came to leave that night Bill thanked them and said that as we had another day planned in Paris – he'd arranged to spend it with Sarre and Chislet's chief technician – what about our repaying their hospitality and taking them out the next evening.'

'*Toujours la politesse*,' I said.

'It seemed the right thing to do ...'

'But it wasn't?'

She shook her head. 'Not really. But we had thought another evening meal together would be rather nice. It had to be in a restaurant, of course ...'

'Anyway, the French tend not to entertain in their own homes,' I said. 'It's one of the reasons why their restaurants are so good.' I didn't like to mention that another of the reasons why French restaurants are so good is that, having chopped off the heads of most of their aristocrats, there was a surfeit of good cooks after the Revolution with nowhere to go, thus starting a great culinary tradition. I don't think she would have been interested. It was last night that she had on her mind, not 1792.

'Bill told me it was usual in those circles, although to be honest it's not really his scene.'

'Quite customary,' I said to hurry her along. 'There's nothing wrong with that at all.'

'His firm doesn't go in for expense accounts much,' she said, still doubtful. 'Their accountant doesn't like them, although Bill thought he'd be pleased enough with the deal he'd struck with Sarre and Chislet ...'

'Accountants don't like anything much,' I said with feeling, 'except a good bottom line. What went wrong last night then?'

'Jules Sarre suggested they brought their wives along to keep me company ...'

'The English are used to being outnumbered,' I said lightly. 'That wasn't a problem, surely?' It hadn't been at Agincourt – or had it been Crécy?

She twisted her hands uneasily. 'And then Philippe Chislet said he thought their technical chief would like to come, too ...'

'With his wife?' I asked, getting the drift.

She nodded. 'It wasn't cricket, was it?'

'Six of them and two of you? No, I suppose not.'

It was the Duke of Wellington who had said that the Battle of Waterloo had been won on the playing fields of Eton but I had never known why. 'No reason why it should be cricket, of course. The *entente cordiale* was over a long time ago and the French never played the game anyway.'

'That wasn't the worst of it.' She looked really miserable now.

'No?'

'First, Bill pranged our car going round the Arc de Triomphe ...'

'Oh, dear.'

'That wasn't as bad as it might have been because we were insured and so we could hire a French runabout while it was being repaired.' She pointed to a nondescript little grey car, pointing north. 'It was the other.'

'The other?' The butter would definitely be melted now.

'Bill left it to Jules Sarre to decide on the restaurant ...'

I whistled aloud. 'I'm beginning to see ...'

'Well,' she said defensively, 'we didn't know Paris well enough to suggest anywhere ...'

'And they did,' I said, with understanding. 'It was definitely one of the best.' A distant look came over her face. 'I shall never forget their *Homard en Chaudfroid* ... I'd never had lobster before and this was done in aspic and a lovely mixture of chervil and chilli.'

'So Sarre and Chislet took you to the cleaners,' I said, hoping to conclude the narrative sooner than later.

'It was out of this world,' she said as if I hadn't spoken.

'One doesn't have lobster every day,' I observed. 'They must have had a very good *carte*, this restaurant of yours.'

'Not *carte*,' she said reproachfully. '*Ecriteau*.'

That told me more than she realised. *Ecriteau* is the older, more elegant name than *carte* for a menu. 'Not that I chose from it,' she said. 'I left it to the others. They all seemed to know what to have.' Their party had certainly been dining high on the hog. Somehow though this last expression seemed altogether too bucolic so I murmured something banal about their probably having been in good surroundings, too.

She wasn't listening. 'Then we had a sort of water ice thing,' she said. 'Sorbet ...'

'I've never had that between courses either.' I resisted the temptation to remark that travel broadened the mind as well as the beam. 'To clear the palate.'

'I wondered what it was for,' she said simply. 'And then?' I asked, pretty sure it would be fowl or flesh rather than good red herring.

She came all over misty-eyed. 'A dear little bird that tasted absolutely lovely – but I would never have had it if I'd known that it was quail.'

'The way of all flesh is to the kitchen,' I quoted. All this talk of food was making me quite hungry myself.

'Then we had something called an *amuse-gueule*,' she said. 'It was lovely.'

'*A bonne-bouche* – a sweet mouthful,' I said, anxious to get on. 'What about the rest of the party? They just had the *menu* did they?'

She grimaced and said bitterly. 'I can assure you that they ate and drank very well indeed. Bill nearly fell over when he saw the cost of it all. They called it *l'addition* but if you ask me they'd just doubled the number they'd first thought of rather than added it up.'

'You checked it, I hope?' I said swiftly.

'Everybody did and Jules Sarre said something that sounded like *faut se plaindre …*'

'Making a complaint,' I said.

'But Bill, being English, thought it wasn't the right thing to do …' She stopped as the sound of a horn came from their little car. 'Oh, look, there he is, ready to be off. He's so upset, poor darling.' The car horn sounded again, louder this time. 'Thank you so much for listening to me for so long. Goodbye – and enjoy the South.'

As soon as they had left I went back to our car to collect the rest of the picnic things. My husband's laptop, his wallet, his precious blackberry mobile phone, my camera and everything else of value in our vehicle had gone.

So had the nondescript little French car.

POPPING ROUND TO THE POST

Peter Lovesey

Look up Keating, Henry Reymond Fitzwalter, in Who's Who *and you will find he lists his recreation as 'popping round to the post.' Not for Harry the impersonality of email. He likes to write a real letter and take a real stroll to what is surely a proper pillarbox. When I was invited to edit this volume as an eightieth birthday surprise I told his wife Sheila candidly that I expected Harry to find out at an early stage. She was confident he would not, even in this age of instant communication. There is a computer in the Keating household, a recent birthday present from Harry to Sheila. Harry looks over her shoulder sometimes, but he has no desire to surf the world wide web.*

A letter from Harry is always a joy. His notepaper is headed with an illustration of a magnifying glass focused on a fingerprint and what I take to be some Indian script. His own handwriting is easily deciphered, as articulate and generous as the man. And invariably he will sign off 'Yours ever, Harry'.

Popping round to the post sounds like a civilized occupation. But in crime fiction nothing can be trusted.

Nathan was the one I liked interviewing best. You wanted to believe him, his stories were so engaging. He had this persuasive, upbeat manner, sitting forward and fixing me with his soft blue eyes. Nothing about him suggested violence. 'I don't know why you keep asking me about a murder. I don't know anything about a murder. I was just popping round to the post. It's no distance. Ten minutes, maybe. Up Steven Street and then right into Melrose Avenue.'

'Popping round to the post?'

'Listen up, doc. I just told you.'

'Did you have any letters with you at the time?'

'Can't remember.'

'The reason I ask,' I said, 'is that when people go to the post they generally want to post something.'

He smiled. 'Good one. Like it.' These memory lapses are a feature of the condition. Nathan didn't appreciate that if a letter had been posted and delivered it would help corroborate his version of events.

Then he went into what I think of as his storyteller mode, one hand cupping his chin while the other unfolded between us as if he were a conjurer producing a coin. 'Do you want to hear what happened?'

I nodded.

'There was I,' he said, 'walking up the street.'

'Steven Street?'

'Yes.'

'On the right side or the left?'

'What difference does that make?'

According to Morgan, the detective inspector, number twenty-nine, the murder house, was on the left about a third of the way along. 'I'm asking, that's all.'

'Well, I wouldn't need to cross, would I?' Nathan said. 'So I was on the left, and when I got to Melrose –'

'Hold on,' I said. 'We haven't left Steven Street yet.'

'I have,' he said. 'I'm telling you what happened in Melrose.'

'Did you notice anything in Steven Street?'

'No. Why should I?'

'Somebody told me about an incident there.'

'You're on about that again, are you? I keep telling you I know nothing about a murder.'

'Go on, then.'

'You'll never guess what I saw when I got to Melrose.' That was guaranteed. His trips to the post were always impossible to predict. 'Tell me, Nathan.'

'Three elephants.'

'In *Melrose*?' Melrose Avenue is a small suburban back street. 'What were they doing?'

He grinned. 'Swinging their trunks. Flapping their ears.'

'I mean, what were they doing in Melrose Avenue?'

He had me on a string now and he was enjoying himself. 'What do you think?'

'I'm stumped. Why don't you tell me?'

'They were walking in a line.'

'What, on their own?'

He gave me a look that suggested I was the one in need of psychotherapy. 'They had a keeper with them, obviously.'

'Trained elephants?'

Now he sighed at my ignorance. 'Melrose Avenue isn't the African bush. Some little travelling circus was performing in the park and they were part of the procession.'

'But if it was a circus procession, Nathan, it would go up the High Street where all the shoppers could see it.'

'You're right about that.'

'Then what were the elephants doing in Melrose?'

'Subsidence.'

I waited for more.

'You know where they laid the cable for the television in the High Street? They didn't fill it in properly. A crack appeared right across the middle. They didn't want the elephants making it worse so they diverted them around Melrose. The rest of the procession wasn't so heavy – the marching band and the clowns and the bareback rider. They were allowed up the High Street.'

The story had a disarming logic, like so many of Nathan's. On a previous trip to the post he'd spotted Johnny Depp trimming a privet hedge in somebody's front garden. Johnny Depp as a jobbing gardener. Nathan had asked some questions and some joker had told him they were rehearsing a scene for a film about English suburban life. He'd suggested I went round there myself and tried to get in the film as an extra. I had to tell him I'm content with my career.

'It was a diversion, you see. Road closed to heavy vehicles and elephants.'

Talk about diversions. We'd already diverted some way from the double murder in Steven Street. 'What I'd really like to know from you, Nathan, is why you came home that afternoon wearing a suit that didn't fit you.'

This prompted a chuckle. 'That's a longer story.'

'I thought it might be. I need to hear it, please.'

He spread his hands as if he was addressing a larger audience. 'There were these three elephants.'

'You told me about them already.'

'Ah, but I was anticipating. When I first spotted the elephants I didn't know what they were doing in Melrose. I thought about asking the keeper. I'm not afraid of speaking to strangers. On the whole, people like it when you approach them. But the keeper was in charge of the animals, so I didn't distract him. I could hear the sound of the band coming from the High Street and I guessed there was a connection. I stepped out to the end of Melrose.'

'Where the postbox is.'

'What's that got to do with it?'

'When you started out, you were popping round to the post.'

'Now you've interrupted my train of thought. You know what my memory is like.'

'You were going towards the sound of the band.'

He smiled. 'And I looked up, and I saw balloons in the sky. Lots of colours, all floating upwards. They fill them with some sort of gas.'

'Helium.'

'Thank you. They must have been advertising the circus. Once I got to the end of Melrose Avenue I saw a woman with two children and each of them had a balloon and there was writing on them – the balloons, I mean, not the children. I couldn't see the wording exactly, but I guessed it must have been about the circus.'

'Very likely.' In my job, patience isn't just a virtue, it's a necessity.

'You may think so,' Nathan said, and he held up his forefinger to emphasise the point. 'But this is the strange thing. I was almost at the end of Melrose and I looked up again to see if the balloons in the sky were still in sight and quite by chance I noticed that a yellow one was caught in the branches of a willow tree. Perhaps you know that tree. It isn't in the street. It's actually in someone's garden overhanging the street. Well, I decided to try and set this balloon free. It was just out of reach, but by climbing on the wall I could get to it easily. That's what I did. And when I got my hands on the balloon and got it down I saw that the writing on the side had nothing to do with the circus. It said *Happy Birthday, Susie*.'

Inwardly, I was squirming. I know how these stories progress. Nathan once found a brooch on his way to the post and took it to the police station and was invited to put on a Mickey Mouse mask and join an identity parade and say 'Empty the drawer and hand it across or I'll blow your brains out.' And that led on to a whole different adventure. 'Did you do anything about it?'

'About what?'

'The happy birthday balloon.'

'I had to, now I had it in my hands. I thought perhaps it belonged to the people in the house, so I knocked on the door. They said it wasn't theirs, but they'd noticed some yellow balloons a couple of days ago tied to the gatepost of a house in Steven Street.'

'Steven Street?' My interest quickened. 'What number?'

'Can't remember. These people – the people in Melrose with the willow tree – were a bit surprised because they thought the house belonged to an elderly couple. Old people don't have balloons on their birthdays, do they?'

'So you tried the house in Steven Street,' I said, giving the narrative a strong shove.

'I did, and they were at home and really appreciated my thoughtfulness. All their other balloons had got loose and were blown away, so this was the only one left. I asked if the old lady was called Susie, thinking I'd wish her a happy birthday. She was not. She was called something totally unlike Susie. I think it was Agatha, or Augusta. Or it may have been Antonia.'

'Doesn't matter, Nathan. Go on.'

'They invited me in to meet Susie. They said she'd just had her seventh birthday and – would you believe it? – she was a dog. One of the smallest I've ever seen, with large ears and big, bulgy eyes.'

'Chihuahua.'

'No, Susie. Definitely Susie. The surprising thing was that this tiny pooch had a room to herself, with scatter cushions and squeaky toys and a little television that was playing *Lassie Come Home*. But the minute she set eyes on me she started barking. Then she ran out, straight past me, fast as anything. The back door of the house was open and she got out. The old man panicked a bit and said Susie wasn't allowed in the garden without her lead. She was so small that they were afraid of losing her through a gap in the fence. I felt responsible for frightening her, so I ran into the garden after her, trying to keep her in sight. I watched her dash away across the lawn. Unfortunately I didn't notice there was a goldfish pond in my way. I stepped into it, slipped and landed face down in the water.'

'Things certainly happen to you, Nathan.'

He took this as a compliment and grinned. 'The good thing was that Susie came running back to see what had happened and the old lady picked her up. I was soaking and covered in slime and duckweed, so they told me I couldn't possibly walk through the streets like that. The old man found me a suit to wear. He said it didn't fit him any more and I could keep it.'

'All right,' I said, seizing an opportunity to interrupt the flow. 'You've answered my question. Now I know why you were wearing a suit the wrong size.'

He shrugged again. He seemed to have forgotten where this had started.

It was a good moment to stop the video and take a break.

*   *   *

Morgan the detective watched the interview on the screen in my office, making sounds of dissent at regular intervals. When it was over, he asked, 'Did you believe a word of that? The guy's a fantasist. He should be a writer.'

'Some of it fits the facts,' I pointed out. 'I believe there was a circus here last weekend. And I know for certain that the cable-laying in the High Street caused some problems after it was done.'

'The fact I'm concerned about is the killing of the old couple at twenty-nine, Steven Street, at the approximate time this Nathan was supposed to be on his way to the post.'

'You made that clear to me yesterday,' I said. 'I put it to him today and he denies all knowledge of it.'

'He's lying. His story's full of holes. You notice he ducked your question about having a letter in his hand?'

'Popping round to the post is only a form of words.'

'Meaning what?'

'Meaning he's going out. He needs space. He doesn't mean it literally.'

'I'd put a different interpretation on it. It's his way of glossing over a double murder.'

'That's a big assumption, isn't it?'

'He admitted walking up the left side of Steven Street.'

'Well, he would. It's on his way to the High Street.'

'You seem to be taking his side.'

'I'm trying to hold onto the truth. In my work as a therapist that's essential.' I resisted the urge to point out that policemen should have a care for the truth as well.

'Are those his case notes on your desk?' Morgan said.

'Yes.'

'Any record of violence?'

'You heard him. He's a softie.'

'Soft in the head. The murders seem to have been random and without motive. A sweet old couple who never caused anyone any grief. In a case like this we examine all the options, but I'd stake my reputation this was done by a nutter.'

'That's not a term I use, Inspector.'

'Call him what you like, we both know what I mean. A sane man doesn't go round cutting people's throats for no obvious reason. Nothing was taken. They had valuable antiques in the house and over two hundred pounds in cash.'

'Would that have made it more acceptable in your eyes, murder in the course of theft?'

'I'd know where he was coming from, wouldn't I?'

'What about the crime scene? Doesn't that give you any information?'

'It's a bloody mess, that's for sure. All the forensic tests are being carried out. The best hope is that the killer picked up some blood that matches the old couple's DNA. He couldn't avoid getting some on him. If we had the clothes Nathan was wearing that afternoon, we'd know for sure. He seems to have destroyed everything. He's not so daft as he makes out.'

'The suit he borrowed?'

'Went out with the rubbish collection, he says. It didn't fit, so it was useless to him, and the old man didn't want it back.'

'Makes sense.'

'Certainly does. We're assuming the killer stripped and took a shower at the house after the murders and then bundled his own clothes into a plastic sack and put on a suit from the old man's wardrobe. Very likely helped himself to some clean shoes as well.'

'I'm no forensic expert, but if he did all that, surely he must have left some DNA traces about the house?'

'We hope so. Then we'll have him, and I look forward to telling you about it.'

'What about the other suspect?'

There was a stunned silence. Morgan folded his arms and glared at me, as if I was deliberately provoking him.

'Just in case,' I said, 'you may find it helpful to watch the video of an interview I did later this morning with a man called Jon.'

*   *   *

I knew Jon from many hours of psychotherapy. He sat hunched, as always, hands clasped, eyes downturned, a deeply repressed, passive personality.

'Jon,' my voice said on the soundtrack, 'how long have you lived in that flat at the end of Steven Street?'

He sighed. 'Three years. Maybe longer.'

'That must be about right. I've been seeing you for more than two years. And you still live alone?'

A nod.

'You manage pretty well, shopping and cooking, and so on. It's an achievement just surviving in this modern world. But I expect there's some time left over. What do you enjoy doing most?'

'Don't know.'

'Watching television?'

'Not really.'

'You don't have a computer?'

He shook his head.

'Do you get out of the house, apart from shopping and coming here?'

'I suppose.'

'You go for walks?'

He frowned as if straining to hear some distant sound.

'Just to get fresh air and exercise,' I said. 'You live in a nice area. The gardens are full of flowers in spring and summer. I think you do get out quite a bit.'

'If you say so.'

'Then I dare say you've met some of your neighbours, the people along Steven Street, when they're outside cleaning their cars, doing gardening or walking the dog. Did you ever speak to the old couple at number twenty-nine?'

He started swaying back and forth in the chair. 'I might have.'

'They have a little toy dog, a chihuahua. They're very attached to it, I understand.'

'Don't like them,' Jon said, still swaying.

'Why's that? Something they did?'

'Don't know.'

'I think you do. Maybe they remind you of some people you knew once.' He was silent, but the rocking became more agitated.

Momentarily his chin lifted from his chest and his face was visible. Fear was written large there.

'Could this old couple have brought to mind those foster parents you told me about in a previous session, when we discussed your childhood, the people who locked you in the cupboard under the stairs?'

He moaned a little.

'They had a small dog, didn't they?'

He covered his eyes and said, 'Don't.'

'All right,' I said. 'We'll talk about something else.'

*   *   *

'You'll get thrown out of the union, showing me that,' Morgan said. 'Isn't there such a thing as patient confidentiality?'

'In the first place, I don't belong to a union,' I said, 'and in the second I'm trying to act in the best interests of all concerned.'

'Thinking he could kill again, are you?'

'Who are we talking about here?' I asked.

'The second man. Jon. He seems to have a thing about old people. He's obviously very depressed.'

'That's his usual state. It doesn't make him a killer. I wanted you to look at the interview before you jump to a conclusion about Nathan, the other man.'

'Nathan isn't depressed, that's for sure.'

'Agreed. He has a more buoyant personality than Jon. Did you notice the body language? Nathan sits forward, makes eye contact, while Jon looks down all the time. You don't see much of his face.'

'That stuff about the foster parents locking him in the cupboard. Is that true?'

'Oh, yes, I'm sure of it. I'd be confident of anything Jon tells me. He doesn't give out much, but you can rely on him. With Nathan I'm never sure. He has a fertile imagination and he wants to communicate. He's trying all the time to make his experiences interesting.'

'Falling into the pond, you mean? Did you believe that?'

'It's not impossible. It would explain the change of clothes.'

'I was sure he was talking bollocks but now that you've shown me this other man I'm less confident. I'd like to question Jon myself.'

'That won't be possible,' I said.

He reddened. 'It's a bit bloody late to put up the shutters. I've got my job to do and no one's going to stand in my way.'

'Before you get heavy with me, inspector, let me run a section of the second interview again. I'm going to turn off the sound and I want you to look closely at Jon. There's a moment when he sways back and the light catches his face.'

I rewound the tape and let it play again, fast forwarding until I found the piece I wanted, the moment I'd mentioned the old couple and Jon had started his swaying, a sure indicator of stress. 'There.' I used the freeze-frame function.

Jon's face was not quite in focus but there was enough to make him recognizable.

'Christ Almighty,' Morgan said. 'It's the same guy. It's Nathan.'

I let the discovery sink in.

'Am I right?' he asked.

I nodded.

'Then what the hell is going on?'

'This may be hard for you to accept. Nathan and Jon are two distinct identities contained in the same individual, a condition we know as Dissociative Identity Disorder. It used to be known as Multiple Personality Disorder, but we've moved on in our understanding. These so-called personalities are fragments of the same identity rather than self-contained characters. Jon is the primary identity, passive and repressed. Nathan is an alter ego, extrovert, cheerful and inventive.'

'I've heard of this,' Morgan said. 'It's like being possessed by different people. I saw a film once.'

'Exactly. Fertile material for Hollywood, but no entertainment at all if you happen to suffer with it. The disturbance is real and frightening. A subject can take on any number of personality states, each with its own self-image and identity. The identities act as if they have no connection with each other. My job is to deconstruct them and ultimately unite them into one individual. Jon and Nathan will become Jonathan.'

'Neat.'

'It may sound neat, but it's a long process.'

'It's neat for me,' he said. 'I wasn't sure which of the two guys is the killer. Now I know there's only one of them, I've got him, whatever he calls himself.'

'I wouldn't count on it,' I said.

He shot me a foul look.

'The therapy requires me to find points of contact between the alter-personalities. When you came to me with this double murder, I could see how disturbing it would be for Jon. He carries most of the guilt. But this investigation of yours could be a helpful disturbance. It goes right back to the trauma that I think was the trigger for this condition, his ill-treatment at the hands of foster-parents who happened to own a dog they pampered and preferred to the child.'

'My heart bleeds,' Morgan said, 'but I have a job to do and two people are dead.'

'So you tell me. Jon thinks he may have murdered them, but he didn't.'

'Come off it,' he said.

'Listen, please. Nathan's story was true. He really did have that experience with the balloon and the little dog and falling in the pond. For him – as the more positive of the identities – it was one more entertaining experience to relate. But for Jon, who experienced it also, it was disturbing, raising memories of the couple who fostered him and abused him. He felt quite differently, murderous even.'

'Hold on,' Morgan said. 'Are you trying to tell me the murders never happened?'

'They happened in the mind of Jon and they are as real to him as if he cut those old people's throats himself. But I promise you the old couple are alive and well. I went to Steven Street at lunch time and spoke to them. They confirmed what Nathan told me.'

'I don't get this. I'm thinking you're nuts as well.'

'But it's important that you do get it,' I told him. 'There's a third identity at work here. It acts as a kind of conscience, vengeful, controlling and ready to condemn. It, too, is convinced the murders took place and have to be investigated. Recognizing this is the first step towards integration. Do me a favour and have another look at Jon's face. It's still on the screen.'

He gave an impatient sigh and glanced at the image.

'Now look at this, inspector.'

I handed him a mirror.

MAYHEM AT MUDCHESTER

James Melville

In invoking his sleuthing charlady Emma Craggs and inventing a daughter for her chum Florrie Milhorne in the little squib which follows I am at once taking shocking liberties and paying affectionate tribute to Harry Keating, whom I have had the pleasure of knowing personally for some twenty years. A fan for much longer than that, I marvelled at his seemingly easy mastery of every type of crime writing, his amazing productivity as a practitioner and critic and, in the latter capacity, his encyclopaedic knowledge of the genre. In person I know Harry to be not only patriarchally bearded but also generous, sympathetic and affable. So I'm hoping to be forgiven ...

'My Julie? She's no trouble really, I s'pose, keeps in touch on the phone and rabbits on but it's mostly over my head. A bit philosophical, is Julie. What's that, Emma? Well, of course I know that's what she's supposed to be studying, but if you ask me she's a bloody fanatic. But then her dad was another: when she was a kid and we lived above the shop he was forever writing up slogans on the wallpaper with red crayons. What? Oh, you know, like 'IF YOU'RE WAITING FOR SOMETHING TO TURN UP, START WITH YOUR SHIRT SLEEVES'. Silly old fool, bless him. Julie must take after him. Another bloody fanatic. Got a scholarship, she did, but earns a bit of extra bunce at college putting in a couple of hours dusting an' cleaning of an evening in what she calls The Command Module ...'

Julie – she didn't much like the name and encouraged her friends at Mudchester Metropolitan University (formerly the Mudchester Polytechnic) to call her Nikki – was sauntering towards the reception lobby while her mother was in mid-flow to Emma Craggs. It was true that the self-contained suite of offices and conference rooms above was known to many as the command module, but a good many of the younger students who barely remembered Star Trek didn't get the reference.

An intelligent twenty-year-old with an enquiring, well-furnished mind, a perky urchin face and radical views, Julie was wearing an old blue tracksuit bottom, a pair of trainers and a faded grey T-shirt washed so many times that the injunction to SAVE THE WHALE! was barely legible. A diligent reader of *Private Eye*, she followed the revelations in its regular 'High Principals' column with mingled interest and disgust, and had a jaundiced view of the occupants of the spacious offices she cleaned but whom she seldom saw, thinking of them as a collective waste of space. The only person she regularly met in the headquarters building and really liked was the evening security man who took over when the reception desk staff went home at five, and remained until the last of the top brass left and the cleaners had finished, usually by about eight. It was soon after half past five when Julie breezed in and grinned at him as he sat there in state.

'Hi, Stan. Fat cats all gone? Home to their gins and tonics?' Stan winked at her and smiled as she headed for the little utility room at the back of the lobby, where the cleaning materials and equipment were stored. 'Evening, Julie – er, Nikki. You're early: as per usual. Only one of the nobs still here. Your boy friend, God's gift to women.'

'Oh Gawd, not the Groper? Just my luck.' The Pro-Vice-Chancellor for Academic Careers and Strategic Planning was arguably – and there were several candidates for the distinction – the most detested man in the university, but seemed to be unaware of the odium in which he was held. Physically unprepossessing, he nevertheless simpered and made incompetent passes at any and every woman he encountered, especially when alone in a room with one. Julie had last set eyes on him a couple of weeks earlier, when with a group of other Students' Union activists supported by sympathisers from the teaching staff, she had attempted to stage a sit-in in the main reception area. They had borne on high placards bearing a variety of slogans: Julie's read 'VC's SALARY UP BY 40%, PLUS PERKS'. Others drew trenchant attention to the fact that, in contrast, resident students had recently been required to fork out stiff additional charges for their rooms. The demonstrators had made a great deal of noise before being turfed out, but to no avail.

*   *   *

'Not boring you, am I?' Emma was enjoying her friend's garbled account of Julie's exploits, and urged her to continue. 'Well, you see what I mean. Anyway, apparently there's this bloke, Julie says he's a geeky nerd, or p'raps it's nerdy geek, well he's got wandering hands! And him very high up in the college, too. Fancies himself no end, even though he's weedy and does that awful thing that balding men do with what's left of their hair. You know, training a few strands across the top of his dome. Pathetic, innit?'

*   *   *

The unsavoury character described, known by repute or through personal experience to all females on campus as The Groper, was one of the two Pro-Vice-Chancellors, academic deputies to the Vice-Chancellor. His particular remit gave him considerable influence over the careers of the teaching staff. Most males among them referred to him as The Creep, a few literary types preferring Uriah because his oleaginous manner was indeed strongly reminiscent of David Copperfield's antagonist.

All reports of the various departmental promotion committees passed through him. These dealt with assistant lecturers hoping to become lecturers, and lecturers aspiring to be senior lecturers and then readers. All of these were at least on prescribed salary scales providing for annual increments until, all too soon, the maximum was reached. Above them were those few with professorial status, and these demigods wanting a rise were required to submit annually a written case for monetary justice to the Vice-Chancellor, who was the ultimate authority. However, before these lengthy documents reached him, they were scrutinised and commented on by The Groper and his only known ally, the Registrar, the University's top lay administrator.

Everybody knew how the system worked, and hated his influence. Moreover, apart from his role in their career development or lack of it, his vapid but pretentious and jargon-ridden Strategic Planning 'initiatives' and the endless time-consuming meetings they spawned were the occasion of much dismay and affront to those senior academics who had to try to put them into effect, and seething rebellion among the secretaries and other support staff who bore the brunt of the consequent dislocation of their work.

Armed with her cleaning gear, the student political philosopher (who was thinking of writing about Rosa Luxemburg and the Spartacus League when the time came to submit her long essay) went up in the lift. Her tutor, a sexy Canadian senior lecturer known to many as Doctor Cool had more than adequate hair and Julie fancied him. She wouldn't have minded a bit if *he* were to make a pass. In the posh regions assigned to her the plain green haircord carpeting of the reception area below gave way to expensive, delicate fawn shag-pile, and the matching walls of the executive corridors were decorated with framed architect's colour-washed sketches of planned new campus buildings. To indicate scale, a few unfeasibly elegant and well-dressed persons were depicted strolling in sunshine under blue skies in their vicinity.

Julie dealt briskly and effectively with the Vice-Chancellor's and Registrar's spacious offices, then headed along the corridor. There was no sound from The Groper's room, but his door was ajar, so she braced herself for a tedious few minutes in his presence. What she saw after knocking and entering momentarily took her breath away. The man was sprawled on the carpet floor beside his desk, a heavy glass ashtray beside him. Julie rather stupidly asked 'Are you all right?' before kneeling down and gingerly taking hold of his right wrist. She could feel no pulse, but kept her head and quickly returned to the Registrar's office, where she picked up the internal phone and rang down to the lobby.

It took Stan a few seconds to grasp what Julie was jerkily telling him. A minute or so after that, he had joined her, surveyed the scene and knelt down. 'I think he's dead,' Julie faltered as the burly security man first shook and then unceremoniously rolled the slumped form over. 'Better make sure before I ring the Medical Centre for help.'

One look at the staring eyes and twisted face she now saw made Julie nearly vomit and she summoned all her strength to retain control of her reactions. Then Stan stood up and gently put an arm round her. 'He's dead all right. There's a lot to be done, love, but first you need a drop of the VC's brandy.' Julie allowed herself to be led from the room, but something made her say 'D-d-don't touch that ash-tray, Stan. It might be evidence.'

* * *

A week or so later Florrie was on the phone to Emma Craggs again, giving her version of Julie's account of the grisly scene she had witnessed, and its aftermath. 'Anyway, the doctor they fetched reckoned it was a massive stroke that did for him, but there's going to be an inquest, because of this heavy glass ashtray or whatever it was. My Julie thought there was something very fishy about it being there. Somebody might have threatened to clobber him with it, and scared him so much it might have sort of frightened him to death, you see? She says so many people at the college hated his guts that there are dozens of suspects ... they say they didn't find any fingerprints on it. Still, Julie says everybody reckons the mystery intruder – if there was one – did the college a good turn. What's that, Emma? Went back and wiped it clean herself? My Julie? Oh, come off it! Got a nasty suspicious mind, you have!'

KEEPING MY HEAD

Andrew Taylor

Three reasons why this is a story for Harry Keating:
   1. Crime fiction has a terrible tendency to become formulaic. The astonishing range of Harry's books, on the other hand, has shown me and the scores of other writers who follow in his footsteps that it needn't be like that – that the genre is as elastic as our imaginations.
   2. Harry once wrote, with characteristic modesty, 'What starts me off writing a crime novel is, almost paradoxically, a philosophical idea. Flying a bit high?' Not in his case, at least.
   3. As the conclusion of this story reveals, it could not have existed, in a sense, without Harry.

They took me out today, dear, to meet a visiting American gentleman, and I happened to see a calendar on the desk. It was my birthday, the 3rd September – and, do you know, I'm ever so old. I don't like to say how old. A lady doesn't. In any case it depends how you count these things. Still, it's cause for celebration. Not that there's much sign that anyone is going to throw me a party.

But I always liked a party. Nowadays I think especially about the one I had on my fifteenth birthday. I was still living at my stepfather's farm in Brooklyn. We had the family and a few friends. I sang and played for them, naturally – even those days there was no doubt about my talent. I had just finished when there was a tapping at the window. It was a tinker, a gypsy, who sometimes mended saucepans or sold my mother clothes pegs.

Mother went out to him and in a moment came back saying that he had offered to tell my fortune because it was my birthday. Mother, who was very superstitious, gave me a quarter so I could cross the man's palm with silver.

The tinker held my hand, palm upwards, in both of his and studied it for what seemed like hours. He smelled rather, and his hair was grey and greasy. He traced some of the lines on my palm with a jagged nail. At last he looked into my face.

'You'll have a long life, young lady.'

'Fancy that!'

'But not how you expect. Many people will be interested in you, they'll look up to you. You'll be known around the world. And for two reasons.'

'I knew it!' I glanced at Mother. 'I told you – I shall be a great artiste. And then maybe I'll marry a millionaire.'

'But you must always beware,' the old man said, lowering his voice to a whisper. 'Beware of keeping your head.'

He dropped my hand as if it had become red hot. I saw the fear in his face. He looked bewildered too, even more than I was. There was a tinkle as the quarter fell to the garden path. He turned and stumbled away. My mother told me afterwards that he never came to the farm again.

I should have taken warning from that. But I was a heedless girl and soon forgot the tinker. I moved to New York and joined the chorus of a music hall. Unfortunately my career did not prosper. Had it not been for the kindness of gentleman friends, I should have had to return home to my family.

The trouble with gentlemen is that sometimes they don't fulfil their promises. (I'm sure *you* aren't like that, dear.) Anyway, so it was that I found myself in an interesting condition, from which there was no honourable outcome. The gent in question, though he reneged on his promises in a very ungentlemanly fashion, at least paid for me to visit a most respectable medical practitioner.

This chap had an assistant, a real doctor like him, a most charming and sensitive man who was very kind to me in those dark days. He had large, luminous eyes and his expression was tinged with melancholy, which I put down to the fact that his wife had died a few months before. So we were two storm-tossed victims of sorrow. His parents had christened him Hawley but I always called him Peter. We found consolation in each other's company, and friendship ripened to a warmer sentiment. I told him he was my rock, my fixed point in this troubled world. Soon we were married in a church in Jersey City.

I can't pretend that my new husband's affairs were as prosperous as I would have liked. First we lived in Philadelphia and then St Louis. We returned to New York where I trained as an opera singer and my husband began his long association with a homoeopathic remedy company. That's why he went to London, in the first place, to set up a branch of the business there.

I'd decided that the opera was not for me and when I reached London, I returned to my old love, the music hall. I can't say my career as a performer went quite as well as I'd have liked. But I became involved in a performers' charity and became quite a leading light in a group of ladies and gentlemen.

All this while, Peter continued working. Although we always lived comfortably, I could not help suspecting that his affairs were not going were not going smoothly. There were changes of office – of job – of the company's name – and I began to wonder whether some of the patent remedies he sold were not quite as efficacious as he claimed.

By now we had moved to a charming house in a very nice part of North London. I remember the very moment when, standing in the kitchen, a pair of my husband's trousers folded over my arm, I began to entertain another sort of suspicion about him. I found a pencilled note in the lefthand pocket.

> *My darling hub, how I missed you when you left me last night, I could not sleep for thinking of you. Your loving wifey.*

Peter was at the office. Otherwise I should have confronted him with this evidence of his guilt immediately. The hours passed as I waited for him to return home. In that time, I changed my mind. My anger did not cool – far from it – but I realised that it would be foolish to lose my head. When Peter returned at last, I acted as though nothing had happened. I have always been a gifted performer, but I believe the performance I gave in the weeks that followed was the greatest in my career.

Now my suspicions had been aroused, it was easy to find ample confirmation of them. I followed my husband on several occasions. I soon realised that the 'wifey' in question must be a little typewriter named Ethel who worked at his office. She was a nasty, sickly little thing, dear – how Peter could have preferred her to me I cannot tell – you'd have needed three of her to make one of me. He'd been conducting the affair under my very nose for years.

There was another problem. Peter's financial affairs were increasingly embarrassed but he still had some money hidden away. If I exposed

him, I should be penniless – and an object of pity to my friends. I
could not bear that. I did not deserve that. As the days passed, another
course of action occurred to me. At first I dismissed it as impossible,
even wrong. Gradually, however, I realised that not only would it be
possible, with a little planning, but also that in a way it would be more
right than wrong. It would punish both my husband and his paramour,
while making sure I'd gain control of what was left of our assets. It
might not be strictly lawful but, as Peter once told me in our courting
days, there is a moral justice that towers above the petty laws of mankind.

The next question was how. Then fate took a hand in the game. As I
made my daily search of my husband's pockets, I found in his waistcoat
a small box labelled Lewis and Burrows, which was the name of the
chemist's shop my husband regularly used for his professional needs.
According to the label, the box contained five grains of hyoscine
hydrobromide.

Since my marriage to Peter, I'd got to learn a bit about drugs.
Hyoscine, I knew, was a sedative in small doses, but fatal in large ones.
In a flash, the scheme unfolded before my eyes. Last thing in the
evening, we often had cocoa. I would place the hyoscine in his cup and
await results. If there were no suspicious circumstances, it might be
assumed that he had died naturally. If the worst came to the worst,
and there was a postmortem, it would be discovered that Peter himself
had bought the hyoscine, and people would naturally assume he had
committed suicide – perhaps out of guilt because of his sordid little
affair with the typewriter. I should be left a sorrowing and, I hoped,
comfortably-provided-for widow.

The fatal moment came on the last day of January. Our friends Paul
and Clara came round for the evening. Though I say it myself, dear, I
was on particularly good form – I gave them a slap-up meal, with plenty
to drink, and afterwards we played cards. I took care to show that
Peter and I were on the best of terms – these impressions are so
important.

Clara and Paul left earlier than I had expected (Paul felt a little ill)
and I suggested to Peter that I should make us some cocoa. I went
down to the kitchen to prepare the drink, leaving him to pour himself
another whisky. I had just added the crystals to the cocoa when I looked
up and saw him, glass in hand, in the doorway.

How long had he been there? Had he seen me?

'Hello, dear,' I said. 'I was just about to bring it up to you.'

Peter smiled and pulled out a chair. 'Let's have it here. It's warmer.'

We sat down, facing each other across the kitchen table. Peter offered me a cigarette, which I accepted. He patted his pockets and said, 'Damn, I've left the matches upstairs.'

I stood up and went to the mantelpiece over the range, where I kept a box of matches. I returned to the table and lit our cigarettes. We sat drinking and chatting in a desultory but fairly amiable way about our little party that evening. I watched Peter sip his cocoa. I found myself laughing rather more than usual. At last he pushed aside the cup and smiled at me.

'Ah – that was good. I'll just go and lock up.'

He smiled at me. I don't know why, but I had a sense that something had gone wrong. He left the room and I cleared the table. There was a tiny chip in the handle of one of the cups. It was a small imperfection but I tended, automatically, to give that cup to myself. Oddly enough, this was the cup that Peter had been drinking from.

I could not be sure but it was *likely* that I would have given myself that cup. Was it possible that Peter, standing in the kitchen doorway, had seen me adding the crystals to the cocoa? Was it possible that he had switched our cups while I was fetching the matches?

I had no way of knowing, not then. I can't pretend that I enjoyed the next few hours, dear. You see, if I asked for help I'd have to admit my guilt.

But I've always been something of a gambler by nature. It seemed to me the best thing to do was to carry on and hope everything was all right. Even when I began to feel sleepy, I didn't abandon hope. After all, I had had a certain amount to drink that evening and it had been a long day. And, by the time I realised that I might be on the borders of a sleep deeper than any other, it was too late.

*   *   *

Not quite sure what happened next. Or of the order. I just couldn't believe it, dear – first that I was dead, and second that I knew I was dead, and third, that I was still at least partly aware of what was going on in the place where people were still alive, the place I'd been before I fell asleep after that cup of cocoa. People are so silly – they think you're either alive or dead. But it's not that simple. You can be neither one thing nor the other. Or a bit of one, then a bit of the other. I don't know. All I know was that at one point I was aware that I was in our cellar at Hilldrop Crescent, and Peter had taken off a lot of my clothes, and there was the sound of sawing, and after a while I preferred not to be aware of what was happening and fell asleep, only I had bad dreams.

*   *   *

Now there's another thing that folk don't know about being dead, or what they call dead. It's not that your thoughts just carry on, and you're sometimes aware of what's happening. When you are aware, or whatever you call it, your awareness is never very far away from your head. You're either inside it or near it. Which is why I have no idea what happened to the rest of me. I stayed with the head.

What I do know is that Peter cut it from my body with the biggest of his surgical saws. He was wearing one of my big aprons and apart from that he was naked. He didn't enjoy it, either. Serve him right. I felt a grudging admiration, too – I never would have thought he had it in him. It's just shows how you can misjudge somebody. After he had finished, he lifted me by the hair – the impudence of it! – and dropped me, or rather dropped my head, into one of my hatboxes. I recognised the box – it was the one that held my Merry Widow hat, which was black and encased in filmy organdie and festooned with lovely floaty ostrich feathers. What's really made me angry, I remember, was the thought that he'd probably given the hat itself to his goddamned typewriter. Pardon my French, dear, as you say nowadays, but she just wasn't the sort of girl who could carry off a hat like that. You need to have style.

After that things went black. Well they would – I was inside the hatbox. I was aware of movements and of being turned upside down. I heard a muffled clang which made me think that perhaps Peter had put the hatbox in a metal trunk. Later still – I don't know how long, it might have been days – there was movement and much more jolting. I heard Peter saying quite clearly and firmly, as if to a cabbie, 39 Yorkley Grove. The mists descended again. Later still he was haggling over money with somebody, perhaps the landlady.

'I am a doctor, madam,' I heard him saying, trying to sound as English as possible. 'Here's my card. Sometimes I work late at the hospital, and it is convenient for me to sleep nearby. I also need to conduct medical experiments in complete isolation. You would not understand it, madam, but the vibrations are very sensitive when one is working under laboratory conditions and sometimes that's simply not possible at the hospital.'

He went on like this for some time, until I fell asleep. I've no idea what he was talking about, and I expect the woman hadn't either. But Peter could sell ice to the Eskimos if he had a mind to. The next time I woke up he was putting me in something that burned. I felt no pain, of course, but some part of me was aware that it hurt.

I think that Peter must have been trying to destroy all possibility of somebody recognising me. Was he boiling me as I used to boil a chicken carcass until the meat fell from the bones? Or was he using some sort of acid? He had always been very interested in chemistry. At least I responded in a ladylike fashion to the horrible predicament in which I found myself. I fainted.

When I regained consciousness – of a sort – it could have been days, weeks, months or even years later. I was quite alone in the soothing dark of my hatbox once again. Everything was quiet. I knew that I was now stripped to my essentials. Though I couldn't see myself, I knew damn well that I was now no more than a skull. That wretched husband of mine was trying to take everything away from me.

Well, I thought, we'll see about that. If he and his wifey think they're going to live in bliss for the rest of their days, then they've got another thought coming. If I had my way, I'd –

* * *

Time began to mean less and less to me to me. I heard two people talking, no idea when, but one of them was perhaps the landlady in Yorkley Grove. The other was a man of the same class as herself.

'Ain't seen hide nor hair of him for two months,' the woman was saying.

'Then you can sell his stuff,' the man said. 'No reason why you shouldn't. It's money owed, after all.'

'I wouldn't like to do that,' the woman said with a hint of a whine in her voice. 'He was such a lovely gentleman.'

I should have liked to scream at her: *He's not a lovely gentleman, he's my husband, and he's a bloody murderer.*

'You can't just to leave his gear here,' the man said. 'I mean you could rent these rooms. You're losing money. Anyway, one of the kids might see what's in that box.' The woman said. 'All right, but I'm sure he'll be back. I tell you what we'll do: we'll put his things in the loft. They'll be waiting here when he comes back.'

'He won't come back, Mother.'

'Of course he will. I've got a feeling in my bones.'

I had a feeling in my bones, too, what was left of them. The feeling in my bones told me that Peter was never coming back, not for me. He'd got away scot-free. He always was a lucky devil.

So they took me up into the attic. Judging by their conversation while they did that, there wasn't much else besides the hatbox, an empty trunk, a few books, and some clothes. And there I stayed, drifting in and out of consciousness, while time passed. Sometimes I heard the patter of mice and rats. That was one advantage of my present state – I could face rodents with a cool head. They could do nothing to me now.

Strangely enough, I was not unhappy, except when I thought of Peter and his typewriter and how he'd got away with killing me, and she was wearing my clothes and my Merry Widow hat and flaunting my jewellery. But life moves on, dear, and so does death. You get used to solitude, you know, you get used to silence and darkness. They have their own pleasures, which is something I would never have expected. Gradually I lulled myself into the belief that life – or indeed death, it depends how you look at it – had nothing more to offer me.

But life is full of surprises, isn't it, dear? – and so is death.

The first I knew of it was when I was moved from the attic along with the rest of its contents by two strange man working under the guidance of one irritable woman. She never stopped talking the whole while.

'Why Granny kept all this rubbish I have no idea. Mind the stairs, George, you're going to bash the newel post with that tin trunk. Oh, for heaven's sake, try to brush off some of that grit before you bring it down the ladder. Oh my God, is that a parrot's cage? Whose was that, do you think? And is that a hatbox?'

The woman lifted the lid. Light and dust poured over me. She gasped, and both men murmured obscenities that would have made me blush, had I been able to. The woman stared down at me, her eyes still wide with shock, but already there was something calculating in her expression.

'It's all right, George, it must have been the doctor's,' she said calmly. 'I remember now – Granny used to rent a room to him and he left his stuff here. She took quite a shine to him.' She tapped the top of my skull with a fingernail. 'Clean as a whistle.'

'Should we have a word with the vicar?' George suggested. 'I mean there must be regulations. It's not fair the poor soul shouldn't have a Christian burial.'

'Don't be stupid. What's the vicar got to do with it? We don't even know this chap was a Christian. Could have been a heathen for all we know.'

A chap? Me? A heathen?

'No, George,' the woman went on, smiling down at me. 'I've got other plans for this one.'

I decided not to listen any more. I cut myself off from what was happening. It would be inaccurate to say that I lost consciousness. It was more that I mislaid it, knowingly, for the time being.

*   *   *

As time goes on – I suppose it must go on, dear, more or less in the way it used to when I was properly alive – everything becomes more and more dreamlike. For example, I remember what happened after Peter switched cups of cocoa quite clearly – too clearly, as a matter of fact. But things get hazier after he moved me into lodgings. Once I went into the attic they get mistier and patchier still. Then there are the occasional moments when everything becomes very clear again but it never makes much sense.

I think the next time things were clear like that must have happened soon after I came down from the loft. I was still inside the hatbox, with the lid back on, but I could hear two women talking, and one of them was the granddaughter. The other had a much louder voice and it made the hatbox itself vibrate. She was a proper lady, too.

'Now it's not every day one buys something like this,' she bellowed. 'And three guineas is a great deal of money.'

'You won't find one any cheaper, ma'am,' said the granddaughter in a wheedling voice. 'Though I say it myself, it's in lovely nick.'

'I'd like to know a little more about its provenance.'

'Come again?'

'How it came into your possession.'

'Oh, that's – it was my gran's. I found it after the attic after she died. One of her lodgers left it there – he was a medical chap, couldn't pay his bills.'

Suddenly light burst into the hatbox as the lid was lifted. A woman with a large round face peered down at me. She was wearing pince-nez which gleamed in the light.

'I thought you might find it useful, ma'am,' the granddaughter was going on. 'You writing the detective stories and all. I see your books everywhere these days.'

Sycophantic cow, I thought. I know *your* type.

'I tell all my friends, I used to work for a famous author.'

The other woman lifted me out of the hatbox. She stared at me and I, somehow, stared at her. We were in the lobby of a hotel. People were taking tea among the palm trees. Somebody was playing a jaunty little tune on the piano.

'Might bring you inspiration, ma'am. Give you a few ideas.'

'Fifty-five shillings,' the author said. 'That's my last offer.'

*   *   *

Well, that gypsy was right. I'm not sure what's happening, or where I am, but I do know I'm very important now. In fact, I'm sort of worshipped. I'm like a holy relic. It's rather nice to be appreciated after all this time.

I don't get out much, mind – as you know, dear, I spent most of my time in the darkness. Every now and then, I wake up. Almost always, I'm the centre of attention at a dinner party. I meet some very nice ladies and gentlemen. I think we were at the Ritz last time. A few years ago it was the Savoy. It's nice to know I'm mixing with genteel people. Every now and then they bring somebody new to meet me. It's impossible for them to shake hands, of course, so they touch my head in a very respectful way.

Of course I have my favourites. Especially you, dear. You remind me of Peter as he used to be, before he met his nasty little typewriter – the same soft voice, the gentle hands, the expressive eyes and the great philosophical brow. You don't have a droopy moustache like him, though – you've got a lovely big beard. I do like a man with a beard.

If only I could speak to you Once you picked me up, and I could tell you felt full of sympathy for my plight. You fondled me in your beautiful hands and tilted me towards the light.

'Alas, poor Eric,' you murmured, in that lovely voice of yours.

Eric? Me?

But I'm not Eric, dear, I wanted to say. I've had a number of names, I admit that, but all perfectly lady-like. My last stage name was Belle Elmore, for example, and you can't get more feminine than that, can you?

But I don't want to have any secrets from you. Let's have it all ship-shape and Bristol fashion between us. My real name is Mrs Cora Crippen, dear, but you can call me Cora.

BEARDED WONDERS

Tim Heald

My first encounter with Harry was in 1973 when, in The Times, *he described my original crime novel as 'a steel-clawed butterfly'. This lepidopterous metaphor proved challenging with subsequent books as Harry felt duty-bound to trawl the nether regions of Noah's Ark in search of ever more exotic creatures to invoke when describing the further misadventures of Simon Bognor. I remember something along the lines of a tungsten-tailed night-moth but after ten novels even the Keating imagination became challenged. Anyway he took a break from* The Times *and I took one from Bognor.*

I first met him soon after the butterfly review when I joined the Crime Writers' Association, of which he was Chairman in 1970 and 71. There have been many enjoyable occasions since then but the one that really sticks in my mind is a chance sighting one morning when I came across Harry and the equally distinguished Julian Symons walking in Kew Gardens with their splendid wives Sheila and Kathleen. The gravitas of the two men was almost tangible. They were discussing what was obviously at least a three-pipe problem and I felt hopelessly jejune and ignorant – like a schoolboy encountering Jung and Adler in the Prater. Their stride was stately, their demeanour wise, but above all it was the magnificent beards that did it. Ah, those beards! Harry's in particular. Almost more than those initials I was awed by those whiskers.

So now, at last, I have written a story in their honour.

They found a beard by the body.

The beard was false, dark and spade-shaped, with hooks to attach it to the ears. The hair was coarse and of a texture which suggested horse. It was cheap, a costume piece, probably made in China though there was no trade mark to say so.

There was no other clue except for the killer bullet which had ended up on the desk top looking deceptively innocent – like a tinsel worry-bead.

Sir Simon Bognor watched them lift the evidence with plastic gloves, bag it, label it and send it away to a safe place. He was ill at ease with corpses and forensics but no longer had occasion to trouble his mind unduly with such mundane matters, not even with plastic gloves. Thirty years since first being employed by the Board of Trade in an investigative capacity for which he was manifestly ill-suited, he now found himself 'running' the department and with a knighthood to prove it. God knows how the knighthood had come about but under New Labour he believed anything was possible. Mind you, he would have fancied his chances under John Major as well. Where the honours 'system' was concerned the chaos was indiscriminate and evenhanded. It was his belief that someone in a high place had got the wrong Bognor. Unless it was a practical joke. Never mind though, Monica enjoyed being Lady Bognor and it helped with credit and at the butcher's.

The beard was perplexing, the body less so. The latter belonged to Bill Brown, originally named Vladimir Hepzi, a native of some obscure Balt state who had changed his name in the interests of assimilation and was the Director of Purchasing at the internet discount company BargainBasement.com. In this and other capacities he was one of Britain's least loved men and in Bognor's estimation much better off dead than alive. His death was no mystery. The only mystery was why it had not taken place earlier. Solving the crime was a problem only because there were so many people with plausible motives and little discernible motive for finding out whodunit. But the beard was a mystery.

Back in the office he took his Shakespeare down and turned to *A Midsummer Night's Dream* where he found Bottom's famous lines on the subject of facial hair. Act Two, the amateur players are all gathered in the house of Quince, the carpenter. On line 93 Bottom the weaver finally agrees to take the part of Pyramus asking only what beard he should play it in. Quince says he can do what he likes whereupon Bottom says, 'I will discharge it in either your straw-colour beard, your orange-tawny beard, your purple-in-grain beard or your French-crown colour beard, your perfect yellow.'

This would have produced howls of mirth from the groundlings because it was a satire, of sorts, on the Elizabethan custom of beard-dyeing. Bognor read it over and over again feeling instinctively that there was a clue lurking there somewhere, then buzzed for his new PA, Harvey Contractor, an Anglo-Indian graduate in semiotics from the University of Wessex and an expert in codes, ciphers, computers and Shakespearean sub-text. He was 'on secondment' though Bognor had no idea where he had been seconded from. It seemed most likely that he had been sent by some other government department to spy on him and report the length of his lunch hours which were deliberately unfashionable. Bognor treated him with caution.

'I'm bothered by the beard by Bill Brown's body,' he said, wincing involuntarily at the unintended alliteration. 'What do you think?'

'Pogonatus,' said Harvey dreamily, 'Constantine IV, Emperor of the East from 668 to 685 was Constantine Pogonatus. In other words Constantine the Bearded. So was Baldwin IV, Count of Flanders from 988 to 1036, Geoffrey the Crusader, Bouchard of the House of Montmorency and, of course, Saint Paula. Socrates was styled Magister Barbatus by Persius because he thought the beard was a symbol of wisdom. Shall I continue?'

Bognor sipped lemon and ginger from his Princess Diana souvenir mug and sighed wearily. He often wondered what they taught on the semiotics course at Wessex.

'No,' he said, 'I'd rather you didn't. But why one has to ask oneself would anybody leave a beard by the newly murdered body of a bent internet huckster?'

'Maybe it fell off in the struggle.'

'There was no struggle, dummy,' said Bognor. 'Brown was shot in the back of the head, execution style.'

They both paused for thought.

'I think it's a calling card,' said Bognor eventually. 'Have we had any results from CCTV?'

'We're not going to get any' said Harvey, dolefully, 'the system was kaput. Had been for several days. It had been reported but no-one had got round to fixing it.'

Bognor sighed.

'And who were Brown's visitors?'

'There were several. The last one signed in as 'John Smith'.'

'And the receptionist didn't have any observations or recollections?'

'None,' said Harvey. 'The receptionist didn't seem very bright and had less than total recall. She said it was a busy morning and she was hung-over from binge-drinking the night before.'

'And Brown's secretary?'

'Day off. He was on his own.'

Bognor sighed again. He seemed to do so even more since the knighthood. It was a habit he really must kick.

That evening over a pre-prandial Uraguayan Viognier he told Lady Bognor of the day's events.

Monica pursed her lips.

'A beard,' she said. 'False. Why would a murderer leave fake whiskers by the body of the person they've just murdered?'

'Some sort of souvenir signature,' said Sir Simon, mouth puckering at the tart wine. 'It's a sort of hairy equivalent of the anonymous heavy-breathing phone call. The murderer is cocking a metaphorical snook.'

'And the answer lies in the beard,' said Lady Bognor thoughtfully. 'I mean it's deliberate. It didn't just fall off. Though if you had just shot someone while wearing a false beard it's perfectly conceivable that the thing might just fall off and in your hurry to get away you wouldn't notice. Or you might not think it mattered. Or you'd realise too late.'

'I think it's deliberate,' said Bognor, 'Whoever shot Brown is trying to tell us something.'

'Up to a point,' his wife agreed. 'Although as you suggest, it's more by way of being a taunt. I think you're supposed to be puzzled. The murderer isn't offering an easy solution. If it were Sudoku it would be fiendish not basic.'

'Perhaps,' he said. 'What's for supper?'

She told him it was steak and spinach. They were on a diet. They always were.

Half an hour or so later they were sitting down to their meal. Monica had filled a jug with tap-water. Sir Simon had opened a bottle of Beefy Batsman Cabernet Shiraz from the Coonewarra and was swirling it round his glass, admiring its colour and savouring its bouquet. The steak and spinach was on the table and as if on cue the phone rang. It was new and made a funny noise. Neither Bognor liked it.

They decided to let it ring and finish their meal in peace. What was the point in a knighthood and a senior position in the Civil Service if you couldn't enjoy a quiet dinner together? They made conversation with the lengthy pauses and silences befitting participants in a long and mainly successful marriage.

Eventually, having agreed to coffee, Sir Simon went to the phone and pressed buttons 1,5,7 and 1, then paused for the disembodied voice he disliked so irrationally and pressed 1 again in order to pick up the new message. It was Harvey Contractor calling from the office. He often worked late. This was partly showing off and partly a rebuke to his boss whom he plainly regarded as left over from a previous regime and well past his sell-by date. Harvey sounded agitated but non-committal. He would either phone again or expect a return call on his mobile.

Bognor sipped black cafetiere Colombian, thought a while and phoned. The trouble with mobiles was that you never knew where the recipient of your call was speaking from. Judging from the noises-off Harvey was no longer in the office. It sounded as if he was in a pub but Bognor was pretty certain that Harvey Contractor didn't do pubs.

'Hi, boss,' said Harvey. 'Thanks for calling. Hang on a second. I need to go somewhere quiet.'

Seconds later he came back with the extraneous noise removed.

'We have another murder, boss,' he said.

Bognor said nothing, just waited.

'Caroline Bartram of Cheapco,' continued Contractor after a silence which he had obviously hoped his superior would fill. 'Same as Brown. Bullet in the back of the head.'

'And a beard by the body ...' It was more of a statement than a question.

Another pause then Contractor confirmed it. 'Yes. The Yard people hadn't clocked it but when I asked they said that yes there was a beard. They seemed surprised.'

'Scotland Yard have everything under control?'

'As much as they ever do.'

'So there's no need for us to get involved till tomorrow.'

Contractor sounded shifty even over the mobile. He was action man. Also concerned to cover his back.

'Guess not,' he said, eventually.

'See you in the office tomorrow then,' he said, switching off abruptly. He went back to the drawing room and told Monica what had happened. She smiled and they watched the news together. Neither murder was mentioned. TV news nowadays didn't report anything unless they had a press release.

'Funny business,' said Monica in bed.

'Yes,' he agreed. It took him a long time to get to sleep.

The sleeplessness yielded no results and meant that when he did finally nod off there were not enough hours left for serious rest so that when the alarm went off he woke tousled and tetchy. Contractor, in contrast, seemed well-creased, bright-eyed, and ready for anything. Bognor told himself that this was a side-effect of youth and that age brought compensations in the form of wisdom and status. He was not actually sure of this, and even less so when just as he had started on his office coffee the Secretary of State rang. He couldn't stand the Secretary of State who was a classic University of Life graduate with a less than complete hold on the English language and a thorough-going contempt for privately educated Oxford graduates such as Sir Simon and indeed his own boss the Prime Minister.

'What's all this then?' he asked. The Secretary of State much enjoyed his reputation for not beating about bushes. He was, Bognor supposed, smiling weakly at the thought, the sort of person who took pleasure in calling a beard a beard.

'What?' riposted Bognor unhelpfully.

'Two murders on your patch in less than twenty-four hours. I've had Number Ten on the line. They want answers pdq. Has anyone been arrested?'

'I don't do arrests,' said Sir Simon wearily. 'You know that. I'm like the Secret Services in the days before people like you stopped them being secretive. I don't exist.'

'You bloody exist as far as I'm concerned. And you haven't forgotten the Brezhnevistan lunch today have you?'

'No,' he lied wincingly. He had forgotten entirely about the Brezhnevistan lunch. The improbable country was some sort of unreconstituted people's republic in central Asia to which the present administration had taken an unaccountable shine. Dachas, dancing girls, oil, perks. Corruption everywhere in some shape or form.

'Dave is very keen to build our relationship with Brehznevistan,' said the Secretary of State.

Dave was the Prime Minister. Bognor, who had once played squash with his uncle, thought Dave a particularly low form of life.

'If I have murders to solve I'm better off not having lunch with the Brehznevistanis,' he said. 'Wouldn't you agree?'

'Absolutely not. Best bib and tucker at the Stein Imperial at 12.45 sharp. Gordon Ramsay's doing the catering. And I want these killings solved by then.'

'Naturally.'

Sir Simon Bognor killed the phone, set it back in its cradle and regarded the back of his hands distastefully, then stroked his chin with their palms. Clean-shaven. He had never gone in for a beard, fearing it would make him look ridiculous. Or, to be more precise, being told so by Monica. He always did as he was told by Lady Bognor. Why would anyone kill two senior directors of prominent British retailers and leave false beards by the bodies? Beards could be used to confer status or as a simple disguise. Which of the two were these beards doing? What was their message?

He sighed and took his Oxford Atlas down from the shelf and looked up Brehznevistan. It was landlocked but riverine. He then consulted his gazetteer. Capital Gromykograd. Pop 800,000. Principal industries: textiles, lead-piping. Under its old identity of Middle Mongolia it had once been the circus capital of the world, renowned for its acrobats, clowns and trapeze artistes. He then leafed through the fading confidential Board of Trade file and discovered some fascinating dispatches relating to the Great Game. In the nineteenth century Brezhnevistan had been on the old silk and spice routes and was regarded by the Russians and British as being of profound strategic importance. There was a short-lived monarchy backed by Lord Palmerston but the King, a buccaneering chancer of mixed parentage and dubious ancestry, was assassinated by local anarchists. The little country seemed to have done a decent line in anarchists – old-fashioned mischief-makers in the tradition of G.K. Chesterton's *The Man Who Was Thursday* – all wide-brimmed fedoras, flowing black cloaks, hand-held bombs with fizzing fuses and, wait for it, beards.

'Hair of man's lower face (excluding WHISKERS and MOUSTACHE)'. That was the Oxford definition. Bognor would have excluded 'moustache' but he was marginally surprised about 'whiskers'. A 'full set' in Royal Navy parlance involved beard and moustache, all whiskery. Then there were secondary non-human definitions: 'chin-tuft of animal; gills of oyster; byssus of mollusc; beak-bristles of birds; awn of grass'. None of these were relevant. Or were they?

'Beards and Brezhnevistan,' he muttered to himself, repeating the words several times. Then he stared into space for a while cogitating inconclusively before buzzing for Harvey Contractor. No point in having young people in the office if one made no use of them. Harvey may have been irritating. He may have been a plant. But he was young and Bognor was old. Well, old-ish. Retirement loomed. He had a guaranteed pension. South of France time. Well, not Eastbourne anyway. He had a mind to take up writing poetry. He would like to have been a poet. With a beard perhaps. He smiled. Monica would absolutely hate that. My husband, the bearded poet.

He was still smiling inanely when Harvey shimmered into the room.

'Any news?' asked Bognor in an authoritative manner befitting a Whitehall mandarin. It was a question expecting the answer 'no' and it got it.

'Cheapco and BargainBasement.com operate on the same sort of principles,' ventured Simon. He left shopping to his wife for the most part and on the rare occasions on which he had haggled he invariably ended up paying more than the original asking price. He simply wasn't one of nature's shoppers.

' "Principles" is rather over-stating the case, sir,' said Harvey. He always said 'sir' when he was being insolent – a habit which Bognor had absorbed but had found no way of dealing with. 'But yes. As the names suggest they flog things for less than anyone else.'

'And make a fortune doing so,' said Bognor. Finance mystified him.

'Yes,' said Harvey, for whom nothing yet thrown at him held any sort of mystery.

'Could there be a link between these deaths and the Brezhnevistan visit?' asked Bognor.

'There could be,' said Contractor, evenly hedging his bets. 'But then again there might not be. If there is one I don't see it.'

'What do we know about the Brezhnevistanis?' he asked.

'Not a lot,' said Harvey. 'Old-fashioned Stalinist-type republic in the middle of nowhere. Rumoured to have large untapped oil and mineral resources. The PM has got wildly excited ever since Camilla Partington took a parliamentary delegation there last year.'

'Camilla Partington?' Bognor sniffed. 'That blue-stocking dolly bird who won the bye-election in the Gorbals?'

'Clackmannanshire actually,' said Harvey.

'Don't split hairs with me,' said Bognor huffily, 'It's all north of the border. Dave's got a suspiciously soft spot for that girl hasn't he? And she's dangerously ingenuous.'

'Seems she was very taken with Brehznevistan,' said Harvey. 'Came back and told her colleagues it was a model democracy. Unemployment nil. First-class education. Nourishing diet. They want to join the EU.'

'They're nowhere near Europe,' complained Bognor with feeling.

'Mozambique was Portuguese', said Harvey. 'Didn't stop them joining the Commonwealth.'

'So,' said Bognor slowly. 'Little Miss Partington wants to cosy up to this unreformed Stalinist basket-case. Premier Dave has the hots for Miss P. All logical bets are off. And this mid-Mongolian so-called trade delegation has come over to do some wheeling and dealing.'

'Yup,' agreed Harvey.

'Meanwhile two wheeler-dealing British cheapskates are found murdered in short order.'

'That is correct,' said Harvey, sounding like a pedantic game-show hostess.

'Coincidence?'

Harvey looked uncomfortable. He was clearly reluctant to commit himself.

'Do you think it was a coincidence?'

'Never answer a question with a question,' said Bognor. 'But since you ask it's at least interesting that senior honchos at Cheapco and Bargainbasement.com should be shot dead while these bandits from outer nowhere are in town as guests of Her Majesty's Government.'

'Sounds like a coincidence to me,' said Harvey. 'But I could be wrong.'

'Doesn't sound like you,' said Bognor snappishly. 'Go and put a bomb under forensics. Likewise the detective wallahs.'

Harvey nodded and exited left with a pseudo-deferential, 'Yes, boss.'

Bognor hated him.

There was a confidential web-page prepared by the Foreign and Colonial Office giving profiles of the visiting trade delegation researched and written by our men and women in Gromykograd, official and unofficial. The Embassy there was tiny and the Ambassador was not up to a lot. It showed. Luckily there was a competent MI6 expert on temporary assignment there. It was obviously he who provided what little substance there was to these potted biographies.

There were two individuals he found particularly interesting. Doctor Luigi Skodt was one and the other was a young woman called Anne-Marie Ng. They made an unlikely pair but they were obviously formidable. Skodt was the brains behind the alleged Economic Miracle of the country. Apparently he was a deaf mute which Bognor would have thought constituted a bit of a problem for an aspiring economic wunderkind but he was the man responsible for ensuring full employment, free milk and a general sense of well-being in what was traditionally one of the most impoverished countries in the world. He was alleged to have degrees from various universities but as these were all in the Third World it was difficult to be quite sure. Even if the universities and their degrees were bona fide it was impossible to say what sort of standards, if any, they aspired to, let alone maintained. Age fifty something. Marital status uncertain.

The woman was the Minister for National Improvement and had, since taking over the job, proved a phenomenal success in the sense that, thanks in part presumably to the efforts of Doctor Skodt, there had been a Great Leap Forward unparalleled in the nation's history. Ms Ng was said to be fluent in a dozen or so languages and to have post-graduate degrees from the Universities of Mexico, Zaragoza, Taipei and the Sorbonne. Aged about thirty-five she was alleged to be famously sensual and a former mistress of the President by whom she was even supposed to have had a child. She drove a white Mercedes Benz coupe and was a leading figure in the night-life of Gromykograd. Whatever, mused Bognor, that might be. She was also a concert-quality oboeist and a celebrated cook. There seemed no end to her talents.

These two not only seemed to work hand-in-glove on behalf of Brehznevistani improvement but also to be the de facto leaders of the country's present delegation even though the nominal boss was an elderly apparatchik called Bolislav Mananin who had once been head of the national security services. Bognor had come across him years ago when he was on secondment to the KGB. He thought him a second-rate stooge.

For the rest of the morning Sir Simon busied himself with his computer; pored over more generally musty files; and made one or two phone calls to a handful of key figures from among his impressive array of contacts. By the time he put on his overcoat and ambled downstairs to his waiting limo some serious suspicions were beginning to form in the Bognor brain.

The Stein Imperial was the latest state-of-the-art South Beach look-alike decorated in a hundred and one shades of white. Sir Simon didn't care for it, preferring panelling and old leather. It was, however, typical of the Secretary of State in show-off mood.

He was shown upstairs to the Berlusconi Suite where the predictable bun-fight was already in progress. At least the nibbles looked good. Bognor accepted something to do with smoked salmon and a flute of champagne. Despite everything life was not, he supposed, entirely bad.

Across the room he saw Brian Maclean, the entrepreneur who controlled 'Something for Nothing', otherwise known as 'Stop at Nothing', the group that had somehow taken lucrative control of the nation's Car Boot Sales. Maclean was an old acquaintance. In former times they had even played squash together. He too now had a knighthood though his was for 'political services' of a different kind, namely financial contributions from SFN.

'Lot of death about,' said Maclean half-way through a Thai prawn.

'Two,' said Bognor.

'Bit of a worry,' said Maclean. 'Cheapco and Bargainbasement.com are the other two in our big three, as well you know.'

'Meaning that you're next on the list.'

'Seems likely,' said Maclean. He grinned wolfishly. 'Though between you and me if it was OUR head of purchasing I wouldn't be altogether unhappy.'

'Who IS your head of purchasing?' asked Bognor.

'Sid Nicholson,' said Maclean.

Bognor said he hadn't heard of him, which was true.

'Old Etonian barrow boy,' said Maclean. 'Not such an unusual combination. The arrogance produces good con-men as well as Prime Ministers.'

'Same thing,' said Bognor, with feeling. 'Do you do beards?'

'Beards?'

'You know. Face fungus. False ones.'

'Why on earth would we?'

'Just a thought. The old Gamages catalogue used to do them. Along with rubber fried eggs, spoons with holes in them, filthy smells, itching powder.'

'I remember.' The tycoon smiled a superior smile. 'Not really our style. We like to think we're above that sort of stuff at SFN.'

Bognor didn't smile. 'I wonder,' he said, 'if that message has quite got through to the remoter parts of the globe. You see, some people equate getting something for nothing with tat. If it doesn't cost anything then it's bound to be inferior.'

'That's not the way we do things. At SFN we believe in VFM.'

'VFM?' Bognor wrinkled his nose. He had hated initialised acrostics since first encountering them in the Combined Cadet Force at school.

'Value for money,' explained Maclean. 'We don't rip people off. It's all good stuff.'

This was a lie and they both knew it.

'Have you ever had any dealings with these people?'

'What, the Brezhnevistanis?' SFN's head honcho looked puzzled. 'Not that I know of. But that doesn't necessarily mean we haven't. If they're in a seller's market then it would be Sid. If we'd got them marked down as a potential market then it would be our sales and marketing guys. But until little Camilla and Dave and your ridiculous Secretary of State got involved with them we wouldn't have identified them as the sort of people who would be into buying things. Not even bargains.'

'Quite,' said Bognor. 'So you don't know if Sid has any plans for meeting anyone from the delegation. Or if he already has.'

'No. I wouldn't. Not unless a deal comes out of it. And a big one at that. I leave little deals to others. That's called delegation in my business.'

'I do delegation too,' riposted Bognor, thinking of Harvey Contractor. 'Like you I get to a certain class of lunch while the others have a sandwich at their desk. That's what I call delegation.'

He deliberately raised his gaze to look over Maclean's left shoulder and scoured the room. 'Ah,' he said, 'there's Mananin. I'd better go and say hello. I suppose that short bloke with the hair and dark glasses is the amazing Doctor Skodt.'

Maclean turned to stare rudely. 'The man behind the economic miracle,' he said. 'That's him. But there's no point trying to talk to him. He doesn't do conversation. Just economic miracles.' He laughed.

Bognor excused himself and pushed through the throng to Mananin who greeted him like a long-lost sparring partner.

'Professor Doctor,' he exclaimed embracing Bognor in a stifling bear hug.

'Bolislav, my dear old thing!' said Sir Simon.

They withdrew a foot or so and told each other how well they were looking.

For a few moments they exchanged pleasantries.

Then Bognor cleared his throat and changed gear.

'So, tell me Bolislav. What is it exactly that brings you here?'

'Oh,' the old secret service operator shrugged expressively, 'a little of this. A little of that. I am just, how would you say, the manager. The real work is Doctor Skodt and Anne-Marie. They are the brains. I carry the bags.' He laughed so that his shoulders shook, drained his glass and plucked another from a passing tray.

'Oh' said Bognor unconvincingly, 'I simply can't believe, er ...' his voice trailed away. He believed all too well. Mananin was the Duke of Norfolk on this tour. Front man. Baggage handler. Schmooze merchant. He was lucky to have survived so far.

'And what exactly do Skodt and Anne-Marie hope to achieve?' Bognor tried to sound merely conversational. He didn't succeed but it seemed not to matter.

The old stooge shrugged again.

'We have factories producing goods which we are world leaders at manufacturing. We have not sufficient demand at home for these things. So we must sell to others. This is what we are here to do. And maybe we have oil. Who knows? Other things. There is a big land mass to be explored. Meanwhile, our factories make what the world does not want.'

'Like false beards,' said Bognor.

'False beards, false moustaches, false wigs. All manner of false things. Costumes for the circus. Disguise. Jokes.' Mananin drained his glass and nicked another from a passing tray. 'I no longer care,' he said.

'And you're here to sell these things?'

The old apparatchik shrugged and gulped. He was becoming expansively inebriated.

'That is what I believe. Professor Doctor Skodt and Madam Ng tell me very little. They have a secret strategy. Perhaps you would like to discuss it with the Doctor? I can introduce you.'

'But they say he doesn't speak.'

'This is true. But I can still introduce you. Then you can make up your mind.' The big man laughed again and grabbed another glass.

'What about Madam Ng?' asked Bognor.

'She is not here. She is never in the same place as the Doctor. They believe that if they were seen together people will talk. They even flew here in different planes. Even so, people are talking.' Mananin winked and put a finger to his nose. 'Gromykograd is a very small place. There are many rumours about the Doctor and Madam Ng. They meet only in secret.'

'Well,' said Bognor, 'you'd better introduce me to your leader even if he won't speak.'

'As you wish.'

Mananin turned and barged towards the small Toulouse-Lautrec-looking figure. 'Professor Doctor,' he slurred, 'I have the honour to present Sir Simon Bognor, Director of Special Investigations at the Board of Trade. Sir Simon is a very old friend and very important in British public life.'

Bognor managed a delicate pinkening of complexion and inclined his head. The little man bowed back but, as predicted, said absolutely nothing. Bognor sniffed involuntarily. Doctor Skodt smelt. In fact he smelt very strongly. Bognor was surprised, inhaled again, just to be sure, but tried to disguise what he was doing. He had no wish to create an international incident particularly on his Secretary of State's turf. Instead he and Mananin exchanged desultory pleasantries and reminiscences, watched in silence by the strange little guru, until, without warning the Doctor bowed again, turned round and departed.

'What a funny little fellow,' said Bognor, involuntarily.

'He is not a joke I see,' said Mananin, with feeling.

A few minutes later, when conversation was not just wearing thin but was evaporating altogether, the two men were saved by the intervention of a woman in a vaguely Muslim outfit which managed to combine a ritual genuflection in the direction of religious convention with a definite dash of haute couture.

'Bolislav, aren't you going to introduce me to your friend?' she asked, in slightly accented English. She was definitely attractive and despite the orthodoxish outfit she seemed made-up, coiffed and scented in a decidedly Western, almost decadent, manner.

Mananin made the introductions and Madam Ng, for it was she, gave him her hand to kiss. Her finger nails were painted. Bognor remembered that Doctor Skodt had worn gloves. No rings.

Bognor asked rather weedily if Madam had been enjoying her visit and she replied that she had very much but that alas all good things had to come to an end and they were flying back East that very evening but she hoped that foundations had been laid for a bright new era in relations between our two countries and she was hoping to return before long so that she and Doctor Skodt could implement many of the initiatives that he had been begun and Dave the Prime Minister was really quite a dish and she had managed to get to the new landscape exhibition at Tate Britain and the food hall at Harvey Nicks was a revelation and she was going to see if they couldn't open a branch in Gromykograd.

All this in a single sentence.

Bognor smiled and said she sounded very busy.

This set her off on an account of the Brehnevistani national output heavy on statistics and low on humour. Sir Simon could see that Madam was a force of nature but he also began to feel sorry for his old acquaintance.

'So do you have a busy final afternoon?' he asked politely.

'I must not say too much,' she said. 'There have been one or two little disappointments along the way but I am ever hopeful. And as you say in your country "Third time lucky".'

Bognor nodded.

'Quite,' he said, and looked ostentatiously at his watch. 'How time flies when one is having fun. That's another old British saying. And now I'm afraid I've got rather a busy schedule. A couple of things need clearing up.'

He embraced Mananin again and kissed Madam Ng's hand.

In the limo on the way back to the office he put a call through to Sidney Nicholson at Something for Nothing. The two had never met but such was Sir Simon's reputation that he had no problem getting through and no difficulty in getting Sid, for all his Etonian spivvery, to answer honestly and at once.

'Just as I thought,' he said to no-one in particular, as he switched off his mobile.

There was no huge hurry but he told his driver to wait outside on the double yellow line while he went inside to collect one or two things and Harvey Contractor. A few minutes later they were on their way to the headquarters of SFN just north of the Circular Road in a grey area between Neasden and Willesden.

'Forget the "for", ' said Bognor with feeling, as they eased alongside row after row of identical anonymous terraced houses 'an "and" would be more appropriate. "Something AND Nothing." Not "Something FOR Nothing." This is nothing territory.' He disliked having to spell things out but felt needs must when it came to Contractor. He was extremely bright but did not move in imaginative leaps and bounds. This was a land of something and nothing. Forget the transfer of one to the other; this was all the same thing. And 'nothing' was the dominant factor.

SFN HQ was an anonymous pile of outsize breeze blocks in a village of similar edifices. One pretentious prefab after another: nowhere-land.

They were expected; they were conducted upstairs; they were greeted; they were shown to a secure but hidden place; they waited.

Presently the important visitor arrived and was ushered into Sidney's presence. There were formalities and pleasantries. Tea was offered and declined; a chair was accepted; murmurings about the ease of the journey and the accessibility of the office were exchanged.

Then the visitor in a thin, nasal metallic voice which had something of the quality of the Daleks on *Doctor Who* only several notes higher, said, somewhat brusquely, 'Deal or no deal?'

It was at this point that Sir Simon Bognor and Harvey Contractor emerged from their hiding place. Harvey held a handgun to the back of the visitor's head while Bognor moved with surprising speed to deftly remove the false beard which had, in effect, been concealing most of the guest's face.

'Ah,' he said, smiling, 'Madam Ng. Or should I say Doctor Skodt?'

The visitor looked back with an expression of pure malevolence.

'Diplomatic immunity and your corrupt politicians will ensure that I am on the plane home tonight,' she said in the same accented English that she had employed at the Secretary of State's bunfight at the Stein Imperial. 'I am able in your country to do exactly as I like.'

'I think not, actually,' said Bognor, 'and I'm certainly not going to let you kill Mr. Henderson here, even if he is a bit of an Etonian wideboy. I'll arrange for some uniformed people to escort you back to the hotel and thence to the airport.'

He smiled. 'I suppose, regrettably, that one or other of Madam Ng and the Professor Doctor will have to be left behind.' He paused. 'How curious that both these unlikely figures should wear the scent. Am I right in thinking it's Chanel Number Five? Old-fashioned I know but curiously enough Lady Bognor's favourite as well. I on the other hand, never touch the stuff.'

Saying which, he told Harvey Contractor to carry on and do the necessary. A week or so later a brown paper package was delivered to Bognor's office. It bore a Gromykograd postmark and a large number of lurid triangular stamps. After being subjected to the usual checks for explosives, drugs or other unsolicited undesirable matter, the package made it way through a series of minions and secretaries to the Director's office.

Sir Simon waited until he was alone before opening his present, conscious, as always, of the unflinching feminine stares from the two photographs, one on the wall of Her Majesty the Queen, the other on his desktop of his wife, Monica, also known as Lady Bognor. He felt, as usual, both diminished and strengthened by their gaze.

The wrapping was perfunctory and old-fashioned, involving brown paper and string. Inside, as he had rather suspected, there were two objects. One was a beard, black, full, Rasputin-like, with two plastic hooks for hanging over one's ears. Holding it out at arm's length Sir Simon smiled softly and half considered trying it on, wondering what he would look like in such a hairy disguise. Then he put it down, gently on his desk, wondering if he might have it framed.

Alongside it was another parcel, though 'parcel' was too grand a word for the little *amuse-gueule* of a gift which was little more than a twist of tissue paper. It could have been a boiled sweet or one of those almond-amaretti biscotti you got in Italian restaurants at Christmas. He had an idea what it was and it certainly wasn't a macaroon.

Untwisting the paper he smiled another little tic of self-congratulation. It was a small-calibre silver bullet.

There was no further message.

SISTERS UNDER THE SKIN

Robert Barnard

Harry Keating detests airports. In this he has the rest of the world on his side. You do occasionally meet people who enjoy being shut in a plane with nothing to see except other detainees and nothing to eat except the inedible. But you really would have to be an expert in haystack needle-searching to winkle out one enthusiast for O'Hare, or Bucharest or (worst of all) Heathrow airports.

What kind of airport-hater is Harry, then? Does he loathe them because he loathes flying? If so, is it death he is afraid of, or terminal boredom? Does he object to being shut up for two hours with wraith-like people who seem to have escaped from an Edvard Munch canvas? Does he resent the fact that even if he wanted to go by surface transport to Australia he could do so only on a cruise, calling only at the world's nethermost hellholes in the company of widows from Los Angeles who have been plastic-surgeried out of mere human existence so that Madame Tussaud's models seem more likely specimens of society?

I shall ask him next time I see him, and will no doubt get a patient, rational and well-argued response. Meanwhile, to salute Harry on the occasion of his Majority, here is a short story that takes off from one of the least desirable locations on the globe.

'I *have* met you before, haven't I?'

The man had come up while Lydia was staring meditatively ahead of her, thinking only of the time when she would be reunited with Brad and the children, when the bustle of O'Hare and the flight were behind her. She raised her head to look at the man.

'I wouldn't say you've met me now,' she said.

'Sorry. But the resemblance is so striking that it must be you. I'm Colin Maudesley, by the way.'

He waited.

139

'Lydia Kingsley,' she said reluctantly. She wanted to say 'My flight has been called', but she was already at the gate for her flight, and nothing was happening. She muttered, heartfeltly: 'God, I hate airports.'

'It was at a party at Professor Smithers' that we met.' Again he waited, but got no response. There was hardly a hair-crack in the ice. He went on: 'Professor of Psychology at Manchester University.'

'And the party was at Manchester?'

'Yes. At the Department, in fact.'

'Then it's impossible we met there. I've never been to Manchester. Tomorrow will be the first time.'

'I just can't ...' He sat down, his face close to her. 'Her likeness to you is so extraordinary – except ten years younger.'

'Lucky her.'

'It was about ten years ago,' he said hurriedly. 'Her name was Beattie. Just a casual meeting at a party. But I've remembered it for all these years.'

There was something in his way of saying it, and in the twist of his face, that intrigued Lydia.

'Why have you remembered it? You don't give the impression that it was a happy encounter.'

'I'm not sure if it was happy or unhappy. But it was odd.'

'Odd crazy?'

'Odd scary. She was so intense. Not cool like you. And she talked in such a way about her husband ... That's why I remembered her.'

Lydia digested this.

'Do you mean that she hated him?'

'Hated, feared, was maddened by him. I mean literally maddened. Every movement was nervy, every expression on her face scared and scary, the whole body neurotic ... That's why I almost believed her when she said she was going to murder him.'

Lydia's eyelids conveyed a flicker of interest against her will.

'I can see why you remember the encounter. You took it seriously, obviously.'

'Oh, I did. It wasn't "I could murder him sometimes." It was a declaration of intent: "I'm going to murder him. I can feel it".'

'Why didn't you go to the police?'

'I don't know ... I think it was a fear of making a fool of myself. Fear that they would take it as just cocktail party histrionics.'

'They could have. You don't as a rule declare that sort of intention to a stranger at a party.'

'You might do, if you were mad.'

'And that's what you assumed?'

'Yes. I'm sorry, it doesn't sound flattering. You are different in every way – body language, clothes, *feel* – but alike in just that one vital way, your face and features, your body itself. There is a total physical likeness. You don't have a sister?'

'I'm an only child.'

'You weren't adopted?'

'If so it's news to me.'

The man shook his head. Lydia got up.

'It's my time for boarding. Thank you for a fascinating conversation.'

She began walking away, but she was pulled up short by the man's voice.

'You have her walk, too. I watched her walk from the house later in the evening and wondered whether she was going straight home to murder her husband. It's just her walk.'

Lydia blinked, swallowed. Walks were a bit of a hobby-horse with her. She often said that a person's walk was as individual to her or him as their fingerprints. She turned round slowly, reluctantly.

'Do you think I could have your card? Or your address, I mean, just in case ...'

She only looked at his card later, when she was settled on the plane. It said he was the Professor of Sociology at Bradford University.

Next morning she was collected by her husband at Manchester Airport at eight o'clock, and was reunited with her children over breakfast at the Radisson Hotel, where they had stayed overnight. Then they set off for an Autumn, half-term holiday in the Lakes. For the first hour she was preoccupied with the children's account of the three weeks she had been away from them, lecturing on Vermeer in East Coast and Mid-West galleries. But as they subsided into the teenage equivalent of car games her thoughts turned to what had been on her mind for the waking hours of the flight. As they neared Carlisle she turned to Brad, her husband, and said:

'Do you think I could have been adopted?'

Her husband was not one for a flip answer. He knew he would be enlightened before long about the reason for the question, so he simply considered the situation itself. A couple of minutes later he said:

'I suppose you could be. Late baby – your mother more than forty. Both of them, by your account, a bit "book-bound" when it came to bringing up a child – trusted to experts rather than their own judgment. That could be the reason.'

They drove on for several miles towards Grasmere, and as they did so the thoughts of both of them were running through Lydia's relatives and before long coalesced.

'Your Aunt Pru would be the one to ask,' said Brad. 'Invite her round one day when the children are back at school.'

'I was going to anyway,' said Lydia. 'I'll explain it all to you later.'

Aunt Pru, when she came round ten days later, was all agog to ask her about her American tour, and it was easy for Lydia, over tea and scones, to lead up to the topic that was now foremost in her mind: 'And the oddest thing happened to me at Chicago airport.'

Aunt Pru, her mother's younger sister, had come into the household on her mother's early death, of cancer, when Lydia was only sixteen. She freely admitted she was not the motherly type, and had merely been doing her duty. But the consequence was a genuine and by now deep affection between the two. As Lydia's narration progressed she saw a worried expression creep gradually over her aunt's face.

'What's bothering you?' she asked.

'Nothing ... Of course I always knew you were adopted. All the family did, such as it was. I was working in Canada at the time, and my father wrote and told me. It didn't seem to me to be any big deal, so I just slotted it into the corner of my mind. A few months later he wrote again that your mother and father were moving south, selling up their chemist shop in Stockport and coming here to Chelmsford. Again, it was just a fact, nothing more.'

'But was it something more? If so, I've never been told what.'

'I really don't know. But when I came to help your father look after you, he told me he'd never managed to tell you that you were adopted. I thought that odd, since you were sixteen, but I went along with the implied meaning, that it was for him to tell you, whenever he decided the time was right. It wasn't a matter of any great interest to me, and when you went away to university I got myself a job and moved out. I'd done my bit.'

'And you did it wonderfully well. I'll always be grateful.'

Aunt Pru smiled.

'I did it as a duty. But love came later. I've never regretted it. But I do wonder now if I shouldn't have taken it up with your Dad, had it out with him that you should have been told.'

'He only died two years ago. He could have found a time if he'd wanted to tell me. Did the subject never come up?'

'I wouldn't say "never", but very, very seldom. I do remember once ...' She shook her head in exasperation. 'It's a long time ago. I can't remember the details, but there was a case in the papers, one of those court cases concerning local government corruption, and your father was reading about it in the *Guardian*. He said suddenly: "I always knew that man was crooked." I said, "Who's that?" "A little bastard called Maclehose. Worked in the children's care section at Manchester. He got his just deserts." I left it a day or two, then asked him what he had against the man. And he said: "He was never crooked with us. Our adoption was always straightforward. But he was a power-freak. He refused to let us adopt Lydia's twin sister. Said that two babies were too much for a couple on the outer edge of the permitted age for adoption to cope with. We were a bit bitter, but we had to accept the decision ..." "But?" I asked. "But we found out later that the baby had been adopted by the man's brother. It was sheer nepotism. The pair were older than we were, and had only registered to adopt in the previous year ..."'

'Do you think that's why they moved south?'

'I don't know. Maybe they were obsessed by the fact that you had a twin in the area, and they didn't want to see how that adoption turned out. Or perhaps they didn't want you to encounter her unexpectedly. Anyway, I didn't ask, because he made it obvious that was a matter he was very reluctant to talk about. I think I rather failed you there.'

'You never failed me in anything, Auntie.'

It took Lydia some days to think up what she might do next, and it was without any great hopes of success that she decided to ring the secretariat at Manchester University. Some blind instinct made her ring during the lunch hour, and she was blessed by her call being answered by a chatty girl who showed every sign of being left in charge without any clear directions of what she should or shouldn't answer. Lydia explained that she was trying to trace a relative by the name of Maclehose, though she thought she might have a later, married name.

'Oh, it's an unusual name, isn't it? Wouldn't want to spell it out, me, every time I had to give it to anyone. It'll be on the wages and pensions computer if we actually employed her ... Wait a sec ... Yes, there was a

Maclehose, B, back in 1985 and on till 1990, when she changed her name to Skelton, B ... Oh yes, and than back to Maclehose, B, for a short time, just a matter of months, from 1998 onwards. After that, nothing.'

'I think that may well be my cousin.'

'We don't have a present address. She's not on a pension, but she seems always to have been a secretary, so that would explain *that* ... You know, the name Maclehose doesn't ring a bell, but the name Skelton does ... Beatrice Skelton ... Beattie Skelton! That's it! Now what ... Oh, I wonder if I should –'

'You've been awfully helpful, and I'm very grateful,' said Lydia hurriedly, putting down her receiver.

She talked the situation over with Brad later that night, and they honed in eventually on the central question: should she take the matter any further? Brad was pretty dubious about the likely outcome, but he tried to hide it, and it was only knowing him so completely that told her so.

'Would I be happier?' Lydia said meditatively to one of his points. 'I really don't know. But I think what I'd be is fuller, more completely in control of myself, more aware of who and what I am.'

Brad thought, then said: 'Then obviously you've got to go ahead with it.'

Lydia thought he said it with reluctance. She went ahead with it with reluctance herself.

Establishing the existence of a Maclehose, B, in the Manchester area proved very easy. She rang Directory Enquiries and grabbed a little card from the mess of her telephone table and took down the telephone number of Maclehose, B. The address she knew they would not give her, but on her next trip to London, mostly occupied with the National Gallery who had sponsored her trip to the States, she went to the London Library, where she found an address in the Telephone Directory for Greater Manchester. She entered it, 37A Peebles Road, on to the card. She thought of giving the number she got from Directory Enquiries a ring, probably with a false accent, but rejected it. It savoured too much of taking what could turn out to be her sister for a ride. She suspected that that was the last thing she should be doing with this particular person. She decided instead to risk being on a wild goose chase and go up to see the person concerned: the rareness of the surname and the correctness of the initial seemed to give her a reasonable chance of success.

When she got to Manchester Piccadilly it was cold and raining, and she got into a taxi and gave him the name of the road, but not the number. It was a long trip, and she often looked at the little card with Beattie's address on it in the palm of her gloved hand. He left her on the corner of Peebles Road, in Salford, as Lydia had requested. She did not want to get out of a taxi outside her sister's home. It was a Council estate, one of the kind that Brad described as 'where they stone anyone who's wearing a tie.' She swallowed, paid her fare, and got out of the cab, wishing she had put on jeans and blouse, rather than the smart suit she had chosen. She walked slowly along, looking for number thirty-seven.

It proved to be a house like all the rest, the little area of front garden fairly unkempt, the paint peeling around the windows. The Directory she had consulted had said 37A, and that was the number not on the front but on a side entrance – the house, she thought, was two flats, and Maclehose, B, was in the upstairs one. She walked through trampled-down grass round to the side, and rang the doorbell. After a second there came some kind of shout from upstairs. She rang again and waited. Then came the sound of heavy footsteps on the stairs, and the door opened.

She looked at a terrible parody of herself – her own face, her own body, but horribly transformed. The first thing that hit her was the smell of alcohol – red wine, she thought. Then she saw her own face – mouth, eyes, cheeks – but transformed by puffiness and dingy complexion into something ugly, unhealthy, almost disgusting. The eyes, though, were still capable of focussing themselves, and the woman let her slack jaws fall open with surprise at what she saw.

'Good God,' she said.

'I'm Lydia Kingsley,' said Lydia, wishing she had made better preparation for the encounter. 'I – I think I may be your sister.'

The woman said nothing, then held the door open and led the way up the stairs into a living room as dingy and unwelcoming-looking as her face.

'I often wondered –' she said, openly staring.

'What had happened to your twin sister?' hazarded Lydia.

'Yes …' An expression of grievance took hold of her face. 'Whether she'd had better luck than I did.'

'I had great good luck,' said Lydia, sitting down at Beatrice's gesture on a sofa whose springs could be felt. 'Lovely people, loving, always anxious to do the right thing.'

'Ha! Have a drink.' She got up and brought a bottle and glasses from the table. Lydia wanted to refuse, but thought it would be taken as a criticism, so she took them and poured half a glass.

'But you weren't so lucky,' she stated. The grievance festered.

'Bastards. Wanted a child, but didn't want the trouble of a child. It was all their fault – one hundred per cent.'

'What was their fault?' asked Lydia, thinking that she could guess.

Beatrice looked at her. 'I thought you knew. Thought that must have been how you found me. I'm notorious. People look at me when I go into a shop. I know as soon as I go out they'll be nudging themselves and talking about me.'

Quite suddenly Lydia felt a surge of pity for the woman – for the neglected girl and the desperate woman. She leant forward and asked gently: 'And what will they be saying about you?'

'That I killed my husband. Everyone knows round here. That's why I thought you knew.'

Lydia was glad she could reply truthfully: 'I didn't know. Was his name Skelton?'

'That's it. Peter Skelton. Senior Lecturer in Biology. Tipped for the top – a chair before he was forty. Only he never sat in that bleeding chair. I saw to that.' She drank her wine to the dregs.

'Why did you marry him?' Lydia asked.

Beattie Maclehose shrugged. 'I was a bewildered girl, no idea where I was going. My parents said I should, it was a wonderful chance, he was a catch, and everyone knew he was going places. There was no way another chance as good as this would ever come my way ... They were desperate to get rid of me, in other words.'

'But you had your doubts?'

'Of course I had my bleeding doubts. I hardly knew the bloke. It was like the fucking nineteenth century, though I didn't realise it at the time. I'd gone to a posh day school where the parents were pressing their daughter to do all kinds of things. I didn't realize that pressuring their daughter to marry someone she'd barely met was a thing of the past.'

'What was the marriage like?'

'Like Hell on earth. He wanted to control everything I did. Made me feel I had to ask permission to pick my nose. If he was in to dinner – which wasn't often, because he was the coming man, wining and dining, being wined and dined, here, there and everywhere – if he *was* home it was as if he was giving me marks out of ten for everything I served up to him. And not many marks out of ten. It was like being back in school – being an eleven year old in a situation that most twenty-five year olds couldn't have coped with.' She poured herself a full glass of red wine and slurped some of it back. 'He liked young girls, and he liked them to be terrified of him. It was bloody murder.'

Lydia could have thought of all kinds of things to say to that, but she just asked him quietly: 'How *did* it come to that? Why didn't you just up and leave him?'

Beattie looked at her resentfully.

'Oh yes, and where was I to go? Back to my devoted family? If I had I'd have been in pretty much the same situation, and they'd have been on at me the whole time to go back to him. No thank you.'

'You could have got a place of your own. You had a job.'

'He'd have come after me – I knew he would. I was like a kid being bullied at school. She *knows* that if she transferred to another school the bully would be outside the school gates at going-home time. She knows it because she knows she's perfect bullying material. I knew that, and he knew it too. I was never going to get away from him except by … putting an end to him.'

'So that's what you did?'

'Yes, with a carving knife. We had a blazing row and I made sure the windows were open so the neighbours heard. The jury brought it in as manslaughter. I think there was someone on the jury who'd suffered just the way I had.' She drained her glass. 'I still don't see what else I could have done. I had no one, you see.'

'You've got someone now,' said Lydia. 'You've got a family of your own.'

It was out before she had had time to think it over. Beattie looked at her, a glint in her eyes.

'Do you mean that? Someone who cares about me? People who will help when things get too much. I wouldn't be a drag. It would be just –'

'A place to go to. In an emergency. That's why I said it.'

'You'll think me a right cow. Not welcoming you, or anything. Not being pleased. Oh Christ! I've got to go to the lav.'

She dashed out into the hallway. Lydia heard the door shut and the lock turn. Then she heard the sound of the floodgates of diarrhoea being opened. She stood up. She had been mad. She, Lydia Kingsley the Ice Queen, who never involved herself in messy emotional situations.

She had seen in the glint of Beattie's eyes what she had let herself in for. She had, quite casually, almost without thinking, taken on an emotional burden that could be life-long. She would be landed up with an incurable drunk who was very probably a drug addict to boot, and she would have to bear all the traumas and wounds that Beattie was so obviously incapable of bearing herself. If she, Lydia, had been a spinster that would have been one thing. But there was Brad and the children. Would her marriage even survive such a deadly weight of responsibility? Would the children, once they had got away to university, ever come and see her? Would they ring in advance to find out whether 'that woman' was there?

It was too much. Too monstrous a load, and one that sprang only from a chance remark, which in its turn sprang from a rare warm impulse she almost immediately regretted. From the lavatory there came sounds of fresh volcanic eruptions. Lydia tiptoed through the hall, down the stairs, and out of the front door, then started to look for the quickest way to get out of sight, to get out of the Peebles estate, then find a taxi or a car-hire firm.

It was not until she was ten minutes away from number 37A and the ravaged, resentful face of Beattie Maclehose that she felt the grip of a November day in Greater Manchester on her right hand. She looked down. She must have left behind her glove on the sofa or the little table nearby. Well, she could afford … Then a thought struck her. Inside the glove, or possibly on top of it, was the card on which she had written the telephone number and later the address of Beattie Maclehose. And on the other side of that card?

It must, she thought, have been one of her own professional cards. She knew she had said nothing about her home town, or given an address. Now she inadvertently had. She was not free of her sister at all.

But when she got home, had come clean to Brad, had said nothing to the children and started for several weeks at every ring of the telephone, gradually she started to feel secure. Beattie had taken her wretched creeping away as a sign she regretted her assurances of concern for her. Quite right too – spot on. She felt guilty, but she also felt liberated.

After a time her sense of self-preservation triumphed over her weaker moral sense, her happiness at her liberation over her intermittent shame at her craven departure from Peebles Street. And when she thought about the incident, all the events which led up to her flight, the picture that came strongly into her mind was the card with Beattie's number and address on it in the palm of her glove on the small side-table. And one day, walking down the road to Chelmsford station, she realised that in that picture the colour of the card was not white but yellow. Not her own professional card then, but whose card? She remembered the card of Colin Maudesley handed to her as she ran for the plane in O'Hare Airport. It was cream-coloured. If Beattie found it, as she surely must have, she would assume that 'Lydia Kingsley' was the name of the wife or partner of Professor Colin Maudesley. She smiled and told herself that if Beattie turned up on the doorstep of that stranger who had intruded himself into her life, there would be a certain poetic justice to it. She walked on with a spring in her step and a fresh accretion of ice in her heart.

INITIAL IMPACT

Simon Brett

Amongst Harry Keating's many achievements, he is one of the few writers who have attempted a crime novel in verse. I know that, because I'm another of that very perverse minority, and on my shelves, along with my own A Crime in Rhyme *and* Lines of Enquiry, *I proudly display a copy of* Jack, The Lady Killer *by H.R.F. Keating.*

So it didn't take long for some masochistic tendency within me to contemplate the idea of writing my contribution to this volume in verse. And then, pondering the fact that Harry was a member of another elite minority – writers known to the reading public by their initials – it wasn't long before I had the idea which turned into the following little frippery …

In the annals of crime that have passed down through time,
There have been many tales of the bad and the base,
But now let's recall the strangest of all,
Which was known as the Farrendale Case.

A body was found, shallow-graved in the ground,
Its throat with a kitchen knife spiked.
His name was Frank Japp, an amiable chap
And – it seemed – universally liked.

But the Scene of Crime crew found a rather odd clue –
A horrible sight to behold! –
Because under Japp's vest, there was stuck to his chest
A card with an 'A' printed bold.

There were police on the spot, but sadly they'd not
Got a clue who had brought the man down,

Who had wanted him dead, or what had been said
That summer evening in Farrendale Town.

So, not being inspired, they researched and enquired
Into Japp's life and personal history.
He was aged about forty, he had never been naughty,
And his life was unclouded by mystery.

The detective in charge was clumsy and large.
Inspector McMahon he was known as.
He was pompous and vain, with a very slow brain,
And one of life's natural postponers.

His mind had no range, was resistant to change
And against new ideas it was walled in.
With each murder that came, it was always the same –
The usual suspects were called in.

His assistant was bright, the young Sergeant Kite,
With a talent that few had expected,
But all a dead loss with McMahon as her boss.
Her suggestions were always rejected.

And so when she tried to say how Japp had died,
The Inspector saw she was ignored,
Treated her as a cipher, and arrested a lifer,
Who'd recently come out of Ford.

So things might have stayed for another decade,
With Kite being doomed to frustration,
Had not poor McMahon been found dead in a barn
In a criminal extermination.

The police force were stretched, so the Sergeant was fetched
To succeed where her dead boss had failed.
Now the case could proceed with rather more speed,
And the killer be finally nailed.

[With this changed personnel, it is timely as well –

Indeed, it couldn't be neater –
To quickly arrange a poetical change –
And give up this horrible metre.
My goodness, that feels better – it's so good we've made the
    shift –
There's nothing like an iambus to give a chap a lift!]
So Sergeant Kite at last took up the case
And tried to make the pieces fall in place.
With the patience of a skilled investigator,
She reassessed all the existing data,
And threw one salient fact into the mix –
That Japp was born in nineteen sixty-six,
When his father who loved him and brought him up
Was ecstatic that England had won the World Cup.
And, throughout his life the murdered man
Had been an avid football fan.
Kite pondered and began to think
That football might provide a link ...
An argument, a punch-up which
Had erupted off the pitch.
A sudden flare-up with a knife
Perhaps had robbed poor Japp of life.
But though Kite questioned everyone in sight,
She found no witnesses to such a fight.
Then, while the case was failing to progress,
Another murder added to her stress.
Another man was hit by something weighty,
A younger victim, born in nineteen-eighty.
The poor young man was known as Alan Storm –
Again no enemies, no past, no form –
But the same murderer – yes, it had to be,
For on his chest was stuck the letter 'C'.
For Sergeant Kite this raised a troubling thought:
Something was missing – yes, there really ought
To be a 'B' between the 'A' and 'C'.
She had a nasty feeling there would be
Another victim found before too long.
And then she thought perhaps they had been wrong
To write McMahon off as a separate case.

She sent the S.O.C.Os back to search the place
Where the Inspector's body had been found.
And, sure enough, beneath a little mound
Of earth outside the barn, just in the yard,
They found another calling card.
A 'B'. The murderer was up to three.
He must be stopped before he got to 'D'.
But how? For Sergeant Kite the leads were few.
To tell the truth, she hadn't got a clue.
At the Memorial Service to her former boss
She joined the other cops to mourn his loss,
Sing stirring hymns and listen to
Encomia that were not true.
Attention wandering, she idly scanned
The Order of Service in her hand,
And read, printed on the front of it, that the late
McMahon had been born in 1948.
But his initials, she saw in that House of God,
Were: C.P.A.G.M.W. – now that was odd.
The strangeness didn't go away
As she sipped a warmish Chardonnay,
And it niggled her acute perception
Over sausage rolls at the reception.
So Kite was still preoccupied
When an elderly man came to her side
And said, 'Gosh, you look out of sorts.
Come on, a penny for your thoughts.'
The stranger, who turned out to be
A former cop, showed sympathy
And Sergeant Kite, feeling relaxed,
Told him all the salient facts
About McMahon's death – and her confusion
About the initials he had in profusion.
The old man grinned and rubbed his chin.
'I'm not surprised the state you're in.
Though you have struggled with persistence,
You really need outside assistance.
I know who'll help you to progress.
This could be a case for the I.S.'

' "I.S."? What's that? It sounds most odd.'
' "I.S." stands for "Initials Squad".
They're always ready, set to go.
They have a specialised M.O.
Their team is small, their cases few,
But when they move, it's P.D.Q.
And, since you seem so at a loss,
I'll send you off to meet their boss.'
The I.S. offices were small and neat,
Set in a suburban street.
To be frank, it should be said
They were nothing but a garden shed,
Where the Chief I.S. Inspector
Worked alone as the director
Of this complex operation.
In his shed the only decoration
Was rows and rows of wooden shelves,
Where rows of books proclaimed themselves
All to be by a certain kind of writer,
Amongst whose names you could not sight a
Single first name. But instead
There were just initials in the shed –
No names allowed, so Ethel M. Dell
Wasn't there – nor Dorothy L.
To be the kind of author picked,
You had to pass – the rules were strict.
You could be 'H.R.F.', but you couldn't be 'Harry'
To join the likes of J.M. Barrie,
C.P. Snow and Wells, H.G.,
The Jameses, M.R. and P.D.,
A.E. Housman, H.E. Bates,
T.S. Eliot, W.B. Yeats,
A.A. Milne, V.S. Naipaul,
A.J. Cronin – that's not all …
C.L.R. James with books on bowling,
J.G. Ballard, J.K. Rowling.
J.B. Priestley playing straight man
To W.C. Sellar and R.J. Yeatman.
Booker winners too were there –

A work by D.B.C. Pierre,
(Who, thanks to Booker nomination,
Is the Keri Hulme of his generation.)
More qualified – you can't deny it –
Were P.G. Wodehouse, A.S. Byatt,
C.S. Lewis – and of course to
Swell the ranks were E.M. Forster ...
G.K. Chesterton, J.L. Carr,
L.P Hartley (but not J.R.!)
In fact the shed was well resourced. If
Books were wanted, quite exhaustive,
A horde of writers it comprised –
But none who weren't initialised.
And overseeing the collection
Was a master of detection ...
An elderly man with a kindly smile,
Who'd been alone for quite a while,
And greeted Sergeant Kite with glee,
Saying, 'I'm D.C.I. M.J.G. Dee.
I'm very pleased to welcome you,
'Cause the jobs that come my way are few.
But now you're here I won't be lax.
I'll help you out. Give me the facts.'
So, feeling more hopeful than of late,
The Sergeant brought him up to date.
When she was done, he grinned, all breezy,
And announced, 'McMahon is easy.
His year of birth? Tell me the date.'
Kite said, '1948.'
'Ahah!' said Dee. 'The truth unveils –
The same year as the Prince of Wales!
MacMahon had parents who were loyal
And named their son for someone royal –
A patriot's gesture nomenclatorial,
As you observed at the Memorial.
On his name the list of letters that begins are
Charles Philip Arthur George Mountbatten-Windsor!'
'So,' said Kite, 'McMahon was named for Charles?'
'Yes. And the murderer's rationale's

Beginning to emerge. We've dealt with "B".
What initials then had "A" and "C"?'
Sergeant Kite supplied the older
Man with details from her folder.
'Japp's initials – gosh, there's lots of them –
A.G.G.R. – and then there is an 'M' –
And after, N.J.R.G.B.B.'
'When was he born?' asked M.J. Dee
'Well that's one detail I can fix,'
Said Kite. 'In 1966.'
'Ahah,' said Dee. 'It's clear as light!'
'It's not to me,' said Sergeant Kite.
'The initials, young lady, logic proclaims,
Spell out the following list of names:
"Alan, Gordon, George, Ray, Martin, Nobby,
Jackie, Roger, Geoff – then Bobby, Bobby."
'But who are they?' The Inspector said, 'By God!
They are the English winning World Cup Squad,
Whose mighty praises everyone has sung!'
He looked at Kite. 'No, sorry, you're too young.
So let's get "C" now … Come on, matey.
He was born in …?' '1980.'
She checked the folder once again.
'His initials were: "C.B.D.N."
J.S.P. –' Dee said, 'Stop it there!
"Clive Woodward, Bill Beaumont, Dusty Hare,
Nigel Horton, John Carleton, Steve Smith, John Scott …"
That's enough – we don't need the other lot.
In 1980 they reigned supreme,
England's Grand Slam-winning rugby team!
A pattern's starting to emerge.
I know what makes him get the urge.
Our murderer goes for – it all makes sense! –
Victims named after big events!'
'I agree,' said Kite, 'with your suggestion,
But do you know why?' 'That is the question,'
Very sagely Dee concurred.
'Till we know that, the picture's blurred.
But don't lose hope. We'll explain his preference

By consulting this fine work of reference.'
He reached and took down from its home
A weighty, thick and well-thumbed tome,
Entitled: *Initials A-Z.*
'We'll find him here,' the Inspector said.
'It's a wonderful volume – it couldn't be better –
And everyone's listed by initial letter.
Cheer up, Kite. We'll soon have nicked 'im.'
'But how did he come to choose each victim?'
She asked. 'Did he wage this awful jihad
Against people who had more names than he had?'
'Spot on,' said Dee. 'Now let me see
What I can find in this directory.
Our murderer's hate is prejudicial
To people who have one more initial
Than he has – two or three or four,
Five or six or even more.
But how many's *he* got, dirty rat?
McMahon had six, so it's fewer than that.'
'Sorry, if I may butt in, sir.
It could be five, if Mountbatten-Windsor
Were regarded as one word, not two.'
'Good point. Well, what shall we do?'
Sergeant Kite looked all reflective,
Then said, 'Start with five.' 'You're a good detective!'
Said Dee. 'What surname – any thoughts?'
'My view of the human mind supports
The image of someone with low self-esteem –
In this case really quite extreme –
So all my instincts would be drawing
To a surname that is really boring.'
Thus concluded Sergeant Kite.
The Inspector said, 'My God, you're bright!
Let's look up Jones and Smith and Brown –
That'll help to narrow our searches down –
And hope we find some lonely male,
Who has an address in Farrendale.'
They searched on through the book until
They found a name to fit the bill.

Among the Smiths they found a score
With four initials, but one more
Was required – or so they reckoned.
Then Kite said, 'Hey, hang on a second.
What about this one?' 'Where?' asked Dee.
She showed him, and announced with glee,
'There – four initials – and a fifth!
Look – P.C.N.D.E. Smith!
I bet that is our lonely male.
See – the address is Farrendale!'
'Yes,' said Dee. 'He fits the spec.
I think we'd better go and check.'
He turned bright red and looked delighted.
'Ooh, I do get quite excited
When this kind of thing occurs.
I haven't left this shed for years.'
Asked Kite, 'You're saying the I.S.
Seldom has cases?' Dee said, 'Yes.'
They set off, Sergeant and Inspector,
To Farrendale's most bourgeois sector
And the address that they had found.
They knocked the door, and heard the sound
Reverberate throughout the house.
It opened and, meek as a mouse,
There stood an inoffensive man,
Dressed in a well-worn cardigan.
His face was pale as the grave,
As though he'd been living in a cave.
'Hello,' he said. 'Who might you be?'
'Are you Smith, P.C.N.D.E?'
'Yes,' he said. 'I can't deny it.'
(His voice was very soft and quiet.)
'We're the police and need to question you
About three murders.' 'Murders? Who?'
'Don't you read the papers? Don't you watch the news?'
But Smith said, 'No, I've been on a cruise.
I only got back yesterday,
So I know nothing, 'cause I've been away.'
'Oh yes?' said Dee in a sceptical tone.

'And did you go on this cruise alone?'
'Indeed,' the pallid Smith replied.
'I go everywhere alone since my mother died.'
'Classic loner,' thought Dee and Kite together,
But they said nothing. 'I wonder whether,'
Dee enquired, 'you might consent
To tell us where your cruise ship went.'
'Of course.' And so Smith went ahead,
And this is exactly what he said:
'The cruise set out from Athens, to which town
I'd flown from Gatwick on a charter flight.
We all embarked and then went sailing down
Through the star-filled Mediterranean night
To visit islands of the Cyclades;
Then Rhodes, site of the mythical Colossus.
Back West we went to sail the Cretan seas
And stopped on Crete to have a look at Knossos.
We crossed the wine-dark sea for many a mile,
Enjoying sunshine on the roomy deck,
Partook of pleasures on the Corfiot isle,
And back in Athens ended up our trek.
To fit that in took four weeks in the sun …
I was abroad when all the crimes were done.'
'Oh well,' said Dee, 'best say goodbye.
It seems you've got an alibi.
Thanks for your time. God bless you, mate.'
And he set off for the garden gate.
Dee was convinced, but Sergeant Kite
Didn't think it sounded right.
'That alibi was prepared,' she said, 'and I'd put money on it.
How many people d'you know who speak naturally in a
     sonnet?'
The Inspector turned, and Smith looked even paler.
'Besides,' young Kite went on, 'you don't look like a sailor.
A month in the sun would surely show –
And yet your skin's as white as snow.
No, Smith, I think your alibi's
Invented – just a pack of lies!'
At this the meek and humble man

Became transformed, and he began
To foam at the mouth and snarl and spit,
And cried aloud, 'Yes, I did it!
I murdered Japp, McMahon and Storm.
Now I've two more murders to perform!'
From his cardigan pocket he drew a gun
And gibbered, 'Yes, this will be fun!
I know who the next two deaths will be!'
And he whipped out cards printed 'D' and 'E'.
He looked along the gun to sight,
But before he triggered, Sergeant Kite
Got him in a hold she could depend on
(One that she had learned at Hendon).
They called to base, and the murdering liar
Was taken off in a Black Maria.
In an interview room Smith confessed,
And he was put under arrest.
Said Dee, 'Strange case. When I review it,
One question sticks. *Why* did you do it?'
Then Smith shrieked a demented squawk
And said, 'I'll tell you. Yes, I'll talk.
Why does murdering people give me such a buzz?
It goes back my childhood.' Said Dee, 'It usually does.'
'My parents lacked the generous touch.
They never thought I'd come to much,
But though they deemed my prospects rotten,
They didn't want their son forgotten.
My only chance, they thought, of fame
Was if I had a special name.
They were called Smith and they knew, like me,
What a boring surname that could be.
So, though of talent I had no spark,
They hoped I still could make a mark
And be remembered – this they bet me –
As unique by all who met me.
They couldn't give me talent, they couldn't pay for toys,
But they gave me more initials than all the other boys.
I was christened Peter Cedric Norman Davenport
Elijah Smith – or Smith, P.C.N.D.E. for short.

But all my life I've hankered for another claim to fame –
To be remembered as a killer instead of for my name!
I vowed that I would, in a glorious bloody spree
Kill anyone who had the nerve to out-initial me!'
So he owned up to the murders, and for committing them,
He was sentenced to detention at the pleasure of H.M.
Smith was sent to Broadmoor where, amidst the convict rabble,
He served his endless sentence playing endless games of Scrabble.
So the Farrendale Case was solved, its success was often quoted.
Dee was highly commended, and Sergeant Kite promoted;
And when the older man retired, no one thought it odd
That Kite was his successor to lead the Initials Squad.
So she lived out her days in that garden shed,
Untroubled by further murders, while voraciously she read,
Sipping a glass of vintage wine,
Books with initials on the spine.

A CASE FOR INSPECTOR GHOTE

June Thomson

Even before I had met him or read any of his books, I knew his name and was impressed by it. H.R.F. Keating. H.R.F. The three initials seemed to have a special resonance of their own, suggesting someone important, of consequence and repute in the, to me then, unattainable world of crime fiction which I longed to be part of.

He was already up there among the greats such as Dorothy L. Sayers and Conan Doyle. So when I was asked to contribute to Harry's eightieth birthday collection of short stories, it was his name which I wanted to feature in some way as a tribute and as a celebration of his life and work.

And also to say, Thank you, Harry, for all the kind words you have written about my own work and especially for creating Inspector Ghote, such a kind, human and humorous man to whom, to a degree, my own Inspector Finch owes his existence.

At the age of seventy-eight, Muriel Stanley decided at last to commit herself fully to the business of retiring. Up to that time, she had, she realised, given it only half her attention, but the moment had now come when she must take the final step and bite on the bullet, as the saying goes.

True, she had already gone quite a long way down that route. Thirteen years before at the age of sixty-five, she had retired from her post of headmistress at Elm Grove Junior School, but as for the rest of it, her house, her car, she had clung on to them like life-lines and might have gone on doing so if arthritis had not got the better of her. First it was the car that had to go; then she had to employ someone to do the housework for her. And that wasn't the end of it. Too much else remained such as the shopping, and cooking meals and, of course, the garden. It was the garden which finally made her face up to the

162

truth of the situation. She could no longer cope. It was time she went into sheltered accommodation and let someone else take care of such chores.

Being a practical, down-to-earth person, she knew exactly where she would go. She had driven past the place hundreds of times on her way to and from Elm Grove Junior. It was the *Laurels* in Westbury Road; rather a pretentious name, in her opinion, considering the only laurels were half a dozen small shrubs planted round the gravelled forecourt. But the building was pleasant. Two-storeyed and built of biscuit-coloured brick, it was set back from the road and had good-sized windows which would let in plenty of light, while its colour scheme, white woodwork and a dark blue front door, reminded her of a naval uniform, all ship-shape and Bristol fashion.

It was an impression which was confirmed when she made arrangements to look round the place before committing herself. Floors shone, glass sparkled, chromium gleamed but any suggestion of a cold, institutional hygiene was dispelled by softly draped curtains, indoor plants and watercolours of English landscapes hanging on the walls.

There were also other benefits, she noted: a hairdresser and chiropodist who called regularly and, should she wish, plenty of activities she could take part in, from social clubs, which took place in the *Laurels* itself, such as weekly whist-drives and a keep-fit class, to outings by minibus to matinees at the local theatre.

By a lucky chance, there was a vacant room on the ground floor which, like all the others, was designed as a bed-sitter. It had a shower-room opening off it and an alcove which housed a small, basic kitchen, perfectly adequate for her needs, as a cooked, mid-day meal was provided as part of the fees and she would only need to make breakfast for herself and tea, or perhaps a light supper of a ham salad or a poached egg on toast ...

However, it was the view from the window which made up her mind for her. It overlooked a courtyard garden, sheltered and sunny, which was planted with ornamental trees and shrubs, interspersed with herbaceous borders. Here and there were benches where she could sit and read. For all the benefits of her house in Cresswell Green that she was going to have to give up, she knew what she would miss most was her garden and its little paved patio outside the dining room where every summer she would set out her comfortable, cushioned lounger with its matching sunshade and, putting up her feet, she would spend long, delightfully warm afternoons reading with nothing and no one to bother her.

Her mind made up, she signed the agreement with the manageress of the *Laurels* and, on returning home, telephoned her solicitor and two or three estate agents to arrange for her house to be put on the market.

It was the 17th of March when she moved into her room at the *Laurels*. It was still too cold to sit in the garden but warm enough some mornings to walk with her stick the short distance to the small parade of shops in Westbury Road which was next door to a branch library, the existence of which pleased her very much. She could change her books there without the fuss and bother of going on the bus to the main library in the town centre. Admittedly, it was small and the choice of books limited, but the building was bright and cheerful and the librarians were friendly and willing to order any books she might want. In fact, the Westbury Road shopping parade catered for a great many of the needs of the local community. As well as the library, there was a newsagent's cum post office, a mini supermarket, a launderette, an Oxfam charity shop and a very attractive baker's, the Sally Lunn, which sold French baguettes and Danish pastries as well as serving morning coffee and afternoon tea. Peering in through the glass door on the second morning after her arrival at the *Laurels*, Muriel Stanley inspected the five small tables covered with blue and white gingham cloths and the blue and white china plates hanging on the walls. It looked very clean and inviting and she promised herself tea or coffee there before too long.

But what pleased her most was the church, St Andrew's, which stood opposite the post office. She had a vague recollection of noticing a church in Westbury Road on her journeys to and from Elm Grove School but had never taken particular note of it apart from registering its existence. Westbury Road was a narrow, busy street and, a careful driver, Muriel Stanley had never allowed herself more than a passing glance at it. She was disappointed to see on closer inspection that it was Victorian Gothic rather than genuine medieval, the period of her old church in Cresswell Green where she used to live.

But, she told herself firmly, architecture was a minor consideration in the grand scheme of things and there were, she discovered when she attended Matins there for the first time on the following Sunday, other compensations. The vicar had a pleasing, well-modulated voice, the stained glass was not as awful as she had anticipated and the lady who played the organ was willing to give her a lift in her car to and from the church when it rained.

However, it was less easy to come to terms with the chestnut trees which lined the broad asphalt path to the main door. Presumably because of some ridiculous bylaw to do with health and safety, their branches had been cruelly lopped back until all that was left were mutilated stumps held up towards the sky as if the trees were amputees begging for mercy. It was because of the trees that Muriel Stanley was not really aware of the churchyard as, eyes lowered, she hurried past them into the safety of the church.

In a similar fashion, Muriel Stanley learned to avoid Mrs Mallinson. At her first encounter with the woman one lunchtime in the dining room of the *Laurels*, Miss Stanley, with her long experience of people – parents, other teachers, school governors, dinner ladies – decided there and then to give the woman a wide berth. It wasn't difficult. Mrs Mallinson walked with the aid of a zimmer frame and therefore had to choose a table that had easy access.

She was a sweet-faced old lady with soft, white hair which she wore fluffed out over her ears and had that fine, powdery skin which has the texture of a moth's wing. And she talked all the time. That in itself was enough to persuade Muriel Stanley against striking up an acquaintance with her. It was easy enough to avoid her. All Muriel Stanley had to do was wait until Mrs Mallinson had settled herself at her usual table and then sit down at another as far away as possible. Even so, she could at times still overhear Mrs Mallinson's voice. It was like a shallow stream which burbles away continuously and, while apparently going nowhere, manages to wear away stones. It was a penetrating murmur, difficult to ignore, and the chief topic of her conversation was herself. Seated one lunchtime with her back to Mrs Mallinson, she counted the number of times the woman used the words I, me, myself and mine in the time it took to eat a plate of lamb casserole, but gave up at one hundred and seven. And there was still apple crumble and coffee to come.

Apart from Mrs Mallinson, life at the *Laurels* passed pleasantly enough although on occasions time seemed to hang rather heavily. When that happened the best way to make it more palatable, she discovered, was to cut it up into small, manageable portions, as she'd done in the past with the school dinner of a child reluctant to eat, so that each day and each part of every day had its own little pleasures and diversions. So, for example, on Tuesday mornings when Mrs Johnson, the nice West Indian lady, came to clean her room, Muriel Stanley took herself off to the library in Westbury Road to give the woman a clear run and, while she was out, took the opportunity to buy the *Daily Telegraph* at the newsagent's instead of having it delivered. She did the same on Friday mornings when she usually allowed herself the special treat of coffee at the Sally Lunn, each time choosing a different cake to eat with it – a Danish pastry one week, a profiterole another. There was often some shopping to buy at the mini-market as well, although, for a small extra payment Mrs Johnson would do that, too, but when it came to certain items, a pound of apples, for instance, or a new air-freshener for the bathroom, Muriel Stanley preferred to do the choosing herself. Then there was church, of course, on Sunday, and plenty of little jobs to be done about her room, such as watering her indoor plants and doing the crossword puzzle in the *Telegraph* as well as programmes on the radio or television to watch or to listen to, not to mention whist on Thursday evenings in the games room and keep-fit on Wednesday afternoons.

But most of all there was reading. She sometimes asked herself what she would do if there were no books and the answer was she really had no idea. They were so precious to her; not just any old books, of course. At the library, she chose those she wanted to borrow with care, mostly history and biography, her favourite subjects, although art and travel were high on her list as well. As for fiction, that was often more difficult. She had brought with her part of her own little library, mainly those well-loved classics which she was happy to read again and again and still find pleasure in them: Dickens, of course, and Jane Austen, as well as Thomas Hardy and a handful of more modern authors whom she could trust. But as for borrowing novels, she was much more hesitant. You just couldn't be sure these days what you might find between the covers, especially when it came to crime fiction, which was another of her favourites. A good murder mystery was pleasurable but one had to be so careful. She really preferred not to read gruesome descriptions of post mortems or forensic evidence, especially when the language used was coarse.

What she was looking forward to with particular anticipation was the pleasure of sitting in her garden with a book on a sunny afternoon. That was one of her chief delights; no, not one of; it was *the* chief delight and every time she went to the library in Westbury Road, she made a short detour through the courtyard garden, testing out the weather and the progress of spring.

The daffodils came and went. So did the tulips. The lilac bushes produced bright green leaves and little clusters of embryonic buds which over the weeks slowly plumped out into tassels of mauve flowers. And, once the threat of frost was over, a small yellow van with the words 'Green Fingers' emblazoned along its sides arrived and two young women in overalls planted the tubs and flower beds with petunias and stocks and geraniums and, best of all, the glorious *nicotiana* which, once the sun grew warmer, would fill the garden with its wonderful fragrance.

And it was getting warmer. Soon she would be able to sit on the bench she had already selected, the one which the sun reached in the early afternoon but which was shaded by a flowering Japanese cherry tree which as she knew from the one she had grown in her own garden would scatter the pink petals of its blossoms like confetti, to be replaced in late summer by bronze-red foliage almost as colourful as the flowers themselves.

In anticipation of these afternoons under the cherry tree, she bought herself a shopping basket on wheels, a contraption which she would normally have despised, but the usefulness of which she had to acknowledge. In it she could put her two cushions, one to sit on, the other for her back, her glasses, perhaps a packet of rich tea biscuits and, of course, the book she was currently reading.

On 10th June, a Saturday, Muriel Stanley decided the weather was at last warm enough for sitting out in the garden and at two o'clock, having had lunch in the dining room, she loaded up the wheeled basket with everything she would need for an afternoon in the sun including her book, David Starkey's excellent and detailed study of the six wives of Henry VIII, due back at the library the following week, and took herself off to the garden.

It was blissful to sit out there under the cherry tree, the sun warm on her shoulders, the air fragrant with the scent of stocks and tobacco flowers, the noise of the traffic along Westbury Road reduced to a low rumble which, after a little while, she was able to tune out completely, like turning down the volume control on a radio. This was what she had longed for all through the chilly days of early spring and now summer had at last arrived! What more could one want than a sunny afternoon, blue skies, the scent of flowers and a good book? Life, she thought, couldn't be more perfect.

At half past three, she ate two rich tea biscuits and made a mental note to buy several of those small plastic bottles of pure orange juice which she'd seen in the mini-market and which she could keep in the fridge until she needed them. And then at a quarter to five, when the sun had moved behind the *Laurels* and the air began to lose its warmth, she decided it was time to go indoors. Packing up her basket, she wheeled it back into the building through the side door which led to the corridor outside her room. She felt full of contentment and remembered pleasure which was as warm and comforting as the sunshine itself.

The afternoon visits to the garden continued for the next six days until the following Friday when the routine which seemed established and which she had come to look forward to with so much pleasure was suddenly broken. Hardly had she settled herself on her bench with her cushions, put on her reading glasses and opened her book than she heard the side door close with a heavy metallic slam and, glancing up, saw the little, white-haired figure of Mrs Mallinson making her way towards the bench with a surprisingly rapid turn of speed, thrusting her zimmer frame in front of her like a small tank.

Oh, damn! damn! damn!

Hurriedly, Muriel Stanley bowed her head over her book, hoping it would discourage the wretched woman from approaching her. But it was no good.

'Do you mind if I join you?' Mrs Mallinson was asking as she lowered herself very carefully down on to the bench.

What could Muriel Stanley say? She could hardly reply, 'Oh, please go away, you silly woman. All I want to do is sit here on my own and read in peace.'

So she was forced to smile as she braced herself for the inevitable ego-centred conversation which was all Mrs Mallinson seemed capable of making. She had not long to wait.

'What a pretty garden!' Mrs Mallinson exclaimed. 'You know, it reminds me so much of my own garden in Woking when I was married to my dear Teddy, except mine had a lovely summer-house in one corner, I used to sit there in the afternoons with my embroidery which I loved doing: *petit-point* mostly; cushion covers and those little mats you put under vases. I must have embroidered hundreds in my time! Everyone said how beautifully I made them. I usually won first prize at the local craft shows, you know ...'

Her voice was like the traffic along the Westbury Road, a low-level distraction which in this case she couldn't tune out. After half an hour, Muriel Stanley, unable to bear it any longer, glanced at her watch and exclaimed with sudden urgency, 'Oh, good heavens! Is that really the time? I must go. I have a letter I want to post.'

She hurried away without looking back, feeling shabby and ashamed at having told a lie and angry with Mrs Mallinson for having forced her to do so. She was angry, too, at the loss of the garden because she knew she would never be able to sit in it again. As soon as she set foot in it, Mrs Mallinson would appear and claim the seat next to her. Her afternoons would be ruined.

Having been forced out of the garden, Muriel Stanley gave serious thought to another location where she could sit and read. There was a bench outside the branch library but the noise of the traffic in Westbury Road and the presence of passers-by made her give up after just an hour's trial. There was, of course, the library itself. It was comfortable and pleasant with a large table in the reference section on which were spread out a selection of newspapers and magazines. There were even a couple of easy chairs nearby constructed from slabs of foam rubber covered with bright blue fabric. She tried sitting on one of them but it was so low she had difficulty getting up from it. As for the newspaper table which had upright chairs, it was popular with people like herself, pensioners looking for somewhere to pass a couple of hours in relative comfort. Sometimes there wasn't an empty seat to be had. Another option was to go back to her room in the *Laurels* but that would defeat the whole object of the exercise. She wanted to be out of doors under the sky, enjoying the sun and the air, considerations which ruled out the Sally Lunn as an alternative.

Which left St Andrew's churchyard across the road from the post office. It was not a choice she would willingly have made, but on the principle that beggars can't be choosers, she set out the following Friday afternoon with her stick, her wheeled basket already packed with the two cushions, the packet of biscuits and a plastic bottle of orange juice, calling first at the library to change her book which she had finished reading.

It seemed that luck was on her side that day in one particular instance at least for, as she searched along the shelves of the trolley on which newly returned books were placed before being reassigned to their proper places, she noticed a copy of one of H.R.F. Keating's crime novels, *Breaking and Entering*, which she hadn't read before. She had always enjoyed his books. She liked his style which was straightforward and descriptive, so vividly evoking the setting of Bombay that a door was opened for her into a new and exotic world which she would never have experienced except through the pages of his books. The sense of colour and crowds excited her, as did the introduction of a new, strange language – *firinghi* for *foreigner* or *chowkidai* for *doorman* for example – and to a world where the familiar and unfamiliar were mixed together to make an entirely new landscape composed of large hotels and holy men, mobile phones and sacred cows. But most of all she liked Inspector Ghote himself. Such a charming and decent man! Gentle, shrewd, intelligent, compassionate and so very human. She understood perfectly his moments of exasperation, his quiet sense of humour and his need for privacy by retreating to his Northern fastness, as he put it. Didn't she herself share this need with him in her desire to read a book under a tree in a quiet garden?

Very carefully, she laid the book on top of the cushions, its cover uppermost so that, as she steered the wheeled basket across the zebra crossing, she could see the title and remind herself of the delights to come.

Although the churchyard was not nearly as pleasant as the garden at the *Laurels*, it was not as awful as she had feared. Normally on her walk to and from the church, she took little notice of it. It was simply an ordinary stretch of mown grass, the headstones removed and propped up against the wall like large playing cards, with only an occasional tree or bush to break the monotony. True, there were benches here and there, one in particular which caught her attention. It was set down on a patch of gravel beside the tower and faced south so that it was in a sunny position and was far enough away from the Westbury Road that, although she could hear the traffic, she could not see it. It also had its back half-turned to the mutilated chestnut trees, thank goodness.

While arranging the cushions on its slatted seat, she noticed a small metal plaque screwed to the back rail which read: 'In Loving Memory of Mary Elizabeth Wishart 1898–1972' and, thinking what an excellent idea it was, she made a mental note to see her solicitor about adding a codicil to her will leaving money and instructions for a similar bench to be set up as her own memorial.

The cushions arranged to her satisfaction, she sat down and, opening the book, began to read with a growing sense of pleasure.

'*Despite everything, Inspector Ghote found his head filled with pleasantly vague thoughts.*'

The opening sentence almost exactly described her own feelings except for one small proviso. Her thoughts were not so much pleasantly vague as pleasantly fluid, flowing out from the central point of the white page in front of her which acted as a focus of her attention to encompass the delights which lay on the periphery of her consciousness. The warmth of the sun was part of that awareness as was the fragrance from a yew tree on the far side of the churchyard and the sunlight twinkling on the glossy leaves of the holly tree next to it as if reflecting it back from hundreds of tiny, green, polished mirrors.

It was all so wonderful! she thought. So peaceful! So perfect!

She made up her mind that, as a celebration, a kind of eucharist, if you like, she would stop at the Sally Lunn on the way back to the *Laurels* for tea and a meringue.

It was about a quarter to four when she was disturbed by the sound of footsteps crunching their way towards her along the gravel path and, glancing round, she saw a young man – well, more of a youth – of about nineteen walking in her direction. His presence disturbed her and she took off her reading glasses in order to see him in sharper focus.

He was thin and weedy-looking with sharp, narrow features which seemed oddly familiar, and was wearing one of those short jackets, the hood pulled up over his head. Something about him, his hunched shoulders, his averted face, gave him a malign air and almost involuntarily she leaned across to grasp the straps of her handbag which lay on the bench beside her. At the same time, she recognised him. Years before, when she was headmistress of Elm Grove Junior School, he had been a pupil. She even remembered his name; it was Johnny Keats. Considering the number of children who had passed through her hands, so to speak, it was a feat of recollection which was largely due to his name. While she was not a great devotee of poetry, several remained very vivid in her memory form her own school and college days. One, *Ode to Autumn*, was by John Keats, and hardly a summer passed and the leaves began to turn yellow than she found herself quoting silently the opening lines.

'*Season of mists and mellow fruitfulness ...*'

So beautiful! she thought. So evocative!

Seeing the name John Keats on the list of new pupils entering her school one year had roused her curiosity and, as she admitted to herself, a sort of soft, poignant sentimentality, quite unlike her usual brisk, no-nonsense attitude to a new intake of children.

But the real boy in no way resembled her image of his namesake. John Keats, always referred to as Johnny, was, not to put too fine a point on it, an unpleasant child. He was pale, undersized and not very bright, both in the intellectual meaning of the phrase but also in the general unwholesome air he gave off, like an undernourished plant which has been raised in a basement room away from sunlight and air. In any other child these disadvantages would have aroused her sympathy but Johnny Keats was a difficult boy to like. He was mean, spiteful, sly, a teller of tales against other children and even at six and a half an accomplished thief and liar. She was relieved when he left at eleven to go to Middleton Street secondary school.

And now here he was, coming towards her, his mean little face tight with malice.

She watched his approach warily, convinced he was up to no good, almost expecting some sort of attack. The danger was there in the look on his face and the tension in his upper body, and her hand tightened on her bag.

And then the threat passed. He drew level with her and even took a couple of steps past her. She relaxed a little, loosening her grip on the leather straps.

It was then that he pounced. Whirling round, he made a grab for her handbag with his right hand, shooting out his other to shove her roughly back by the shoulder. For a long moment, the two of them hung together in a silent struggle, Johnny Keats' left arm extended like a battering ram, his right clutching the handbag while she struggled to maintain her grip on it, her other hand scrambling out to reach her stick which was propped up against the bench.

As if she were listening to someone else's voice, she heard herself call out in those clipped, sharp tones she always found so effective against recalcitrant pupils during her time as headmistress at Elm Grove Junior, 'Johnny Keats! What on earth do you think you're doing?'

And suddenly she realised he now knew who she was. The moment of recognition was stamped on his face as clearly as those on the features of a witness at some disaster. Shock was there and fear and something else which for a moment she did not recognise as hatred. But that's what it was. Hatred. Simple, unadulterated hatred.

The next moment he had snatched his hand away from her shoulder and in a movement which was too fast for her to take in properly, it disappeared momentarily from her field of vision before re-appearing again a second later as a fist clutching a knife.

Someone screamed; herself, she assumed, although she was oddly distanced from what was happening to her. She did not even feel the blade enter her body, only a blow against the wall of her chest as if someone had punched her. Then he was gone. At least, she could no longer see him although she could hear the sound of rapid footsteps flying away in a shower of small stones down the gravelled path.

Her own movements were much slower; almost gentle. Very quietly she slid sideways toward the left until her face was resting against the slatted seat of the bench. She saw in close-up the book she had been reading and which she must have put down there when she first became aware of Johnny Keats. It had sprung open at the title page and the printed words *Breaking and Entering* stood out very clear and black against the white paper with the name H.R.F. Keating just below them. And then something else appeared on the page which puzzled her at first. It was a round, red drop like a bead which, as she gazed at it, was joined by another and then another.

Blood, she realised. Her blood.

How extraordinary!

She realised something else as well with that certainty of knowledge that allows no contradiction. In that moment of perfect clarity, she knew she was going to die and what she had to do.

Stretching out her right hand, she dipped her little finger into the drops of blood and very, very carefully, like a child writing for the first time, she crossed out the initials and last three letters of the author's name and traced the letters 'J' and 's' in their place.

J. Keats.

It wasn't much of a clue to the identity of her killer. She could only hope that, when they came to take away her body, someone would have the perspicacity to notice the title-page and appreciate its significance.

Inspector Ghote would have been aware of it; of that, she was quite sure.

FRIENDS OF THE GARRICK

Michael Z. Lewin

My sharpest memories of Harry in action were as President of the Detection Club but my first outing with him was in 1992. He, Bob Barnard and I were guests of the Scandinavian Crime Writers at their annual conference. The event that year took place in a small Norwegian town, a small plane ride from Oslo.

A very small plane ride – four seats, with the luggage stuffed behind the two in the back. There's more room in a Mini. But while Bob and I cowered in the back, Harry chatted away with the pimply pilot, taking advantage of the novelty of being in an airplane cockpit and not even put off when we dropped down through the clouds so the kid could compare the landscape to the roadmap on his lap. But that's Harry – always looking to find the 'interesting' in any situation. He is genuinely good company.

Even by the gossipy standards of the Garrick Club, the event was shocking. More dirt than dinners may have been dished up by the friends of David Garrick and those who followed them over the years, but *murder?* Within hallowed halls hung with mementoes of Britain's highest cultural achievers? No, no. Truly, shocking.

That the desecration should have taken place at the Annual General Meeting of *The Detection Club* made at least a speck of sense. Comprised of authors spanning the spectrum of crime fiction, the organization's members are at the peak of their game. Three times a year they gather as a *club* to eat, drink and, yes, gossip. Not that just any crime writer may attend. Consideration of suitable new members is one of the main features of the annual meeting, which precedes the Summer dinner.

However theirs is a 'club' without its own premises. They are but guests at the Garrick and if *detection* be the subject at which they are meant to be so jolly good, it's curious that they did not declare a solution to the murder themselves. Not that they didn't try, mind, while the body festered.

The body in question was that of a matronly member called Hattie Butt-Known. She had no sooner tabled an amendment requiring the word 'extremely' to replace the word 'very' in the motion, 'We, The Detection Club, agree that we are very serious,' than she collapsed in fits. Her death soon followed, being painful but quick.

Several of those at the meeting table readily agreed that her symptoms pointed to strychnine as the mortal agent. But no one admitted to having slipped the poison into the unfortunate woman's fruit juice, either by design or accident.

Events relating to her demise *were* considered, although since Ms Butt-Known was a stickler for procedure they waited until AOB as a matter of respect. When at last President Simon Thorough-Brett opened the floor to a solution of the murder, it was Baroness P.E. Gyms who asked the first pertinent question. 'How was it, do you think, that Hattie didn't taste or smell the poison as she drank it?'

'Perhaps,' Peter Lusty suggested, 'what actually happened was that someone slipped a masking chemical into the fruit juice she took before the meeting convened. I happen to know for a fact that Hattie had some lemonade because as I reached for the last glass on the tray she whisked it away for herself. So if someone had, say, added a pinch of propalomine to her glass while she was looking in another direction, it would have deadened her taste and olfactory senses to a degree sufficient to obliterate her ability to detect the strychnine. I used such a plot device in a story of my own once.'

'So did I,' called three other members, although none, including Lusty, could remember the title of his or her work.

'Even if some of the strychnine taste did remain,' Lusty completed, 'it could easily have been missed in the heat of the moment.'

'There was bound to have been plenty of heat in the moment,' HRT Keats noted.

'Nothing Hattie liked better in an amendment than heat.'

'Unless it was rigging the outcome ahead of time,' Dick Assisi muttered.

A hearty hear-hear followed this remark, for no one in the club manipulated events behind the scenes more enthusiastically than the late Ms Butt-Known.

'So,' President Thorough-Brett said as he took a wine bottle out of one pocket and a glass out of the other, 'is the floor now saying that we must look for two occasions on which substances were added to Hattie's drink rather than one?' He poured himself a glass, then emptied it quickly as a security measure.

'As our beloved Agatha showed so often, a second murder often simplifies the solution of a first murder,' Bob Barn-Owl noted, wide-eyed as he turned his head.

A hearty hear-hear followed this comment, but Susan Gloomy asked, 'Are you suggesting that we hang around until someone else is murdered? Because if so, I'd rather be elsewhere. Like, Australia.'

'My point,' Barn-Owl said with a hoot of derision, 'is metaphorical rather than literal. If we think of the additions to Hattie's glass as the murders, then having had a second addition might make it easier. Slut.'

'Pardon?'

'It's Norwegian for the end.' Barn-Owl spent some of his formative years in Norway. Not many people know that.

Silence greeted this 'explanation' until Lida Cozy said, 'That sounds like legalese to me. Would someone fucking translate, please?'

'Feisty lass,' Ian Rankling remarked, nudging his neighbour.

'I wouldn't raise it with her if I were you,' Paula Goose advised.

There were several legal or legalish minds among the company and eyes turned to Frances Fi-Fo-Fum (known to her friends as Fee). 'Perhaps,' she said, 'the proper place for the wig of suspicion is on the heads of the members who are *not* here.'

'Ooooo,' many said, pleased and impressed by Fee's arcane acuity.

'After all,' she continued, '*we* turned out for the meeting. *They* didn't.'

'I don't quite take your point,' James White-Whale said. 'However,' he began diplomatically, 'once, when I was flying between Japan and the Court of St. James –'

'My point,' Fee said sharply, 'is that one must ask why the absent ones stayed away. Did they, perhaps, loathe Hattie so much that they couldn't stand to be in the same room with her? If so, I put it to you that whoever murdered the woman – and someone most certainly did – it is more likely to have been one of them than one of us. So I ask you to consider, who is *not* here?'

Many members looked around to see who was not sitting at the table. 'Baroness Vine!' Timon Heraldry shouted. 'Anyone who supports New Labour ...'

'I think this logic must be followed farther,' Reginald Fell insisted.

'If they're not here, how could they have put the poison, or the masking chemical, into Hattie's drink?'

Mutters of 'Never thought of that,' and 'Good point,' and 'Worthy of Andy Dalziel himself,' followed, but Fee's sly smile showed that she was ready for the question.

'I put it to you,' she said, 'that the correct place to turn our attention is ... to the club's *servants*'

This suggestion was very welcome and comfortable to the assemblage.

'I did that in a novel of mine,' five members were heard to say, but none offered a title.

'I put it to you,' Fee continued, 'that one or more absent members bribed, blackmailed, tortured or asked one of the Garrick's serving staff to administer the contents of one or more vials into one or more glasses that went into one or more hands of Hattie Butt-Known.'

All eyes now looked around the room for a sheepish servant.

'But aren't all the help-persons required to leave the room before we begin our AGMs?' July Tomtom asked. Ever since her writing had embraced Sherlock Holmes, July had been perfecting her powers of observation.

'Good heavens, yes,' several members recalled. 'The secrecy of our proceedings is paramount. Are the doors locked?'

A silence followed the question. It was broken only when Mike Loon said, 'Why is it, do you think, that Yale got all the locks? You'd think Harvard would do it better.'

A further silence followed. Loon was, after all, American.

In a startled moment, Anthea Freezer woke up and said, 'I've just had a dream the plot of which indicates we should look for a wider perspective on the matter.'

'Such as?' President Thorough-Brett asked.

'Well, we *do* have among our number an expert on Romanology and it's well-known that the Romans poisoned everybody they didn't stab.'

Eyes turned to Linseed Daffs, but she just shrugged. 'That was a long time ago. Who cares?'

'We haven't even necessarily identified the correct method,' said Catherine Broadcast. 'Especially when you take into account that propalomine is a chemical unknown to science. Like Dame Agatha, I have experience of working in a pharmacy.'

'Mmmmm,' many mused.

'An alternate scenario,' Broadcast continued, 'is that Hattie was given the strychnine in a capsule that would dissolve only in the presence of acid. So perhaps there is someone in her life outside the club who knew her well enough to know that while she was here she would be drinking *lemon*ade ...'

'You mean ...' many susurrated, 'the murderer might not have been a member at all?'

'Exactly,' Broadcast said.

'Ahhhhh,' many agreed.

'Are you truly suggesting that there could be *anything* erodable by acid that would require additional lemonade inside Hattie?' Michael Tickerland asked from his background of espionage and its chemical manifestations. 'Talk about unknown to science ...'

'Did she, by any chance, have an identical twin?' Jonathan Slash asked in the momentary silence that followed.

Blank faces answered his question.

'It would mean the dead woman might not be Hattie at all.'

'So ...?' the blank faces asked.

Slash shrugged, his point tailing away as he thumbed through an antiques journal.

'It does raise a perennially pertinent question with an historical context,' Andy Tailor bespoke. 'Who benefits – signally benefits – from Hattie's lamentable, deplorable and mysterious death?'

The group considered the question.

'Besides all of us?' Lionel Goliathson asked.

Then Len Ipcressfile made a tart suggestion, possibly first seen in the cookery column he once wrote in *The Observer*. 'Perhaps,' he opined, 'the truth of the matter is that the late Ms Butt-Known *had* detected the poison in her beverage – how could she not? – and that she did, in fact, consume it on purpose. Indeed, quite possibly, she even administered the dose herself. That would be a *lemon* twist, eh?'

'She knew quite a lot about being a dose,' several Scottish members said together.

'Are you,' asked Ambridge Dextrose, cupping his hand to his ear, 'saying that Hattie killed her *self*? I didn't quite hear.'

Several members across the table from him nodded. Since finishing off Morse the poor man had little excitement in life except the Archers.

'But why would she do that?' he asked. 'She was, after all, female and therefore a bit of a babe in my book. In fact maybe someone should check whether she's really dead.' He rose from his chair and went to

Hattie's body. He felt for a pulse in several locations while the rest of the membership looked away.

Just at that moment a key was heard being inserted into a lock and the door to the meeting room flew open. 'My Lords, Ladies, Baronial persons and miscellany, dinner is served.'

'Crikey crumbs,' President Thorough-Brett said. 'What do we do now?'

'Eat, obviously,' Lord Bertie Jeans said. 'Otherwise the food will get cold.'

'But... What about Hattie?'

'I believe you'll find that she's not very hungry.'

The cat, however, was soon well and truly out of the bag. At the behest of the serving staff who cleared the meeting room, a call was made to the police and Detective Xena Home – from Scotland as well as the Yard – was soon on the premises.

During the meal Home moved from table to table examining members and their guests. By the time coffees were served her investigations were finished. Her conclusions were as potentially scandalous as they were potentially shocking.

'I fear,' she declared at the dining room door, 'that I shall be unable to allow *any* Detection Club member to leave the premises tonight. The reason is that I am now going to arrest *all* the attending members for conspiracy to murder Hattie Butt-Known. It is clear to me that instead of you all seeing, hearing and knowing nothing about the poisoning – a quite unbelievable plot line in a locked room – you conspired *together* to rid yourselves of the victim and then to feign subsequent ignorance.'

Guilty gasps were heard all around the room, seven for having already used the plot device in a novel.

'Therefore I'm now going to read you your rights and –'

But at *that* moment Detective Home was knocked to the floor as the door behind her flew open. Two men entered, led by Lord Jeans, the Garrick member at whose invitation *The Detection Club* enjoyed Garrick facilities. Bertie, anticipating trouble, had slipped away during a conversation about the growing of figs under the guise of being a smoker.

Detective Home struggled to regain her feet. 'I was just about to arrest –'

'Forget it,' Bertie said. 'The Garrick Club did not achieve its unique status in London society life by allowing its private business to be bruited in the outside world, even private business involving commoners.'

Home took a closer look at the man next to Lord Jeans. 'Sir?' she said.

'Your transfer has just come through,' the Commissioner said. 'Xena Home, you're off to Skye, effective immediately.'

'Sky, sir?' Home considered. 'To make crime documentaries?'

'If you expect your police career to be exhumed, X. Home, you'll be more mindful in the future of the big picture in any investigation you conduct. That's why I'm sending you someplace small. So, be off with you.'

The Commissioner flicked his head and Detective Home departed.

'And now, as for the rest of you,' the Commissioner said sternly to the Detection Clubbers, 'I deduce from your actions tonight that you do not have in your membership any serving police officers.' He looked around the room. The silence which greeted him confirmed his observation. 'As it happens, I once wrote a short story and, as I understand that you now have an unexpected vacancy on your membership roll ...'

BUNDOBAST ON VOYAGE

Jonathan Gash

Some years ago, catching a plane home, Harry remarked, 'In India, we say ...' His words stuck, for some writers have the gift of saying the best words in the best order. This tale is prompted by the casual comment about imperial slang, and concerns the reminiscences of an old expat, such as I, on a voyage home from India. With appreciation to H.R.F. this story is dedicated.

The P&O ship *Melissa* was days out of Bombay when I finally opened Hal's letter. I still can't work out if there was a crime, and if so was I to blame. Somebody must be, a death is a death. I still believe Hal's missive had something to do with it.

Coming aboard, I'd been dead beat after the journey down-country, as we used to say. A strange inertia takes hold until about the third day, when you begin to take notice of other passengers. Fogies like me can't help noting blokes who'd once been in the regiment in the old days or, more likely, some boxwallah recognised from the maidans and godowns where the business of India is done. There's a definite pukka-cutcha status among us retirees, in case you're one of those who never got his knees brown. Cutcha is the dregs, pukka the carriage trade. It applies to merchandise as much as people. You get the idea.

Eventually I read Hal's scrawl in Tiffany's, the usual bar at six o'clock. On the *Melissa*, this favourite bar's design was in the form of a wide balcony (marble of course) with gleaming brass rails, couches, and stairs sweeping down to the shops. Stewards were ever eager to bring ladies teas, and drinks for us leathery old re-pats. You had to watch yourself, for lounge gossip is terrible. Quite the worst aspect of tittle-tattle, I think, is that it calls for judgement of the most self-righteous kind. Truly a thing of horror. If you didn't want to fan its terrible flame you could just listen.

I made a mistake, that third day out. Looking back across the years, I still cannot see if I condoned a crime. The primary cause was the cunning of a lady. I sent a steward for my drink, and settled to read.

> *Dear Jonathan,*
>   *This note is to say so-long. Keep a weather eye out on the voyage for T, a youngish chap from that QM mob in Pindi. Word is he's being bowler-hatted. Something of a poodle-faker, he will be with a Lady A twice his age. Some bundobast I simply cannot understand.*
>   *Safe voyage, friend. Not many of us left now from the days of the old Raj. Sorry you're gone on the 'Long Walk To Wimbledon' as it were.*
>   *My regards to home. See you, in'shallah.*
>   *Your old oppo,*
>   *Hal*

For some reason, I was physically tired. Swim at seven, breakfast at eight, walked, wrote, went to a talk on gardening, then scanned the jewellery exhibition. Lunch, the art auction, seeing ballroom dancers practising, then to the casino to ogle the blackjack players hard at it. I don't play myself. Throngs everywhere, for Melissa carried some 2,000 passengers, a crew of 863, was 78,000 tons burthen. I could have avoided the man T and Lady A if I'd considered Hal's words.

My mistake was to pause longer than usual. I fancied some Gunpowder Green tea, an old Hong Kong habit, with one of those crumbly cakes that leave bits in your teeth. I sat on a couch, back to the blue sea, nodding at passengers – you get to know people smartish – as they strolled by. I was in a reverie, trying to compose a message to my woman, perforce in England.

Gossip began on the next alcove. It was loud and unconcealed.

To clarify, Tiffany's has nooks against the sea windows, with small brass-and-glass tables and matching leather armchairs to allow foursomes. People don't congregate.

There are other bars for huddles or general wassailing, or even to rest should the pace of total idleness wear you out. Myself, I'd come to like the Corniche restaurant for tiffin (one o'clock lunch, to my generation) but eleven other places offered dining should anorexia or sobriety threaten before four bells. You needed strength for voyaging on the *Melissa*.

There is much to be said for cruising. My pleasure lies in those chance encounters that can take whole mornings and, while not exactly wasting your time, somehow distract you from whatever you intended to get on with. Hence Tiffany's lounge. I liked the glimpses of glamorous passengers. One has choice, you see, of actually finishing those letters, or not.

And here it came, the first unavoidable eavesdrop of the day.

'There they go.' A lady's voice, next alcove to mine. 'Just look!'

'Revolting!'

'It's nothing less than insolence.'

'Not a shred of decency. It makes you wonder.'

'You'd think he'd have some pride. She must be twice his age.'

'Definitely senile. Have you seen her when she's asleep?'

'On a Riviera Pool recliner. Isn't it Deck Fourteen?'

'He puts her on the Promenade Deck. Seven, I think, wherever there's shade.' The aggressive woman gathered herself. Her voice quietened. Shamefully, I found myself trying to listen. (This is what ships do to morals.)

'What?' her gravelly-voiced companion asked, meaning get on with it.

'I saw her. You remember the deck-quoits competition? You weren't there. He put a blanket over her, tucking it well in.'

'She must pay him. Rich bitches can buy anything.'

'Listen.' The informant was back to audible strength, her pitch flutey. 'He said to her, "All right, Amy?" and she said, "Yes, Terry." She hardly read a line before dropping off.'

'How old *is* she?'

'She lay there with her mouth open, quite like somebody's great-grannie. Seventy.'

'God! Really?'

'She can't be less. Her shape's all shrunk; you know how they get.'

'He'd make three of her.'

'It makes you wonder ... you know?'

'If they do it?'

'Well, yes.'

'They're in a grand suite. Shameless. They have their own stewardess, not just one girl for ten cabins like on Formosa Deck. She tells Jill – she knew her on the *Arcadia*, wears turquoise, had that row?'

'Jill with the teeth? What did the stewardess say?'

'They really *do*. Jill wants to complain.'

'Can you do that?'

'You have a perfect right. Look at those families who fought so. I forget which ship. The captain had them put ashore in Durban. They had to fly home at their own expense.'

'I wouldn't want to be involved.'

'Well, somebody has to.'

Their conversation then became general, contumely over contract bridge and arguments in the General Knowledge Quiz. I sipped my tea, made notes, and waved hello when greeted.

The two unseen gossips I dubbed Flute and Gravel. They meant a couple easily identified by their incongruity. T and A gave me a clue. He was over six feet and beefy. He dressed casually in sandals, khaki shorts, safari shirts, but went to dinner well turned out, shoes shone, trousers knife-edged, shirts a-gleam, and walked with his chin raised as if expecting problems. He had an elderly lady on his arm.

A man walking a lady reflexively adjusts his stride to allow shorter paces, and if she's of an age he naturally goes steadily so she doesn't have difficulty where carpet edges give way to marble flooring, the usual hazards. It suggests care. I've gone on about him because I possibly put myself in his shoes, the way a man imagines.

Not to put too fine a slant on it, the woman interested me.

She was almost spindly, having developed that droop of the head elderly women get from, what, some skeletal atrophy? I'm only guessing, but you often see it. She dressed with elegance in styles appropriate for the day's Dress Code. This is a major consideration on the P&O Line, and is the first thing passengers look for in the daily *Melissa Today* newspaper. Suggested Dress was taken as a mandatory. Formal meant 'dinner jacket or tuxedo for gentlemen' and 'formal evening or cocktail outfit for ladies'. Casual implied whatever you liked, and Informal meant jacket and tie for the men, and left women to compete to their hearts content. This lady dressed impeccably, and drew envious glances by reason of the quality of her attire – never trousers, culottes or slacks. Her jewellery was envied, before gossip added a new perspective.

Without doubt she must have taken a rich woman's steps to retard the effects of time. I guessed seventy, but would not have argued had I been years out. Her grey hair was not quite ironed to inflexibility in those arcane hairdressing mysteries women find indispensable.

By the fifth day, I noticed that this couple sometimes went down my corridor from the lift down to Deck Five and the Atrium. Once or twice I greeted them on the way to dinner. The Rigoletto Restaurant is on the same deck.

This in itself was an oddity, for passengers in a grand suite could elect to dine there, with any menu they chose. I had visited one of those suites by invitation, and they were quite splendid. This set me wondering if they relished the challenge of confrontation, to show defiance to other diners. Yet why on earth should they be furtive, and where was the harm? I didn't know their circumstances, of course, and I was assuming the chap was the one mentioned by Hal in his letter. A bundobast, incidentally, is Anglo-Indice for official Revenue settlement or some shifty arrangement. It can even be a plot. Lots of tales from the old Raj use the term as our own, like so much Hobson-Jobson slang.

Early one evening, I was dutifully plodding round Deck Seven in the sunshine ('3.27 times round the deck equals one nautical mile', a notice claimed) feebly trying for a sensible balance of kilojoules and activity, when I realised I must have passed the very couple twice before noticing. They were on deck loungers – yellow and blue striped mattresses on wooden frames; folk with ghoulish humour call them melanoma makers. She was fast asleep in the attitude described by the gossips. Without having to gape, I saw as I trundled by that he had a hand on her thigh in a proprietorial way. Her hand lay on his wrist, suggesting compliance and even possession.

Close observers can read too much into gestures. Possibly I was guilty of stretching my chance observation beyond sense. Yet their postures – her asleep, him reading – was quite moving. I realised as I went by that I was taking their part against malice, for by now there was plenty. No actual complaint had been made, however. Indeed, why should there have been? And isn't misbehaviour, like beauty, often merely a trick of the light or in the eye of the beholder? So what if she was frail and he in his prime? Age is only an ascription, an allotting of numbers to assign superiority over others. Whose affair was it but their own?

Foolishly I forgot them and the animose gossipy syndicate, and sank into the kaleidoscopic pattern of shipboard life. As I say, my assumption was made in ignorance. I'm good at that.

Two days later the trouble began. War was declared.

*   *   *

A slight squall had made the decks uninhabitable for an hour. Seamen worked on the swimming pool and were busy drying the deck loungers. Passengers had been driven indoors and deck games cancelled. Line dancers occupied the Atrium floor, music was troublesomely loud, and people found lounges and engaged in prattle. I found my usual alcove invaded by two ladies in their mid-thirties, say, with brighter colours than they would have worn at home at that hour. As soon as they ordered coffee, their voices told me they were none other than my Flute and Gravel chatterboxes. In appearance, they seemed less malign than I had judged. I introduced myself.

'Oh, no need,' said one. 'I'm Jane, incidentally. This is Beryl.'

'No need?' I was startled. Had they detected my eavesdropping?

'You spoke on the QE2.' She explained to Beryl, 'This gentleman spoke on antique frauds. And Victorian wedding furniture, wasn't it?'

'Thank you,' I said weakly. 'I'm going straight now.'

My jokes always become feeble quips and sound inane. Worse, my smile becomes a pale imitation suggesting I'm hounded. This weakness is a handicap you have to live with and can never quite hide.

'Then he's just the person,' Beryl said, full of meaning.

Jane's brow cleared. 'Why yes! I hadn't thought.'

A terrible suspicion grew. I wanted to run away calling excuses over my shoulder. They were clearly up to something. Jane leant forward and said, 'You should complain about that couple. Everybody's talking.'

I tried for ignorance. 'Couple?'

It was no good. They took turns describing the pair.

'I think I've seen them,' I said vaguely. 'Complain why?'

'Their behaviour.' Jane was reasonable beyond patience with someone she now thought an utter cretin. 'It's disgusting. Passengers have been put ashore for less.'

Beryl chipped in, 'No thought for the sensitivity of others.'

'I'm sorry.' I slowed myself on this slippery slope. 'Complain about what exactly?' I would insist on precision, otherwise how to tell them no? Too many negatives rest on illogicality. Mine wouldn't, mustn't.

'Everybody's up in arms.' Beryl looked desperate for a fag. Soon she'd be drumming her fingers. I could see my sloth maddened her.

Jane added, 'Yesterday she asked him did he intend to go to the chef's exhibition of ice carving. You know what he said?'

'No.'

'He told her, "I want you in the cabin first, then we'll decide." You see?'

'He could have meant anything.'

'Oh, sure,' Beryl gravelled out. Bitterness seemed her thing. I began to wonder what she did for a living, and for how long she and Jane had endured friendship. Had she known T before?

'They're all over each other, *in public*.'

'Lots of people hold hands.'

Good old Beryl stuck viciously to her plan. A teacher, perhaps? I wondered if Jane could be got to withdraw.

'He uses her. It's indecent.'

'Are they married?' More innocence

Beryl ground out, 'An old married couple? No, they certainly are not. He is recently divorced. Look.' Her exasperation was now of a headmistress driven beyond tether. She even tapped the table. I'd not seen that done for years, and then only in a pub. 'Passengers have a right to decent standards.'

'You are right. Everybody does.' I made some excuse to leave. Their faces closed in anger.

* * *

Some days later, my scribbling was interrupted by Beryl. She found me at a library writing table and sat, suddenly there. Nobody within earshot so I was trapped by circumstance.

'I want to tell you we've all decided to shun the couple.'

'The man with the lady?' I didn't know what to say.

'Can you believe it? They want to arrange some ceremony and are asking around for witnesses among other expatriates. They've seen the captain. Jane said you lived overseas for quite some time?'

She was worse than any interviewer. I said nothing to this, and tried to wait her out.

'The point is,' she pressed, 'we all want them boycotted.'

'Who is this we?'

'Everybody.' Her voice took on that querulous sound I'd first used to identify her.

'There will be a chance to make them leave in Egypt. We dock in Alex.'

'What is the point of that?'

She thinned her lips. I had made an enemy. I wondered how and why exactly. Matters like this can wear you out. After all, I did not know the disparate couple and certainly didn't want further acquaintance with his vengeful lady.

'Decency!' She almost shrilled the word. A passenger looked in and hastily withdrew. 'It is high time action was taken on things like this.'

'What things?' I can be pedantic to the point of lunacy when it is called for.

She showed only contempt. 'People like you make me sick. You are too lily-livered to stand up for what is right. No wonder nobody *ever* reads your books!'

She rose, quivering. 'And don't think they'll go through with their idiotic ceremony. We'll stop it, just you see!'

Becoming interested is always a danger. From the way Beryl had spoken, I got the notion she knew the man, and not just as a casual acquaintance. I tried to get back to my scribbles and failed. I was glad when the library girls came to close the library until after supper.

*   *   *

Next morning, I made the Horizon lounge feeling like a shipwrecked mariner reaching shore. It is my practice to read over my tiny spidery scrawls before getting to where new words are needed. I have spectacles now. I was just getting there when I became aware of someone standing nearby, and looked up. It was the man.

'Excuse me. Can I interrupt?'

Which proves an interrupter already has. I've never heard of any writer actually saying no outright. I didn't know whether to close my notebook and put my pen away. Would he see it as a silent rebuke if I did?

'We – I – couldn't help overhearing. Those ladies.'

'Sorry.' I felt uncomfortable. I didn't want much more of this. 'I don't really know them. They just introduced themselves then rather led off.'

'Look.' He knew he was being assessed. His eyes had that looking-in-the wind appearance. 'Would you be free some time? A drink, maybe?'

'If it's another row, I'm afraid I'm done for. I drain easily.'

He seemed puzzled. 'No. Nothing like that. I've learned a lot.'

A curious remark. Learned what, and from whom? I wondered if silence would be interpreted as surliness. I didn't want that, so accepted. He gave me a card with his suite number. 'Any time. Someone'll find me smartish.'

I imagined scampering serfs.

'Thank you,' I said, the usual English reversal, receiving notice of another chore with thanks normally kept for a gift. 'Can we decide now?' I actually meant to get this over with.

He left seeming pleased. After a few moments I went back to my cabin. I didn't want more gossip for a long, long time.

*   *   *

A butler, no less, opened the door. The stewardess was a Thailander in full fig. I tried not to watch her, seeing she was reputedly a gasbag. Terry, eager to please, introduced Amy who was seated near their balcony. Coffee was served. Amy instantly dismissed the two helpers – it seems wrong these days to call folk servants – and we settled.

To my alarm he went straight in. I'd been prepared for a gentle discourse on the crops and the weather.

'I'll assume you know nothing about us,' he began, and I didn't correct him. 'I'm Amy's friend. I am divorced. My previous relationship was, frankly, hell.'

'Sorry.' One never knows quite what to say. It's a gap in etiquette. Regret seems the most apt, though why, if Terry rejoiced?

'Please don't be.' He took Amy's hand. 'Amy has been my salvation. May I speak bluntly?'

What else was he doing, for God's sake? His place, after all. 'Please.'

'We know passengers complain about us. Letting the side down and all that.'

'Terry had the ghastliest time imaginable,' Amy said in a rusty voice. I could see that other women would have envied her looks when she'd been younger. Her eyes still showed a lovely brightness, with a level of perception often absent from more youthful faces. 'His wife – she joined the ship at the last moment – was most aggressive.'

Joined which ship, exactly? I wanted to ask, but didn't dare. Compassion, if not exactly sorrow, did seem apt. I sipped the coffee and tried not to judge. People often accuse me of 'collecting material' – as if any writer worth a groat would know what the hell that means.

'Terry started visiting after his break-up. He knows about plants and helped my malee with the garden plants.' Terry made a disclaiming shrug. 'He did my accounts with the Customs, the dustoori.'

Customs in old Raj days had that nickname, which signified official

Revenue business with the double meaning of sticky fingers. I smiled, keeping well out of it.

'And Terry probated my husband's will.' She fixed me with her beautiful old eyes. 'I am explaining so you have a fair choice.'

Choice? This had become stickier than I'd imagined. Was Terry's former wife on *this* ship?

For some reason I envisioned Amy in a capellone hat and elegant dress, turning with her trug and secateurs as she found her favourite blue Ectromelia weeded to its demise, crying, 'Oh, Terry! What have you done?'

'I did extra work for Amy.' He smiled and gave her a gentle tap in rebuke. It was a shared joke, and she seemed pleased with herself at having scored.

'My people back home knew Terry's father,' she said. I understood that was their exposition, and I would get no more. Fair enough.

Amy's smile had an immediacy of the kind only infants and women possess. Men can't do it except on rare occasions. I began to like her.

'At least we give the ship's gossips the chance to make jokes about ladies and employees! I sent Terry to my lawyers for advice on his divorce. Of course the whole district knew.' She sighed. 'Gossip is a bane, don't you find?'

'Sometimes.'

She smiled. 'As long as somebody can keep up with it! What *do* people get out of inessentials?'

'We started seeing one another.' Terry was determined to stick to the issue. 'I paid my ex-wife off before deciding to go home.'

'By then we were lovers,' Amy capped unexpectedly. To her credit she did not wait for a reaction, just smiled on Terry. 'It rather took me by surprise, all these years.'

'Amy was like the sun coming up. To have friendliness, love, was beyond any hope I ever had after Beryl, and there Amy was.'

'People say the cruellest things. I suppose it's inevitable, seeing our age difference.'

'There's no such thing,' I said. I really do believe this. 'If an espousal – I hate the word relationships – is fitting, arbitrary numbers don't come into it.'

'I was charmed to overhear you say so.' Amy gave me a shy look, and I saw a new reason Terry had gone to her. 'Espousal is close to the mark, isn't it, darling?' Her look became mischievous. 'Do you notice how brave I am with terms of endearment? Quite as if I had confidence!'

'Stop it.' Terry was kindly but gruff. It was evidently old ground. Maybe she had expressed early doubts about his constancy, something like that? 'Amy wondered at first,' he admitted, as if I had spoken my thoughts. 'But a man doesn't cut his lifeline, which is what she is. I wake every day and thank God I have Amy and Beryl is in the past.'

That name again.

'Look,' I said, uncomfortable at the turn the conversation had taken. 'I can't see why you are explaining. You overheard my opinions. Live and let live should be enough. Women can do without a man. No man can do without a woman. That's the basis of all, gloss it as you wish.'

Terry leant forward. 'We've talked it over and want you to be our witness, please. Will you?'

'Please do,' Amy said. I sat transfixed, those lovely eyes.

Astonished, I waited for more. Witness what? I imagined some legal thing, but they were too intent and I was forced to ask, 'Witness what?'

'Our vows.'

Like a marriage? I knew cruise liners had chapels, and it pleased some passengers to renew vows before the captain. 'Doesn't the ship have to be registered at home? I'm not sure.'

I am such a worm. Every word sounded like I was edging to the door. Amy saw my plight and took over.

'There's a hitch, you see. Terry's divorce has proved ... hard to enforce.'

'I thought you said ...?'

'I can't shake Beryl off,' he said, looking for Amy's nod before continuing. 'She stalks, creating new obstacles every month. It's a mess.'

Amy added, bitter for the first time, 'We want to make betrothal vows.'

'Why? Would it be legally binding?' I asked feebly.

'Not really. I've spoken to the captain and he will comply. It's just a ceremony.'

She said comply, not that the skipper agreed. I wondered if Lady Amy was a massive shareholder in the company. As usual, I didn't dare ask why they were so set on an actual ceremony.

'Would you?' she asked. 'I've looked it up in the ship's library. Please?'

'Last resort?' I tried to joke, wondering whom they had already asked. I knew I would stay up late, writing imaginary conversations among their fellow diners bent on refusal.

'Well, yes. Thank you.' I'd hoped to flannel my way out, but sensed that Amy would be a better friend than foe.

'We may consider a firmer union once we're home in England. I have estates. Possession in my family descends through a lengthy line. Terry can remain safe with me, and his odious ex will be laughed out of our lives.'

'How?' I can be very stupid.

'That will be taken care of.' Amy gave me innocent eyes.

Doctors say women blink three times more often than men. I knew how my daughters wheedle me. Like I say, I can be mightily thick.

Terry spoke on the telephone about details while Amy chatted of her home in Hyderobad. I thought, this is one mischievous lady, though like a dolt completely missed her concealed intention. By now my liking for the lady swayed my judgement. A woman, after all. If Terry alone had approached me, my answer would probably have been different. I drew breath to demur, but paused. This is always fatal. I too intended to consult the library, find out the various rubrics.

'One other thing. Could you plan a certificate for us? One that is apt,' Amy said.

Fiction is my game, I thought wearily. By then I had succumbed, and with relief went into conversation about the merits of this ship, that ship and where they planned to sail again. Amy was entertaining, and Terry did his best not to show anxiety, obviously wondering about the doubt he spotted in my manner.

Next day I sent a note saying I would comply.

*　*　*

Two days later I stood witness for them in their suite. The purser read vows, and two female officers attended. (I'm old now, so female P&O officers still seem curiosities, yet I observed all proprieties.) I stood as principal witness, though strictly speaking we were all superfluous. I had concocted a grand certificate that called for enough formalities to fit the circumstances. I rather think everyone except Terry and Lady Amy thought it a hoot. Flowers were everywhere and the ship's printers had done a good job. I always think printers are obsessional neurotics. Twice they'd rung me to check type faces, when words are what matter.

The stewardesses and the barman entered into the spirit of the thing. The wine was almost silly, so much choice and no guests.

Once the officers had left, I wondered openly how the ceremony would be heard among the passengers. Amy simply smiled when I said this. She replied, 'Please do not concern yourself. It's all in hand.' I felt relieved, trusting her.

The barman was a Gomantak – Goanese, with his characteristic tattooed cross on his wrist (they do it at the age of seven to boys). He was happy to be there, and I saw to it that he and the stewardess received a fair tip for their trouble. It went off pretty well, the 'subcheese' as we used to say for the whole shooting match, just right. Amy and Terry retired for the afternoon, insisting that I return later for a sundowner about five-thirty. I tried excuses but they joked they would hunt me down. Ever the ingrate, I turned up and we toasted their future.

That would have been everything except for the crime, if that it was. We docked in Alexandria, Egypt, and trouble occurred.

The *Melissa* had done her usual stint, getting passengers ashore on those appalling floating gangways, our Ghurkas checking to make sure nothing unusual came aboard. The ship was to sail at six o'clock local time. I walked ashore in the city, not risking hours of exhaustion on an impossibly long journey to the Pyramids, though I believe they use air-conditioned charabancs now. The ship was quiet, and I saw my two betrotheds – I thought of them so – walking arm in arm along the waterfront into the drab shopping area. They would return soon, I told myself, because the horse-and-carriage touts would drive them mad, pestering and calling, 'Hey, Captain McGregor!' as if we're all named that. Terry could take care of himself, and Amy was sufficiently experienced and good-humoured to carry anything off. Also, she would quickly tire in the heat.

The ship sailed that night full of tired passengers all talking about their experiences ashore and purchases risked.

Next morning I was invited to call and see the happy couple's photographs. Amy herself welcomed me in a state of some excitement, eyes shining, features animated. She looked attractive, hair done and a double set of pearls, the central one a large baroque. She certainly knew style. No wonder Terry looked gratified.

'We're missing Haifa this cruise, aren't we, darling?' She insisted on serving me coffee herself, the stewardess trailing in support. I'd become a friend of the family, it seemed.

'Yes. I'd have liked to see it, but, well.'

'The troubles,' Amy explained. 'I shan't be sorry, all those plastic bags blowing about Palestine. Any housewife would tidy it in a trice. The duty officer phoned to say we shall put in at Rhodes.'

Did he, indeed, I thought. Not everyone gets this service.

She sent for the photographs and sat beside me. 'Now don't be diplomatic.'

The portraits were mounted in ship photographer's silver frames with the P&O logo. They must have been taken soon after I'd left. Two photos, one in colour.

'My opinion will end our friendship,' I jibed. 'The black-and-white one is better.'

'There, Terry!' She clapped her hands. 'I *said*, didn't I? Why?'

'Was the coloured photo taken second?'

'Why, yes.'

'Your eyes seem focussed on an event beyond the scene, like ...'

'Like what?' Terry asked, frowning. Amy inclined the picture more her way.

'As if you suddenly thought of something disagreeable. Silly of me, really. Is it the light? I'm no photographer.'

We spun out the moments after that. Perhaps my careless remark had put a damper on their elation. After that, I was never asked back. I was slightly troubled so didn't mind, though I saw them about the ship as the voyage home went on.

It was the day following Alexandria that I heard a rumour of the kind you hope to forget. A lady was taken ill and had had to be invalided ashore to a Cairo hospital, so the tale was. Somebody told me it was one of the two ladies. I dug at the rumour as diligently as I could, and for the first time since leaving Bombay feeling a profound sense of foreboding.

One chap – gangling, always in the bars, worked in the docks in Honawur – was my eventual source.

'Didn't you hear? Some daft woman. Only thirty-six, in her prime and she does such a thing? Overdose.' He smoked and kept flicking ash.

'Was it serious?' Obliquity rules in gossip.

'Dead, that's all. Can you imagine? Men all over the bloody ship and she goes and does that? She didn't leave a letter. Nobody guessed.'

'Poor woman. Bad news from home, I suppose.'

'She was friendly with another lady. Her friend had gone ashore on the Sphinx trip and couldn't raise her when she got back. Tablets, they're saying. Ship's quack hit panic stations, no bloody good.' He looked about conspiratorially and said, 'Divorced husband's on board, I heard.'

Now I felt almost ill but kept on, strike while you can. 'The husband must be pretty cut up.'

'Dunno. Divorce happened to me, but not like this. Kids are the worry.'

I got him a complicated brandy thing as if in payment and left him in his carcinogenic cloud. The ship's photographer was quiet that afternoon, and I asked the spotty youth if he'd taken Lady Amy's pictures, adding I thought they were excellent. He brightened.

'Me and my mate. Good, eh?'

'Only, I was witness. Sorry, but I didn't quite like the coloured portrait.'

His girl assistant emerged from where they do the developing. 'You liked the black-and-white? I thought it was better. The lady sent the coloured print to her friend, though.'

'She did?' I tried to show surprise. I'm no actor, but gave it a go. 'I suggested the plain one.'

'She took ten of the coloured, four of the plain. We mounted them straight away.'

'Are you sure it got there? Only, I may want one. Would that be all right?'

By checking his order form, then the voyage brochure in the Atrium, I made sure. The woman who had taken 'too many tablets' was Beryl, recipient of the portrait photograph. I went to Reception and asked if there was a problem with a lady friend's telephone, as I'd been unable to reach her since Alexandria.

The purser's shroff hesitated when I gave her the cabin number. Diplomatically she explained that a lady was taken ashore at Alexandria, 'because she became quite poorly. The doctor thought it best.'

'I hope it's nothing serious? I don't really know her well. Just a book I'd promised her.'

And left, sick at heart.

Deliberately I lurked to encounter Amy, and eventually came across her on the lee side, Deck Seven, and said hello. Terry would be back before long and I needed to speak, wanting to judge the extent of her manipulation without too much innocence around.

'I thought you'd come by.' She lay back and closed her eyes, closing her book. She still managed without spectacles.

'Was it all accidental, Amy?'

'Beryl? The bitch is made of teak. Why can't you men see the obvious? You know what consoles me, my dear? I would have hated her even if I had met her in different circumstances.'

I didn't want endearments from her. I wanted her to open her eyes and look at me, not hide away as she was doing.

'How did you engineer Jane's absence ashore?'

'While I sent our betrothal portrait to Beryl?' She smiled. The effect of a smile with the eyes closed can be particularly insulting. 'Opportunism, of course. She teaches Ancient History, and collects snapshots to illustrate her lectures.'

'You chose the colour portrait deliberately.'

'The black-and-white is for friends.' She spoke with relish, almost purring. The effect, with that closed face, was utterly malign. 'Beryl had to be shown that her delaying tactics would come to nothing. Five minutes on the waterfront, she could buy whatever tablets would do the trick. And Jane would be ashore for, what, twelve hours? Women can't stand defeat.'

It wasn't malignity, I realised, those closed eyes, her inwardness. It was the absence of rapport. I began to wonder about her determination to acquire Terry, and in what order those past events had occurred. Did she simply work things out, and decide to form a plan that, if successful, would achieve success over some rival? It was beyond me.

'It wasn't just luck, darling,' she said as if dreamy. 'I didn't dare hope Beryl would go too far. Terry is rather shaken. He had an interview with the Executive Purser, poor lamb, but what could he do? The formalities had to be settled.'

'And now?' I stood, wanting never to see her again.

'Now?' She sounded surprised by that and finally squinted up at me. 'Why, we shall be married at home. I shall insist on your certificate being registered, though.'

'Leave me out of it, Amy,' I said. 'Goodbye.'

As I turned away she said after me, 'It's only proper. Oh, regards to Hal.'

That last remark stunned me. She knew my friend Hal? Had he perhaps told her I was someone who could be easily got onto their team if there was need? Even thinking this now sickens me.

The ship berthed at Malta two days later. I left the *Melissa* there, changing my itinerary, and completed my sessions on antiques and art frauds on the White Sisters, ships of the same line.

It seems odd to me now, that I have made a successful career by my skill in matters of fraud, while wholly lacking the same talent when it comes to gossip. I truly wish I were perceptive.

One thing, though. I shall find it hard to forgive Hal.

DIFFERENT TIME, DIFFERENT PLACE

Michael Hartland

Inspector Ghote was an inspired invention. I was an admirer of Ghote – and of his creator, H.R.F. Keating – for twenty years before I first met Harry in the 1980s. He was then – and has always remained for me – a master of the craft, whom I respect for his narrative skill, human perception and poetic economy with words. And, of course, he writes a darn good crime story.

Later, Harry was the President who welcomed me to the zany but warm fellowship of the Detection Club. He and Sheila became good and loyal friends. Rites of passage are as important to writers as anyone else, so it is a privilege to help mark the eightieth year of a gifted writer who has left a significant print on the crime writing of his time.

She knew they would shoot her at the end of the journey. As the prison wagon jolted over the rails, her mind was a turmoil of bitterness and fear. It was too cruel, after surviving the camp for nearly thirteen years. She knelt on the floor of her swaying cell and beat her fists against its splintered wood, weeping with frustration.

When her hands ached and were bleeding she stopped, but stayed huddled on the floor because the tiny space had no seat – nothing, not even a slop bucket. A grille of steel bars separated it from the corridor. Her only luxury was solitude, not being crammed in with the sweaty bodies of a dozen others; but there could be only one reason for that.

*   *   *

The day had ended like any other. After twelve hours in the mine she had marched back to the camp with her shift. It was dark, as it had been when they marched out in the morning. There were only a few hours of daylight in February and in the mine you missed them. Vorkuta was north of the Urals and well inside the Arctic Circle. The temperature was below freezing.

Supper had been the usual runny stew. It tasted of the disinfectant used in the kitchen and dripped over the edge of the flat plates – there were no bowls for the prisoners. Later, she had been lying on her bunk trying to read in the dim light, which flickered every time the thud of the generators slowed. Suddenly the hut door burst open and two guards stamped in with a flurry of snow.

'Levshina! Get packed and bring your things. You're moving.'

She was only five feet tall and the two men dwarfed her as she trotted between them, the wind cutting through her cotton trousers and worn padded jacket. The office was warm, with a roaring stove. An officer she did not know sat behind a metal desk.

Two bluecaps stood silently behind him. The officer glanced at some papers, as if to remind himself who she was.

'Levishina, Anna Petrovna. …' he muttered. 'formerly doctor of medicine … age now forty-seven. Sentenced to twenty years' deprivation of liberty, Article 58-1a, Criminal Code of 1926. Moscow District Court, May 3rd, 1961.' He looked up. 'Your sentence has been reviewed. You are being moved. There is a train going tonight.'

One of the guards gestured to Anna to pick up her brown paper parcel of belongings. She brushed his hand away and took a step towards the desk.

'What do you mean, *reviewed*?' She did not want to seem afraid, but her voice shook and her hands were trembling.

The officer shrugged. 'I have no instructions on that. You will be informed in due course.'

One of the bluecaps laughed. The officer cut him short with a gesture and the room felt very quiet. 'But where am I going?' she cried. 'For God's sake, where am I going?' No one answered. Two guards took her arms and hustled her out.

A prison van was waiting, but she pulled away from the guards and pointed back to the hut which had been her home for a quarter of her life. 'Please. There are people there who are my *friends*. At least let me say goodbye to them!' The guards said nothing, gripping her arms more tightly and pushing her into the van. She sat alone in the back as it bumped over the track away from the camp.

She was dazzled by the blaze of lights when the van stopped and the rear door clanged open. The inner gate of steel bars remained shut – but, peering through it, she could see a train of four *stolypin* prison wagons and a heavy locomotive. It had started to snow again and a white layer was settling on the roofs of the train and the station buildings. A guard with a sub-machine gun unlocked the grille and ordered her out; she huddled her coat around her against the cold.

The steps of the *stolypin* were covered in ice and she slipped as she tried to pull herself up to the door. She fell heavily, the sharp flints of the rail track cutting into her hands. The parcel vanished under the train. The guard pulled her sharply to her feet and pushed her back up the steps.

'But my things ...' she cried, pointing under the wheels. 'They're all I've got. Let me get them. Please let me get them!'

'You won't need them.' He jabbed her in the ribs with his gun barrel, stamping his feet and obviously anxious to get back into the warm.

Inside, the car was dim. She was hurried down a narrow corridor past four or five grilles of open bars. She was conscious of a crush of silent forms behind them: empty eyes in shaven heads. The end cell was empty and she was locked into it, alone. With a grinding of wheels and a jerk which threw her to the floor, the train started to move.

The train rolled southwards for three days. Anna had forgotten how excruciating travel by *stolypin* could be. The cell was too low for her to stand up properly – there was another above it – and she alternately knelt, crouched on all fours and sat with her back against the wall, hugging her knees. Her back and shoulders ached and knots of cramp in her legs made her twist in pain.

She was allowed out to the lavatory once a day, separately from the other prisoners. Twice she was given a handful of dry fish and some rye bread. The fish was very salty and tormented her with thirst until she was given a mug of dirty water several hours later. The second time she pushed the fish into her pocket and ate it when the water arrived.

Sometimes the train stopped and there were jerks and clanking, as wagons were coupled on or shunted away. Eventually it stopped for a longer time and the barred door was unlocked. She slithered down the steps to the ground. It was snowing heavily, but she did not care. She stretched her arms, jumped up and down and felt almost happy to be in the open again, out of the narrow little cell and the stench of the *stolypin*. The train was in a siding of a marshalling yard: a huge, white expanse broken up by the black shapes of freight cars and shunting engines. There were factory chimneys in the distance. It could have been the suburbs of Moscow.

Once again she was pushed into a prison van and they drove for several hours. Anna felt hungry and cold. She was very thin and her body began to ache from contact with the iron seat. But, as they drove, her physical discomfort was overtaken by a wave of black despair, of fear for what was to come. For twelve years she had tried to keep her health and sanity, so that when the nightmare was over she could start some sort of life again. Now she knew that it had been futile.

She had escaped death, all those years ago in Magadan, by losing her true identity. Now someone in a ministry with a thousand windows and a million files had caught up with her. They would torture her by leaving her in doubt until the last minutes. But the bluecap at Vorkuta had looked at her as if she were already dead, like an executioner. The bluecap *knew* ...

How would they do it? Was it true that they took you down to a cellar and made you undress, so they could give your prison clothes to someone else? That they made you kneel down; and shot you in the back of the head? She supposed it wouldn't hurt much, but even after twelve years in the camp she didn't want to die. She couldn't imagine being dead. For a few minutes she pulled herself together and tried to be composed about it. Then she slipped from the seat and huddled on the floor like a trapped animal.

When the van finally stopped she could not contain her fear. The steel door clanged open. As the guards hauled her out she screamed and struggled violently. Outside the van one of them tried to lock his arm round her neck, but she sank her teeth into his wrist and he pulled it back sharply.

They flung her to the ground and she flailed with her legs to keep them away. She heard confused shouting. Other people came running – blue uniforms, a white coat.

Hands seized her and she felt a prick in her arm, then another in her thigh. Her head swam. She felt sick and lost consciousness.

*   *   *

When she awoke she was in the back of a car. A woman she did not know sat beside her. They were driving down a country road in sunlight.

There was snow on the hedges, but it felt quite warm. The leather car seat was soft and comfortable.

'Where are we?' she asked.

'In Hungary. You were very foolish to struggle at the airport. We had to make you unconscious. You stayed asleep all through the flight to Budapest.'

'But why are we here? Where are we going?'

The woman looked at her sharply. She wore a blue jacket with a sergeant's chevrons on the sleeve. 'Don't you know?'

Anna shook her head.

'How odd – someone should have told you. You are going to be exchanged at the border – for a Soviet citizen imprisoned in Britain for alleged espionage.'

Anna's head swam again. 'You mean they're letting me go? I'll be *free*?' Her voice sounded strained and far away. 'But why me?'

'I do not know. The orders came from high up.' The woman clearly disapproved of them. 'As a political criminal with seven more years of correction to serve you are very lucky – although now, of course, you will not be able to take your place in Soviet society again. You are deprived of your citizenship.' Her mouth closed like a gin-trap.

Anna's mind filled with too many thoughts to cope with. She sank back in the seat in a daze.

They stopped beside a concrete building where a red and white barrier blocked the road. A red, white and green flag flew over the building. A hundred yards away was another barrier and another building, with a different flag. Two cars and a knot of people stood beside it. The woman reached into her pocket and handed Anna a headscarf. 'You might want to put this on.' She looked embarrassed.

Anna blushed and knotted the scarf under her chin. She had forgotten that her head was still shaved. Ruefully, she glanced down at her soiled clothes and bony ankles. She felt light-headed, as if she might faint at any moment. They got out of the car and she walked shakily towards the other barrier, between the woman and a border guard. Three figures ducked under the barrier and came towards them.

The two groups met in the middle of no man's land. A strip of brown scrub a hundred yards wide stretched away to right and left, separating the rusty chain-link fence on the other side from the coils of barbed wire and high watchtowers she was leaving behind. No one said anything. A woman in a dark overcoat detached herself from the other group and walked swiftly past them, back into Hungary. For a moment Anna thought she recognised her face, from somewhere long in the past, but she was too confused to be certain.

Someone took her arm and led her towards the other barrier, saying in Russian, 'Dr. Levshina – welcome to Austria.'

The speaker was a girl in her twenties – not much above Anna's height, with long dark hair and a cheerful face more round than oval. Her Russian was terrible, as if she had just learnt a few words for the occasion, but she had striking amber eyes, set wide apart – and kind. 'I'm Ruth Ash. And this is Mr. Mayhew. We're from the British Embassy.' A tall, stooping man in a grey suit shook hands gravely.

Anna ducked under the barrier and stood in silence, looking down into Austria. She did not look back. Ahead, the road ran down into a valley of snow-covered fields. The sun was shining on a village, clustered round a turreted castle and a pink church with an onion-topped tower. It looked like a child's drawing of a fairy tale. Suddenly, she began to feel steady and composed.

'Where are we going?' she asked. For the first time in twelve years she asked it with no fear.

'To Vienna, first. In a day or two, to London. I expect you'd like to rest and get a change of clothes?'

The tall man ushered Anna towards a car. He spoke for the first time as he opened its door. 'By the way – I do hope you had a good journey to the frontier?' He said it in English; she was surprised to find that she remembered enough to understand and reply.

She smiled at him. 'Yes, I had quite a good journey, thank you.'

*   *   *

It was a body. Undeniably a body. The young WPC nearly tripped over its legs, clad in jeans and frayed trainers, sticking out from the bushes where it had fallen. She was patrolling across Hackney Downs, looking for a lost child in the darkness just before dawn. Another uniformed officer was searching a parallel path a hundred yards away. She called to him and together they turned the body over. Too big for a child. The beam of the torch showed an elderly woman, wearing a Barbour above her jeans. Sue felt the neck. There was no carotid pulse and the skin of her face felt cold. 'She's gone? A heart attack?'

'Probably. No sign of violence or a struggle.' Her partner was radioing for an ambulance.

*　　*　　*

In A & E at Homerton hospital, the old lady was declared dead. A gentle Bengali doctor called Tahmin signed the certificate – 07.20 hrs, 6 November 2006, myocardial infarct, 79 years old – and the body was wheeled away to the mortuary. They knew her name, address and insurance number from the pension book in her pocket. A phone call gave her date of birth. Sue had also found a set of keys. 'Her place isn't far away. I'll go round there later, when we've finished on the Downs. See if I can trace any relatives.'

*　　*　　*

The flat was in a beaten up council estate, with broken glass and rubbish in the stair wells. Sue asked for directions from a group of Somali men squatting around a fire in an oil drum in the car park. They grinned and waved in a friendly way but did not understand her. Most of the faces she saw came from the Horn of Africa, the women graceful and veiled as they hung out plastic baskets of washing. Anna Levshina's flat was on the fourth floor. It was off an open walkway, the only one with a neatly painted red front door and a doormat. Sue turned the key.

There was a small living room, with a balcony. Sue opened the metal-framed glass door: outside were a white plastic table and two chairs for the summer. She turned back and looked around. There were shelves and rows of books with Cyrillic and English titles. They all looked well-used and quite a lot of the English ones were medical textbooks. The dead woman seemed to have come from Russia. That became clear when Sue opened the drawers in a bureau. Anna Levshina had preserved a letter from the Home Office, faded and thirty years old, recognising her as a refugee. It was clipped to a naturalisation certificate dated seven years later.

Sue had never been to Russia, the Soviet Union had passed into history, but she badly wanted to know who this old woman had been. She had looked peaceful enough in the hospital. But she had died of a heart attack. She had died alone. She seemed to have lived all alone too. There were no family photographs, no photographs at all. A few letters in Russian in another drawer. A neat bedroom. How had she got here? Why had she come? All those years ago there had not been many refugees and they were all fleeing real persecution. She must have escaped from the Gulag and the terror. She must have had a remarkable story to tell.

In the bedroom there was a neat row of small notebooks on the window sill – everything here was neat. They had hard covers and each was labelled. Sue opened one. It was written in Cyrillic handwriting, short paragraphs with many dates. She could not read a word. She was interrupted by a banging on the front door and went to open it.

Outside was a young man with wild Rastafarian locks and two others in blue overalls. 'I'm from the Council.' He noticed Sue's uniform. 'You on duty or a relative?'

'On duty. I found the body and I'm trying to discover if she had any relatives that should be told she's dead.'

'You finished?'

'No, not really.'

The Rastafarian nodded to the others, who went through into the bedroom. 'Stay as long as you want, but we gotta clear the place. It's needed for a family from Eritrea later today. Asylum seekers – they've been living in B & B.'

There was a crash from the bedroom and Sue hurried back through its door. The window was open and the men in overalls were dropping clothes from the wardrobe out of it. She looked down. The stuff was going into a skip in the yard. The bed had already gone, so had the notebooks. She felt a wave of anger. Perhaps she could retrieve them? Even if she did she couldn't read the bloody things. It hardly mattered.

The Rastafarian smiled sympathetically at her as more furniture crashed into the skip. 'Sorry, but I got a job to do'. He nodded at the books now going through the window. 'Russian, was she?' He shrugged. 'Same old problem. Different time, different place.'

Sue shook her head. No, not the same old problem. But, yes. Different time, different place.

ARKADY NIKOLAIVICH

H.R.F. Keating

Sheila Keating writes:

In choosing one of Harry's numerous short stories for inclusion in this anthology I thought it was appropriate to have one which featured his almost lifelong companion, Inspector Ghote. From the early sixties to the mid-nineties he was the seventh permanent resident in the London house where our four children grew up and India provided the income necessary for our survival. But in 1992, when Harry was already beginning to leave the sub-continent behind and had begun to explore the intricacies of the world of British police detection leading to the series centred on Harriet Martens, he wrote this short story. It gives us a glimpse of a very young Ghote, possibly at his most naïve and, as usual, beset by problems. To some who know him, Harry has an outgoing and relaxed personality, but to those who know him best there are many parallels between the writer and his character – at least in the author's mind – and it is not difficult to understand how he came to say in an interview, Inspector Ghote, c'est moi.

Gorby for Bombay. Each of the city's newspapers had hit on precisely the same headline. How could they have done anything else? Saying that one thing was to say everything. The hero who had brought the magic word *glasnost* to Russia, to the world, was to spend a day in Bombay during his visit to India. If there could be another avatar of God Vishnu, here he would be. If the Sikhs were to have an eleventh Guru, Gorby Singh would be his name.

Within a day of the announcement seats at every window along the route of the triumphal procession had been snapped up at black market prices. Loafers and vagrants of all sorts had been hired soon after for day and night occupation of the best places on the footpaths, on high ledges, even on climbable trees.

But, poised between these two financial extremes, Inspector Ghote of the Bombay C.I.D., burdened with family expenses, had felt unable to command even the least of these luxuries, avid as any though he was to have *darshan* of the great, magnetic man. For a little while he had actually toyed with breaking the rule of a lifetime and seeking a nice fat bribe somewhere, enough to enable him to join the bribers, the blackmailers, the tax-dodging businessmen, the rich and the nouveau riche who would crowd those desirable windows giving a full view of the hero of the Socialist world. But when it came down to it he could not bring himself to go that far. There was, however, one not entirely honest action he did feel he could rise to.

On the day itself he dressed not in his customary C.I.D. walla's shirt and trousers but in full uniform. An inspector of police could surely bark and bully his way to the front of the crowd at a good spot, however shoulders-jammed it might be. Then behind him, a little rowboat in the wake of an angry steam-tug, there could come his son, his Ved. He would have liked to attempt to bring in his wake, too, his wife. But, to his shocked surprise, Protima had said that she did not see that a politician being Russian made him any less of a politician and that she was not going to go one step beyond her door to look at one of those.

Thus it came about that Ghote standing, Ved tucked in beside him, in the very first rank of a squeezed coagulation of Bombayites yelling 'Gorbyji, Gorbyji' at just the place where the great man had elected to take one of his famous, hands-grasping walk-abouts, saw not two yards away a figure from his far past whom he at once recognised. There, loping along at the head of the posse of more or less overwhelmed bodyguards, was a man it had been all of a quarter of a century since he had last set eyes upon and whom he had never expected to encounter again. But at once he had known him.

'Arkady Nikolaivich,' he shouted.

It surprised him that he even remembered those twin names, or how to pronounce them. But the impact of that face so near his own, the broad, frown-creased forehead, the flaringly prow-like nose, the wide but iron-set mouth, the chin like an assertive fist, and that distinctive little black gecko-lizard shape high on the right cheekbone – how could he ever have forgotten that? – at once brought back to him a sweeping, eddy-checked flood of memories. Events he had done his best over the years completely to blot from his mind sprang back there in full, appalling detail.

It had been when he was still at the National Police Training School. In his last term. One day a notice had appeared on the board in the Mess. There was to be a Youth Police Congress in Moscow. Young men and women about to become fully-fledged police officers from all over the world were invited. India was to send one delegate.

Who among all the Probationary Sub-Inspectors would go? It had been decided to select the lucky man by lot. Anyone from the final term could enter, 'provided record is unblemished.' But there would be a fee of Rupees 10 to participate, monies to go to the Flood Relief Fund. He had read the notice, but had decided not to put in his ten rupees. Wonderful though a three-week stay in the Soviet Union would be, he foresaw as many difficulties as rewards. Probably more. The responsibility of being India's representative among so many foreigners would, surely, hover over him like a storm-tingling monsoon cloud.

But the Mess president had noticed just before the draw was due to take place that he was the only one who had not stumped up. Pressure had been brought to bear. And, of course, who should get the lucky ticket but himself, the reluctant payer?

So he had found himself in Moscow. In February. In his first hours there all he had been able to think of was the intensity of the cold. Even indoors it had seemed to pry into the very middle of his being, and outside it occupied every thought, every movement. The River Moskva, glimpsed on the way from the airport, had been a solid, shining, unmoving mass of dull ice. Every tree along its banks had branches rime-coated into twisted, glittering bars. The very mucus in his nostrils had congealed into iciness in the short time he had been outdoors.

The night temperature would reach minus forty, his guide from Intourist, a formidable young woman not much older than himself – Anyuta Vassilovna, the name came back to him – had told him, with plain boastfulness. Even the tea, which he drank at every opportunity to dispel his inner chill, came not in the familiar milky stream from a pot, but was trickled from a samovar into a glass, milkless and inky.

Nor was the ever-present sun of home the only thing he had missed in those first days. He had become hour by hour more miserable from the lack of animation everywhere. Among all the people he saw tramping the slushy streets he never seemed to catch a single smiling face, when at home even the poorest of the poor smiled and smiled as they made the best of their lives. And colour. Colour of any sort seemed, too, to have been driven out of the scene. Gone were the bright shirts and vivid saris of home. Instead, men and women alike appeared to be clothed in the drabbest of materials. And nowhere to be seen were anything like the huge brightly-painted film posters of Bombay. Even the hundreds of portraits everywhere of General Secretary Khrushchev were monotone and unexciting. Only the splashes of red stars and all-red flags straining in the ice-cold wind made small bursts of brightness amid the universal dark browns, dark blues, and worn blacks of the people, the dull ochre of the buildings, and the greyness of the air, heavy with still-unfallen snow.

Gradually, however, he had become more accustomed to it all, and had begun to lift up his head. If not standing out among the hundred or so other delegates to the congress, he had contrived once or twice actually to ask a question. And he had received replies that had indicated he was not utterly foolish.

All might have been well, in fact, had it not been for the ever-looming presence of Intourist's Anyuta Vassilovna supervising his every move outside the lecture rooms and meetings of the congress. Every time she opened her mouth and issued some commandment of the Socialist way of life she had made him feel pathetically small. And he had felt yet smaller when he had ventured to open his mouth and she had stayed stonily silent in disapproval. She was in every way a young woman with no time for human frailties. Even the snorting cold she had – his first introduction to her had been interrupted by a series of body-shaking sneezes, utterly ignored – had done nothing to stem the vigorous and unrelenting statements of Soviet achievements and Soviet aims she had bombarded him with.

There had been, he remembered vividly now, the first evening he had felt able to combat the all-pervading cold and had gone out to see the sights. Noticing a street vendor of the dolls-within-dolls called matryoshka, the only utterly Russian things he could think of to take home to his sister's children, he had eagerly advanced towards the stall.

'Halt,' Anyuta Vassilovna had snapped.

He had come to a full stop, slithering in the frozen slush, arms waving wildly for balance.

'Those are black market,' Anyuta Vassilovna had pronounced. 'Just now such toys are being under-produced. Selling them in the open market is sheer adventurism. You know that profiteering from the needs of one's fellow citizens is a crime in the Soviet Union? Whatever is done elsewhere.'

Disheartened, he had turned away. And had caught sight of a passing pair of grey-uniformed militiamen. He had been unable to resist at least indicating them to Anyuta Vassilovna with a raised eyebrow. If the doll-seller was committing a crime, why was she not pointing it out to the police?

'Adventurism,' she had said stonily, 'is, of course, a political offence.'

'But –'

'So it is a matter for the K.G.B.'

The K.G.B. That had sobered him into silence for the whole of the rest of the evening.

So, next day, when in place of grim-faced Anyuta a new Intourist guide had come unannounced to look after him, a girl he had at once taken to, a short, plump creature with a pink-and-white complexion that had reminded him irresistibly of sugary *barfi* on Bombay sweetmeat stalls, he had felt suddenly that life after all had become tolerable. Giggling almost before she had ceremoniously shaken hands, she had explained that Anyuta Vassilovna had been rushed into hospital with a high fever and she was taking her place for the rest of his stay.

Larissa Mikhailovna, her names were. But in no time at all he was calling her, at her own request, blue eyes sparkling, by the diminutive, Larechka.

The truth of it was, he supposed looking back, that, just only half-ripe as he had still been at that age, almost as soon as he had set eyes on the bouncing, cheerful creature, seemingly so different from himself, he had fallen in love. It was little wonder, really. There he had been, lonely, far from home, bewildered and a prey to constant worry that he might not be showing India in the best possible light. And there was this girl, interested in everything he said, full of questions about himself and his country, and so pretty. It could have happened to any young man.

'Your film star, Raj Kapoor, we love his films here, you know. He is so sweet, so nice, so innocent. So Russian.'

'Oh, yes. He is very, very good. I am laughing and laughing always at his many jokes and capers.'

'And snakes, are there snakes in India everywhere you go? Oh, I would not like that.'

Her English was very good.

'No, no. In Bombay you are not seeing one snake from year end to year end only.'

'But elephants? Do you all go to work riding on elephants?'

He had spluttered with laughter. And she had responded in an onset of giggles so overwhelming that she had had to clutch at him in an effort to keep upright.

'No, no, no. Bombay is not so different from Moscow. Except it is nice and hot, and here it is so cold.'

'But do you have everything we have?' She cast her eyes around. 'The Metro? Mailboxes? Buses?'

'Buses, yes, some with trailer buses attached. Metro, no. Post-boxes, of course.'

She looked at him then.

'And your mail,' she asked, a hint of daring coming on to her plump, pink-cheeked face, 'is that censored? We have some not-so-nice things in our country, you know.'

What a difference between my Larechka and that terrible Anyuta Vassilovna, he had thought then. To dare to utter such a thought.

My Larechka. Oh, how young he had been.

'No, no, no, no,' he had assured her. 'In India there is not at all any censorship of the mails.'

It seemed as if it was almost from that moment on, their love affair had shot up to, to him, dizzy heights. Of course, it had not gone as far as illicit relations. Although the thought had distinctly entered his head, in those days there had seemed to be an enormous gulf between thoughts and actuality. So Larechka had never so much as entered his room at the hostel. How young he had been. How very young.

But in quiet corners there had been embraces.

And there had been the confidences and exchanges. By the dozen. By the hundred. More than once, indeed, he had been terrified by the things Larechka had said to him. Disloyalties to the state. Jokes about Party officials. Even jokes against Mr Khrushchev himself. He had felt the wings of the K.G.B. spreading over them, for all that he had never to his knowledge so much as seen one single K.G.B. officer. Much less at that time the powerful, gecko-marked face of Arkady Nikolaivich Volkov, Major Volkov.

Yet he had been enchanted by Larechka's every word, even the most daring. That he, Ganesh Ghote, should be the recipient of her confidences. What trust she must have for him. What love for him.

The days had gone whirling by. Although he had a notion that he was acquitting himself reasonably well in the public discussions of the congress, he really had hardly paid them attention. His thoughts had been of nothing but his Larechka.

His Larechka.

He could see her now, twenty-five years and more on, as he stood in the jam-packed crowd in Bombay's steamy heat. That deliciously plump young figure. That wonderful pink-and-white flesh that he had wanted and wanted to pinch between finger and thumb, and quite often had. Those blue eyes alive with mischief.

And those ever more dangerous confidences.

'You know, Ganeshji' – he had taught her the Hindi name-tag, an exchange for that diminutive Larechka – 'there are so many forbidden books in the Soviet Union. Books young people ought to be able to read. The works of your own Mahatma Gandhi, George Bernard Shaw, Ayn Rand. We ought to be able to read everything. Don't you agree?'

'Yes, yes. Those are very, very good books. Ayn Rand especially.'

'Well, so what we need, this little group of students and ex-students I have spoken to you about – Ganeshji, you will never ever tell anybody that we exist, will you? Will you?'

'Never, never. Not under tortures even.'

'Well, what we need in our group is a way of getting hold of such books. They can come from America, but we have to order them. We can pay, even. We are willing to pay. For just one copy of each. We will pass each book round, you see.'

'Yes, yes. That would be a good way to be doing it.'

'But there is this difficulty.'

'Yes? What? If there is any way I can help I would do it to my last breath.'

She had broken into a fit of giggles then.

'Oh, Ganeshji, you are so sweet. But it isn't a question of any last breaths. All it is, is just posting a letter for us. A letter to America.'

'But why cannot you –'

'But I told you, Ganeshji. We have censorship of the mails. Any letter going to America is most likely to be opened by the K.G.B. And if that were to happen … You know about Siberia, Ganeshji, the camps there?'

'Yes, yes, I have heard. Terrible. Terrible.'

'And colder even than Moscow. Much colder.'

'So,' he had said, 'what you are wanting is for me to be posting your letter when I am getting back to India.'

'Yes, yes. You have guessed. Clever boy.'

He had received a kiss then. A smacking, wonderful kiss. And a warm senses-arousing hug.

But not many days later a shock awaited him. Larechka, standing ready to escort him to the morning session of the congress as he had come out of the hostel into the icy air, slid her hand inside his coat not for the purpose of giving him a delicious squeeze but instead so as to slide into his inner pocket a thick envelope.

'What is it?' he had exclaimed.

'Sssh.'

'Yes, but what?'

'The letter. In two days you are going back to India. The letter for you to send for us.'

He had not, somehow, realised that the time had grown so short. Dull, downwards-spiralling dismay had abruptly invaded him. Larechka, when would he see her again? They had never talked about what would happen after the congress. Their days had been all concentrated into one present. But when, now, would he see Larechka again? Could she get an exit visa? It struck him with blank certainty that she could not. Could he come and live in the Soviet Union, in Moscow? But what would he do? He could not join the police here. They were going to be parted. Perhaps never to see each other again. In two days only.

His mind blank, he had hurried back into the hostel and hidden the secret letter safely in the folds of his second-best uniform.

But in the event the dread parting from Larechka had come that very day.

When he had emerged after the congress session was over expecting to see her waiting for him as she always had been on the snow-swept steps outside, she had not been there. But someone else had been. Anyuta Vassilovna. White-faced and washed-out from scarcely ended illness. Sternly resolute as ever.

'You,' he had almost shouted in dismay as she had marched up to him. 'What is it you are doing here? Where is Larech – Where is Miss Larissa?'

'Comrade Larissa Mikhailovna is under arrest.'

'What? What? But – But – But why? Why?'

'I think you should very well know that, Probationary Sub-Inspector Ghote.'

'Me? Why? Why me? Why should I be knowing?'

Then from inside her thick grey coat Anyuta Vassilovna had produced the fat envelope with the American address on it he had hidden in the room at the hostel.

He had experienced a great wave of rage that had blotted out for that instant every other consideration.

'You took that from my room,' he had stormed. 'You entered my room and searched my cupboard.'

'Of course. It is my duty to see that any foreigner in my charge is not acting in an anti-State manner.'

'But that letter is private. Private.'

'A letter addressed in Larissa Mikhailovna's own writing to an address in America? Private? I do not think you can know what you are saying, Probationary Sub-Inspector Ghote. Perhaps it is different in India, but here the interests of the state come before those of any individual.'

But by then all the implications were beginning to sink in. He had almost seized the white-faced girl in front of him by the shoulders.

'Larechka,' he must have shouted, 'where is she? Arrested, did you say? Where has she been taken?'

'Doubtless to the Lubyanka. Her offence is a political one, of course.'

'The Lubyanka?'

'The K.G.B. headquarters,' Anyuta Vassilovna's eyebrows had risen in despair at such foreign ignorance.

'Where is that? Where? I must go at once. I must explain everything.'

'Well, I am going there myself. I have to hand over this evidence.'

Anyuta Vassilovna sternly held up the thick envelope with its American address.

Ghote in his flood of revived memories even recalled flashes of the journey they had taken by trolley to Dzerzhinsky Square, for all that it had passed for him in a state of numb misery. He could see again now in his mind's eye, even after those more then twenty-five years, the forbidding yellowish building. Anyuta Vassilovna had led him up to, head high with her own importance, and the huge thirty-foot-tall portal they had somehow gone through.

But once inside, again dazed numbness had set in. Had they been told to report to an upstairs floor? He had a vague recollection that they had and that there they had passed through several tall glass doors, twice his own height and more, with yellow curtains over them. Or were those the products of a later nightmare? And there had been, yes, a waiting room in which he had sat for hours – Anyuta Vassilovna had left him by then – with a huge map of the Soviet Union on one wall and a table with two or three yellowing magazines, the Russian names of which he had been unable to make out. There had been two other people waiting there, too. Or had it been three? Certainly one of them had been an old woman, her feet in clumsy felt boots. He had wondered what political crime such an ancient crone could have been involved in.

And then, almost as if he had been lifted bodily and transported elsewhere, he had found himself sitting in front of a large desk behind which, upright and implacable, uniform tight and spotless, had been the man he was to learn was called Major Arkady Nikolaivich Volkov.

The very face, hardly changed by the years, that he could see just two yards away from him at this very instant. The identical black gecko-shaped mark high on the right cheek, the broad forehead, frown-marked, the powerful flaring nose, the wide hard-set mouth, the chin like a fist.

'Arkady Nikolaivich,' he shouted again. 'It is I, Ganesh Ghote. You remember, the Lubyank –'

It was clear, however, from the look on that assertive face that Major Volkov, plainly rising star of the K.G.B. a quarter of a century ago, had already somehow remembered the Indian police trainee he had had on the other side of his desk in the Lubyanka in those distant, different days.

'We must meet,' Ghote shouted. 'We must. There are things I must … I would come to the President Hotel. After the big dinner.'

All Bombay knew that the whole of that towering hotel at Cuffe Parade had been taken over for Gorby's one-night stay in the city. They knew, too, that the great man was to be entertained that evening at a dinner given jointly by the state chief minister and the chairman of the Bombay Municipal Council at the Taj Mahal Hotel. Entire Bombay invited, or entire Bombay that possessed any of that magical thing, influence.

Arkady Nikolaivich looked for a moment acutely unwilling to agree to the meeting. But at once second thoughts must have prevailed.

'Yes,' he shouted back. 'Come tonight. Come, if you must.'

And then he turned again to his impossible task of protecting from assassins the great man who would insist on multiple hands-shaking amid the tumultuous, cheering, jam-packed, flag-waving, hooters-squealing Bombay crowds.

Standing altogether unmindful of the world figure he had cheated and cajoled to get a view of, Ghote let his mind recreate the scene twenty-five years before in that office in the Lubyanka. The piled grey cardboard files on the green baize-covered desk, the sprawl of notebooks, the ashtray filled with the cardboard filters of the curious *papirosi* cigarettes the Russians smoked, the half-empty bottle of Bronozhi mineral water. And there had been a cupboard with its door leaning a little ajar. And a coat-rack beside the door with Major Volkov's heavy uniform coat and fur hat on its wooden hooks. It all came back to him.

Little wonder, he thought. However much, on orders, he had tried to suppress what had taken place in that office, everything had been so laden with threat and revelation that he could not possibly ever have really forgotten.

What he could not recall – and again he thought there was little to wonder at in that – was just what he had said to that implacable figure sitting unmoving on the far side of the desk. Once he had realised that this grim figure spoke excellent English, he must have pleaded with him for all he was worth. He must have attempted to point out that the offence Larechka had committed would be no offence at all in the country he himself came from. He had probably, too, spouted some phrases from the great Englishmen of the past, half-remembered from dull college lectures. 'A good book is the bloody – no, is the life blood of a master's spirit.'

But he could recall, with horrible distinctness, the exact moment when Major Volkov, having let him blow himself out of all his protestings, delivered the bombshell.

'Young man,' he had said, although he himself had dimly realised this formidable figure could not be all that much older than he was, however far up the ladder of promotion he had raced. 'Young man, do you really believe I am not aware of the contents of that letter you were attempting to smuggle out to America?'

With a swift gesture then he had jerked open a drawer on the desk, whipped out a small sheaf of papers together with the envelope with Larechka's handwriting on it and, swivelling the whole round, had thrust them under his nose.

He had read. He could not help it. And at once he had realised that there was nothing in the papers about ordering single copies of books by Mahatma Gandhi, Ayn Rand, or George Bernard Shaw. Instead they consisted of a long and detailed order for clothes, principally blue jeans.

He was unable to make much sense of the commercial jargon, but the gist of it all was clear. Larechka's 'group' was no more than a gang of crude profiteers, the sort of people Anyuta Vassilovna had contemptuously labelled adventurists. There was not a shred of idealism, of spreading the notion of freedom, of high intellectual ideas, in anything they were doing. They were out, in just the way a Bombay smuggler might be, to make as much money as possible by whatever quick means came to hand. That and nothing more.

All of his disillusionment must have shown on his face, clearly as if pictures from a slide projector were being flashed up on to it.

Major Volkov had looked at him with clear contempt.

'So,' he had said, 'that pretty young creature had got you just where she wanted you, had she? And in double quick time, too.'

'But – But – But I thought … No. Yes, she had. I see it now. She was asking me even, just only after we had met, whether mail was censored in India.'

He had groaned then, actually groaned aloud.

As he groaned again now, as loudly, at the thought of his youthful self. That self who was – it could not be otherwise – still a part of himself. But, amid all the hubbub following the great Gorby's onward progress, no one heard, not even Ved still tucked in beside him.

'You realise that, though a foreigner, you are nevertheless subject to the laws of the Soviet Union?' Major Volkov, that implacable rising star of the K.G.B., had gone on to say. 'The penalties for profiteering are severe, and rightly so. At the most the offence incurs the death penalty.'

Death. By shooting. To him. Here now, far from home. Alone. Perhaps never to be heard of more.

Cold, quaking fear clamped down on him.

But something else just found room in his mind as well.

'And her. Larech – Comrade Larissa Mikhailovna?' he had heard himself asking, croakingly. 'She would be shot also? But that is wrong. It is unfair. Smuggling blue jeans from the West is bad, yes. But it is not so very bad. It is not doing harm to anyone. Not directly. Not serious harm. Please, to shoot someone for that, it would not be right.'

Major Volkov stared at him, blank-faced, as if he was some unfathomable form of life. An ant carrying a burden uselessly.

In face of that pitiless solidity, he had found in himself yet greater determination.

'Please,' he said. 'Please, I know that it is looking bad about her. Damn bad. But, you see, I am knowing her. Knowing her very, very well even in just only such a short time. She is a good person. Yes. Yes, she is. I know it. Yes, now I am seeing what it is. She must have been led astray by evil companions only. Please, do not punish Larechka. Punish me. Punish me, if you must. Send me to Siberia. I would endure the utmost of cold. But let her go.'

And then an extraordinary thing had happened. On to Major Volkov's stone face there had appeared something he himself had hardly once seen in Russia. A smile.

Giggles he had heard in plenty. Larechka's delightful giggles. Occasionally, too, he had heard wild, raucous laughter, though he suspected that was mostly from drunks. But smiles, smiles such as most Bombayites flashed, white-teethed, almost constantly despite all their troubles, he had hardly once seen all the time he had been in Moscow. Yet now on Major Volkov's inflexible countenance there was something that could not be described other than as a smile, for all that it did not cause his firm-set mouth to alter very much or take away one frown-line from his broad forehead.

Smiling he was. Definitely. And then he had allowed to escape a single small sigh.

'Oh,' he had said, 'you silly boy. Look, go home. Go home even before your congress is over. I will see you get on the next flight to India. And, all right, I will let that girl of yours go, too. You neither of you deserve it, but – but, really, you are too silly. Off you go. But listen. You are to forget that any of this ever happened. Forget it utterly. To let it be known that a K.G.B. officer behaved ...'

He had broken off in exasperation, though whether it was exasperation at his own sudden human generosity or over the idiocy of the young Indian who had come before him Ghote could not make out. Neither at the time, nor at those moments in after years when he had been unable totally to obey the order to obliterate the scene from his mind.

He had risen from his chair then and stammered out the first words that came into his head.

'Sir. Sir, you are a truly good man, sir. Truly good. Please what is your good name? I am wishing always to remember same.'

'I am Arkady Nikolaivich,' the rising K.G.B. star had replied. And at once had looked as if he regretted even this small further sign of humanity, because he had added at once, 'Major Volkov, that is. Major

Volkov, of the Komitet Gosudarstvennoy Bezopasnosti. But you are to forget that. Forget everything about all this. It is to be as if it had never been.'

Bemused incomprehension had descended on him then, once more, from the moment he had turned away from the major. From Arkady Nikolaivich, as he could not prevent himself naming in his mind ever afterwards the man who had committed that unexpected act of humanity.

He had had little idea what had happened until he had found himself back once more under the blissful Indian sun, even if this was at distant Delhi airport rather than in Bombay.

And now, utterly unexpectedly, he had come face to face with Arkady Nikolaivich once more. And had an appointment to see him at the President Hotel that evening, however much agreed to with that disconcerting tinge of reluctance.

So at a time in fact well before Gorby's motorcade had left the Taj Hotel after the big dinner, Ghote was there at the appointed place awaiting the great man's return, together with that of his bodyguard led apparently by Major – but by now surely he must be much more senior than that, perhaps a major-general – Arkady Nikolaivich Volkov.

Then, at last, the great Russian hero arrived, was swept up to his private suite attended still by all his bodyguards. And then, some fifteen minutes later, out of the lift in the hotel's grand foyer, there stepped Arkady Nikolaivich.

He came striding over to Ghote, looking, except for the changes made by twenty-five years of living, almost exactly as he had done when he had been seated on the far side of his green baize-covered, files-untidy desk in the Lubyanka.

'Arkady Nikolaivich,' Ghote exclaimed, rushing forward.

'Yes,' said Arkady Nikolaivich, without even a trace of that suspicion of a smile that had moved a little of the corners of his wide, hard-set mouth twenty-five years before. 'Yes, I remember you. I even remember you name. Ghote, was it not? Ganesh Vinayak Ghote?'

Arkady Nikolaivich looked at him with no change of expression.

'Well, Mr Ghote, I am afraid I cannot share your enthusiasm. I seem to remember that my parting words to you all that time ago were that you should forget everything that had passed between us. You do not seem to have done so.'

'But how could I, Arkady Nikolaivich? How could I forget the humanity you showed to a silly young Indian boy who had got himself into much, much worse trouble than he was having any idea of? I can remember I was altogether failing to thank you then. I was so young, so pleased to be escaping from the fate awaiting me, so delighted that you were extending your kind mercy to that girl, Larechka, also, that I said not one word of grateful.'

He felt the tears of thankfulness that should have come from him in bitingly cold Moscow, but had not, prick behind his eyes now.

'So let me say it,' he rushed on. 'Arkady Nikolaivich, I thank you from the bottom-most core of my heart for the humanity you were showing to me and to the girl I was then so foolish as to be loving.'

He expected at that moment to find Arkady Nikolaivich's arms round him, to feel a hug of warm human-to-human friendship. Instead he saw the Russian standing stiff as an ice-bound tree at the worst of the Moscow winter.

The stone eyes in his stone face were directed briefly onto the three pips on Ghote's uniform epaulettes.

'Inspector Ghote,' the unyielding figure said. 'I wish you to understand something. I regretted that foolish and impulsive action of mine almost from the moment you left my office at Number One Dzerzhinsky Square. It was wrong. Not the action of a true Party member and true officer of the Komitet Gosudarstvennoy Bezopasnosti. I regretted it so bitterly that, like yourself, I was unable ever to forget I had committed such a crime.'

'Crime?' Ghote burst out, horrified. 'But – But, Arkady Nilolaivich, that was not at all a crime. It was showing the common humanity we are all sharing. It was in the one hundred per cent spirit of *glasnost*. Just as Gor – Just as Mr Gorbachev himself has taught us.'

'Gorbachev,' Arkady Nikolaivich almost spat out.

He took a quick look round.

There was nobody at all to hear them in the big, glittering lobby, neither Indian nor Russian.

'Listen to me, you idiot,' he growled. 'What do you think my whole life has been? From the moment I joined the K.G.B. thirty years ago I devoted myself to ensuring the safety of the State. It was my task in life. Do you understand? My task. And in all those years I never deviated from that task. Except once. Except when, for some goddam reason or other, something a blubbering young Indian said or offered to do made me forget all the pledges I had made of unswerving service to the State and its interests. When I let him and his criminal girlfriend go free. And that was you. You.'

'Yes, I am well knowing, Arkady Niko –'

'Thirty years of service. Thirty years with one tiny blemish and no more. And then what happens? Mikhail Sergeyevich Gorbachev comes along, and everything I had believed in, everything I had done in all those thirty years, except that one foolish act of weakness, all is thrown onto the scrap heap of history. Gone. Wasted. Finished.'

His face had come closer and closer to Ghote's own, burning with fury and bleak disappointment.

'Why even do you think I am here in this stinking hot country of yours?' he demanded. 'Why? Because in the days of damn *glasnost* they have no use for anyone at Number One Dzerzhinsky Square who believes in the old things, the old ways. So I am shunted out to take charge of a bodyguard in a country where anyone could assassinate the man I am meant to protect, a country without order, without discipline, without anything.'

His face was now within an inch of Ghote's, and Ghote could think of nothing to say in answer. For a moment he had thought of flinging back at that enraged face the simple retort, 'Yes, but a country with love.' But at once that reply had been stilled on his lips. Stilled by the troubled, swirling sympathy he had not been able to prevent rising up in himself for this man who had lost all he had believed in, who felt that in all his life he had committed but one crime against his conscience. The crime of letting a silly young Indian go free when he ought to have been hurried away to the depths of Siberia.

So that all in the end he managed to croak out were the words, 'Arkady Nikolaivich. Oh, Arkady Nikolaivich.'

COPYRIGHT ACKNOWLEDGEMENTS

THE VERDICT OF US ALL

The Verdict of Us All, Stories by the Detection Club for H.R.F. Keating, edited by Peter Lovesey is set in Baskerville Old Style. It is printed on sixty-pound Natures acid-free, recycled paper. The cover painting is by Carol Heyer and the design is by Deborah Miller. The first edition was printed in two forms: trade softcover, notchbound; and three hundred numbered copies sewn in cloth. Each of the clothbound copies includes a separate pamphlet, *The Justice Boy* by H.R.F. Keating. *The Verdict of Us All* was printed and bound by Thomson-Shore, Inc., Dexter, Michigan and published in by Crippen & Landru Publishers, Inc., Norfolk, Virginia.

CRIPPEN & LANDRU, PUBLISHERS

P. O. Box 9315, Norfolk, VA 23505
E-mail: info@crippenlandru.com; toll-free 877 622-6656
Web: www.crippenlandru.com

Crippen & Landru publishes first edition short-story collections by important detective and mystery writers. The following books are currently (November 2006) in print in our regular series; see our website for full details:

The McCone Files by Marcia Muller. 1995. Trade softcover, $19.00.

Diagnosis: Impossible, The Problems of Dr. Sam Hawthorne by Edward D. Hoch. 1996. Trade softcover, $19.00.

Who Killed Father Christmas? by Patricia Moyes. 1996. Signed, unnumbered cloth overrun copies, $30.00. Trade softcover, $16.00.

My Mother, The Detective: by James Yaffe. 1997. Trade softcover, $15.00.

In Kensington Gardens Once by H.R.F. Keating. 1997. Trade softcover, $12.00.

Shoveling Smoke by Margaret Maron. 1997. Trade softcover, $19.00.

The Ripper of Storyville by Edward D. Hoch. 1997. Trade softcover. $19.00.

Renowned Be Thy Grave by P.M. Carlson. 1998. Trade softcover, $16.00.

Carpenter and Quincannon by Bill Pronzini. 1998. Trade softcover, $16.00.

Famous Blue Raincoat by Ed Gorman. 1999. Signed, unnumbered cloth overrun copies, $30.00. Trade softcover, $17.00.

The Tragedy of Errors by Ellery Queen. 1999. Trade softcover, $19.00.

The Velvet Touch by Edward D. Hoch. 2000. Trade softcover, $19.00.

McCone and Friends by Marcia Muller. 2000. Trade softcover, $19.00.

Challenge the Widow Maker by Clark Howard. 2000. Trade softcover, $16.00.

Fortune's World by Michael Collins. 2000. Trade softcover, $16.00.

Long Live the Dead by Hugh B. Cave. 2000. Trade softcover, $16.00.

Tales Out of School by Carolyn Wheat. 2000. Trade softcover, $16.00.

Stakeout on Page Street and Other DKA Files by Joe Gores. 2000. Trade softcover, $16.00.

The Celestial Buffet by Susan Dunlap. 2001. Trade softcover, $16.00.

Kisses of Death by Max Allan Collins. 2001. Trade softcover, $19.00.

The Old Spies Club by Edward D. Hoch. 2001. Signed, unnumbered cloth overrun copies, $32.00. Trade softcover, $17.00.

Adam and Eve on a Raft by Ron Goulart. 2001. Signed, unnumbered cloth overrun copies, $32.00. Trade softcover, $17.00.

The Sedgemoor Strangler by Peter Lovesey. 2001. Trade softcover, $17.00.

The Reluctant Detective by Michael Z. Lewin. 2001. Signed, numbered clothbound, $42.00. Trade softcover, $17.00.

Nine Sons by Wendy Hornsby. 2002. Trade softcover, $16.00.

The Curious Conspiracy and Other Crimes by Michael Gilbert. 2002. Signed, numbered clothbound, $42.00. Trade softcover, $17.00.

The 13 Culprits by Georges Simenon, translated by Peter Schulman. 2002. Trade softcover, $16.00.

The Dark Snow by Brendan DuBois. 2002. Signed, unnumbered cloth overrun copies, $32.00. Trade softcover, $17.00.

Come Into My Parlor: by Hugh B. Cave. 2002. Trade softcover, $17.00.

The Iron Angel and Other Tales of the Gypsy Sleuth by Edward D. Hoch. 2003. Signed, numbered clothbound, $42.00. Trade softcover, $17.00.

Cuddy – Plus One by Jeremiah Healy. 2003. Trade softcover, $18.00.

Problems Solved by Bill Pronzini and Barry N. Malzberg. 2003. Signed, numbered clothbound, $42.00. Trade softcover, $16.00.

A Killing Climate by Eric Wright. 2003. Signed, numbered clothbound, $42.00. Trade softcover, $17.00.

Lucky Dip by Liza Cody. 2003. Signed, numbered clothbound, $42.00. Trade softcover, $17.00.

Kill the Umpire: The Calls of Ed Gorgon by Jon L. Breen. 2003. Trade softcover, $17.00.

Suitable for Hanging by Margaret Maron. 2004. Trade softcover, $17.00.

Murders and Other Confusions by Kathy Lynn Emerson. 2004. Signed, numbered clothbound, $42.00. Trade softcover, $19.00.

Byline: Mickey Spillane by Mickey Spillane. 2004. Trade softcover, $20.00.

The Confessions of Owen Keane by Terence Faherty. 2005. Signed, numbered clothbound, $42.00. Trade softcover, $17.00.

The Adventure of the Murdered Moths and Other Radio Mysteries by Ellery Queen. 2005. Numbered clothbound, $45.00. Trade softcover, $20.00.

Murder, Ancient and Modern by Edward Marston. 2005. Signed, numbered clothbound, $43.00. Trade softcover, $18.00.

More Things Impossible by Edward D. Hoch. 2006. Signed, numbered clothbound, $43.00. Trade softcover, $18.00.

Murder, 'Orrible Murder! by Amy Myers. 2006. Signed, numbered clothbound, $43.00. Trade softcover, $18.00.

The Verdict of Us All, Stories by the Detection Club for H.R.F.Keating, edited by Peter Lovesey. 2006. Signed, numbered clothbound, $43.00. Trade softcover $18.00.

FORTHCOMING TITLES IN THE REGULAR SERIES

Thirteen to the Gallows by John Dickson Carr and Val Gielgud

The Archer Files: The Complete Short Stories of Lew Archer, Private Investigator, Including Newly-Discovered Case-Notes by Ross Macdonald, edited by Tom Nolan

The Mankiller of Poojeegai and Other Mysteries by Walter Satterthwait

A Pocketful of Noses: Stories of One Ganelon or Another by James Powell

Quintet: The Cases of Chase and Delacroix, by Richard A. Lupoff

A Little Intelligence by Robert Silverberg and Randall Garrett (writing as "Robert Randall")

Attitude and Other Stories of Suspense by Loren D. Estleman

Suspense – His and Hers by Barbara and Max Allan Collins

[Untitled collection] by S.J. Rozan

Hoch's Ladies by Edward D. Hoch

14 Slayers by Paul Cain, edited by Max Allan Collins and Lynn F. Myers, Jr. Published with Black Mask Press

Tough As Nails by Frederick Nebel, edited by Rob Preston. Published with Black Mask Press

You'll Die Laughing by Norbert Davis, edited by Bill Pronzini. Published with Black Mask Press

CRIPPEN & LANDRU LOST CLASSICS

Crippen & Landru is proud to publish a series of *new* short-story collections by great authors who specialized in traditional mysteries:

The Newtonian Egg and Other Cases of Rolf le Roux by Peter Godfrey, introduction by Ronald Godfrey. 2002. Trade softcover, $15.00.

Murder, Mystery and Malone by Craig Rice, edited by Jeffrey A. Marks. 2002. Trade softcover, $19.00.

The Sleuth of Baghdad: The Inspector Chafik Stories, by Charles B. Child. 2002. Cloth, $27.00. Trade softcover, $17.00.

Hildegarde Withers: Uncollected Riddles by Stuart Palmer, introduction by Mrs. Stuart Palmer. 2002. Trade softcover, $19.00.

The Spotted Cat and Other Mysteries by Christianna Brand, edited by Tony Medawar. 2002. Cloth, $29.00. Trade softcover, $19.00.

Marksman and Other Stories by William Campbell Gault, edited by Bill Pronzini; afterword by Shelley Gault. 2003. Trade softcover, $19.00.

Karmesin: The World's Greatest Criminal — Or Most Outrageous Liar by Gerald Kersh, edited by Paul Duncan. 2003. Cloth, $27.00. Trade softcover, $17.00.

The Complete Curious Mr. Tarrant by C. Daly King, introduction by Edward D. Hoch. 2003. Cloth, $29.00. Trade softcover, $19.00.

The Pleasant Assassin and Other Cases of Dr. Basil Willing by Helen McCloy, introduction by B.A. Pike. 2003. Cloth, $27.00. Trade softcover, $18.00.

Murder – All Kinds by William L. DeAndrea, introduction by Jane Haddam. 2003. Cloth, $29.00. Trade softcover, $19.00.

The Avenging Chance and Other Mysteries from Roger Sheringham's Casebook by Anthony Berkeley, edited by Tony Medawar and Arthur Robinson. 2004. Cloth, $29.00. Trade softcover, $19.00.

Banner Deadlines: The Impossible Files of Senator Brooks U. Banner by Joseph Commings, edited by Robert Adey; memoir by Edward D. Hoch. 2004. Cloth, $29.00. Trade softcover, $19.00.

The Danger Zone and Other Stories by Erle Stanley Gardner, edited by Bill Pronzini. 2004. Cloth, $29.00. Trade softcover, $19.00.

Dr. Poggioli: Criminologist by T.S. Stribling, edited by Arthur Vidro. 2004. Cloth, $29.00. Trade softcover, $19.00.

The Couple Next Door: Collected Short Mysteries by Margaret Millar, edited by Tom Nolan. 2004. Trade softcover, $19.00.

Sleuth's Alchemy: Cases of Mrs. Bradley and Others by Gladys Mitchell, edited by Nicholas Fuller. 2005. Trade softcover, $19.00.

Who Was Guilty? Two Dime Novels by Philip S. Warne/Howard W. Macy, edited by Marlena E. Bremseth. 2005. Cloth, $29.00. Trade softcover, $19.00.

Slot-Machine Kelly by Dennis Lynds writing as Michael Collins, introduction by Robert J. Randisi. 2005. Cloth, $29.00. Trade softcover, $19.00.

The Detections of Francis Quarles by Julian Symons, edited by John Cooper; afterword by Kathleen Symons. 2006. Cloth, $29.00. Trade softcover, $19.00.

The Evidence of the Sword by Rafael Sabatini, edited by Jesse F. Knight. 2006. Cloth, $29.00. Trade softcover, $19.00.

The Casebook of Sidney Zoom by Erle Stanley Gardner, edited by Bill Pronzini. 2006. Cloth, $29.00. Trade softcover, $19.00.

The Trinity Cat and Other Mysteries by Ellis Peters (Edith Pargeter), edited by Martin Edwards and Sue Feder. 2006. Cloth, $29.00. Trade softcover, $19.00.

FORTHCOMING LOST CLASSICS

The Grandfather Rastin Mysteries by Lloyd Biggle, Jr., introduction by Kenneth Lloyd Biggle and Donna Biggle Emerson

Masquerade: Nine Crime Stories by Max Brand, edited by William F. Nolan, Jr.

The Battles of Jericho by Hugh Pentecost, introduction by S.T. Karnick

Dead Yesterday and Other Mysteries by Mignon G. Eberhart, edited by Rick Cypert and Kirby McCauley

The Minerva Club, The Department of Patterns and Other Stories by Victor Canning, edited by John Higgins

The Casebook of Jonas P. Jonas and Others by Elizabeth Ferrars, edited by John Cooper

The Casebook of Gregory Hood by Anthony Boucher and Denis Green, edited by Joe R. Christopher

Ten Thousand Blunt Instruments by Philip Wylie, edited by Bill Pronzini

The Adventures of Señor Lobo by Erle Stanley Gardner, edited by Bill Pronzini

Lilies for the Crooked Cross and Other Stories by G.T. Fleming-Roberts, edited by Monte Herridge

SUBSCRIPTIONS

Crippen & Landru offers discounts to individuals and institutions who place Standing Order Subscriptions for its forthcoming publications, either all the Regular Series or all the Lost Classics or (preferably) both. Collectors can thereby guarantee receiving limited editions, and readers won't miss any favorite stories. Standing Order Subscribers receive a specially commissioned story in a deluxe edition as a gift at the end of the year. Please write or e-mail for more details.